It was all quite by accident ... the conservationist discovered what he first mistook to be a bag of garbage. Swearing under his breath at the carelessness, no, filthy ways of lazy pigs that use the bay shoreline as a dumping ground for their discarded lunch, condoms, beer bottles, and whatnot, he grabbed at a black plastic bag with two slender fingers and a surprisingly long thumb. The heft stunned him. Good God, this could crush the life out of the tender grasses. What was wrong with people? Did they care so little about the planet that... He let out a stifled scream when he realized what he had between his fingers. The plastic bag was barely covering something horrific. Jumping back, he tripped over his own feet and fell bottom down into the still, cold water onto the very grasses he was trying to protect. Flailing, his heart pounding, he stumbled with great difficulty out of the water, tearing out the grass beneath his waders.

Numb with fear he stomped in a circle, pounding his fists on his thighs, issuing expletives he knew but had never spoken before. Tears rolled down his gaunt cheeks in his rage. His rage was twofold. First he would never ever get that image out of his head, but more pressing was the fact that he was now placed in a situation in which he had no desire to be. That dead person and the grass were secondary to the fact that he was now going to be the center of unwanted, unasked for attention that would undoubtedly result in hives.

SHE'S DEAD, WHO CARES?

BY RANDYE LORDON

GORDIAN KNOT BOOKS

For Henry Morrison, friend, guide, agent, and force of nature
Jack deLashmet who is no doubt making the heavens shake with
laughter
and Roberto, a not-so-secret light

PROLOGUE

Corliss Blines was always racing from one moment into the next, as if she were somehow late to live her life. This hurry was, no doubt, at the root of her memory fog. The often-repeated phrase, "Gee I don't remember that," frustrated her—perhaps even frightened her—but drove her gallery assistant, Ruggiero, to the brink. "How can you possibly conduct business when you can't remember shit?" He had finally exploded and then answered his own query. "I'll tell you how: me!"

She now kept copious notes for business.

It was not early onset Alzheimer, as she had feared. "It happens as we age," her very young doctor had assured her with a shrug and a lopsided smile Corliss wanted to slap right off the young Harvard graduate's face. But instead, she too smiled and said, "Whew, that's a relief." No need to show the rage that simmered constantly just below the surface. The entirety of her inner workings had become, as she saw it, a freak show brought to her by the sponsors of menopause: the bearded lady, the human sauna, and yes ladies and gentlemen, the elastic woman whose skin … well best not to think about that.

But now, after a lifetime of Peggy Lee's "Is That All There Is?" riffs, she had found something she wanted to savor, to take time with and relish each and every moment, not race off into the next. Perhaps that was the problem all along; there had been nothing to fully engage and excite her. Yes, she was a powerful art rep and gallerist, and yes she could walk into just about any major museum and be welcomed with open arms (oftentimes fists curled at the end, but she didn't care), and yes she even had a dog, Beanie, whom she really did like. She provided Beanie with all the expensive toys and blankies, designer sweaters and coats, a concierge vet and groomer, but she never seemed to have that *"My dog is my life"* connection with the mutt that most other people seemed to have. In truth Beanie didn't seem to cotton to Corliss either, but they lived together amicably, one wishing she's gotten a cat and the other thrilled to be out of the old lady's house from which she was rescued that smelled like urine, which would have been fine except it was cat urine.

But things were changing now. Now Corliss had a raison d'être. From now on she would, as she had been doing for the last few months, take her time and fully experience one moment before hurling herself into the next. And it felt good.

CHAPTER ONE

It had been a good run on a beautiful morning. Corliss had had a totally Zen jog, managing to block out everything except the high from her exercise, the warm air on her skin, the smell of the ocean, the wet strands of hair on her neck—chilling proof of a good workout.

She paused in her driveway, closed her eyes, raised her shoulders and dropped them several times, and then rolled her head from side to side easing the tension in her neck. Inhale. Exhale. Inhale.

But before she could fully exhale she was blindsided by a force so powerful it felt as if her body would split in half. She opened her mouth to retrieve the air that had been knocked out but it was useless. There was a moment of searing pain when the tip of the hunting knife made initial contact with her tongue, but it all happened so quickly that she barely had time to gurgle "*Oh*" before her knees buckled and she fell back into a dense row of holly bushes crowded with brambles, hawthorns and gooseberry shrubs that hid her property.

An unexpectedly perfect hit.

It was late June and the homes along the road with its breathtaking view of the ocean were not yet filled with the owners and renters. That would come July Fourth when second homeowners and entitled visitors alike would descend on the area like locust in such density that the natural beauty of the land would be momentarily lost in the influx. Only Corliss's killer saw her face shift from its normal state of haughty contempt to surprise. The executioner couldn't help but notice that death had an altogether softening effect on the internationally renowned art dealer who was nothing more than a wolf in lamb's clothing, a crook whose misbegotten wealth was built on the bones of trusting fools. Her rigid mouth was still, and her lips looked almost tender wrapped around the black, non-slip handle of the dagger.

No one would know that the last thing Corliss saw in clear consciousness was a seagull gliding overhead, wings still, a vision of grace and beauty in a clear summer sky. Just as no one would know what she was thinking when blissful unconsciousness brought her the first and only moment of absolute inner peace she was to know in this life.

When she finally departed this world it was oddly without so much as a glance back, completely unconcerned with the fifty-five years of experience she had just left behind. Even released inmates turn around to see what it looks like from the other side, but Corliss Blines was out of here in no time flat, taking with her the name of her killer and the recipe for her orange/cilantro scallops.

However, unlike Corliss, her killer was entrenched in the here and now, senses jolted into a state of hypersensitivity that was frighteningly pleasurable. This enhanced sharpness embraced all of the senses: the smell of sweat mixed with Corliss's shampoo and her fear; the taste of bile; the sound of the ocean, and the almost electrical, physical charge that zapped the killer's body at the moment the blade met Corliss's tongue and glided effortlessly to the back of her head.

The killer looked down at her slender, light body fisting the fabric of her t-shirt in one hand, holding her up, and ran a gentle finger along her left cheek with the other.

Without rushing the killer was able to get Corliss under a tarp in the back of the vehicle and cover all tracks.

Two pickups passed the driveway before the killer felt cleared to enter the road unnoticed.

One stop first but soon enough they were on Old Stone Highway, a winding road that runs through the bay side section of Amagansett into Springs. They pulled into the Old Stone Market, a deli many still called Marty's from the old days when Marty and his wife lived in half the space of the corner store. Ordering coffee, an egg sandwich, and two doughnuts, the killer lingered at the deli, engaging the woman behind the counter in mindless conversation, not wanting to get to Landing Lane before all the contractors who breakfasted at the bay had finished their coffee, read their papers and started their workdays.

If the killer hadn't lost the Cuddy cruiser in a stupid bet there would have been no problem getting rid of Corliss. A quick zip out into the ocean to toss her overboard and that would have been it. Without a boat, options were limited. But with time to plan and creative thinking the killer had devised a perfect send-off for a woman whose foundation was based on the principle, "Screw others before they screw you."

Corliss would have her ultimate send-off from the shore. Landing Lane, an indented boat launch facing Accabonac Harbor with spits of beach like Louse Point and Gerard Drive, seemed to be the most sensible place. It was surrounded by marsh with dense, high beach and cordgrass and there was one spot forty feet off the road where no one except deer would venture, and none of the nearest houses would have clear sightlines.

In truth this watery necropolis was an all-too-idyllic setting for a woman as underhanded and greedy as Corliss, but the killer—really a softie at heart—smiled at this final act of kindness.

CHAPTER TWO

A s concierge to the rich and the richer, Mary Moody's day started early. By seven thirty in the morning she had been to the gym, downed half a pot of coffee and completed her email responses.

Now as she pulled onto Further Lane with its views of the ocean, she felt a fleeting sense of well-being. Possibly the past was finally fading. Her once hectic life as a preeminent divorce attorney was solidly behind her despite the periodic calls from her old employer, reminding her that she always had a home at the firm. She had long been tired of the cut-throat gamesmanship of winning obscene amounts of money for her clients, but had put off leaving the practice until after she and Marshal were married, after they knew what kind of life they wanted to pursue. The plan had been to get pregnant as soon as possible and take a leave, but those plans had shattered, as plans so often do.

Be here now, she thought as she drove past pristine estates where caretakers lived year-round, and owners visited rarely. She shook her head, amazed at the journey her life had taken during the last three years. A journey she hadn't even orchestrated. No, this journey had been conducted by fate, friends, and fortunate finances.

First there had been the jarring discovery of finding her fiancé Marshal in their bed with one of the co-op's doormen, who was dressed like Liza Minnelli.

This was shortly followed with the epiphany that she was a fraud—how could she possibly represent anyone when she had been so blind to her own life? She who had always been so in control, the one that everyone turned to for levelheaded advice: how could she have not seen this coming?

That's when the depression set in. She lost interest in everyone and everything and spent hours watching HGTV and obscure Netflix movies. For the most part she ignored calls, e-mails, mail, and the doorbell. It was comforting. Neither family nor friends could make a dent. She kept the maid, paid her bills, went to the supermarket, and on a very rare occasion to a movie with one of her closest friends. This might have been perfectly normal for others, but the once-vibrant woman, the woman who was always at the top of her game, had faded and the stranger who remained was clearly on a bad path. If it hadn't been for her dog, Otis, she might have gone for days without ever stepping outdoors.

Then one day her three best friends—often at odds with one another—had arrived unexpectedly, all with a common goal in mind: they had banded together to bring Mary back to life. She opened the door to them in soiled sweats and no makeup. She smiled, recalling how Ellen blurted out at seeing her, "Holy cow you look just like Jenny!" Jenny was Ellen's tough sister who owned a moving business and shaved her upper lip rather than waxed. Unconsciously Mary had run her fingers over her mouth.

After making her dress to go out for dinner, Ellen Wright, her zaftig friend since high school and now a respected book publisher, peeked in her garbage and saw all the clues she needed: empty containers of cookies, ice cream, Chinese food, and wine bottles. Diane Ajam, an ex-client and renowned filmmaker, turned on the TV and found it on *Love It or List It*. Camille Logan, who had met Mary at college and went through law school with her but now made her living as a model, simply waited patiently on the sofa and watched the other two poke their noses in and out of Mary's personal detritus as if she were dead, not depressed. That the three of them had agreed on anything was nothing short of a miracle, but they had a plan, and it was a good one.

At the end of dinner Camille pulled a flimsy hat from her bag and set it on the table. Each woman then pulled an identically

folded piece of paper from their wallets and placed them in the
hat. It was Ellen who explained.

"Mare, it's like this. You can't keep on the way you are. We
all understand six months of depression, but we've decided
enough is enough. You need to take control of your life and we
think we have the perfect structure for that. Right?" She had
looked at both Diane and Camille, who nodded their agreement.
"In this hat are three very different locations, all places you love
and all places you have said you would move to if ever given
a chance. Well now you have your chance. We are asking you
to agree to our only stipulation, which is that you move to the
chosen location for at least a year, and in the scheme of things
that's no time at all, right? Right. You can keep your apartment,
rent it or sell it. If you have any concerns financially, we have all
agreed to pitch in with no expectation of being paid back. This
is because we love you and hate to see you stuck where you are.
Okay?"

"You want me to leave?" Mary asked softly.

"We want you to *move*," Diane said. "Just ... move. Start
fresh somewhere else."

"Without a plan?" Mary asked.

Camille lifted a slim shoulder and said, "Actually I think it's
a great idea. What's the worst that can happen? You don't like it
and you come back."

"But in the meantime you have an immediate task," Ellen
explained.

Diane added, "It makes you focus outside rather than in,
and that's the point. It couldn't hurt to try, no?"

After a long pause and without a word, Mary wiggled her
fingers into the hat, caught a piece of paper between her middle
and index fingers and handed it to Camille to read her fate.
Three years later life was indeed different.

Now Mary pulled into the circular driveway, parked behind
a champagne-colored Escalade and cautioned Otis, her sixty-
pound, twelve-year-old mutt, to "Behave. I'll be right back."

He raised his brows from the back seat and watched as she
strode to the front door.

She rang the bell as she tapped a reminder to herself in her cell phone: CONFIRM BRANDIN AUGUST HOTELS.

After checking two texts she realized Corliss hadn't answered the door. She rang again. The front gate had been left open just as Corliss had said it would be, but that didn't mean she was home. It was likely that she was out for her morning run, but Mary rang several more times before using the key she had been given several days earlier.

Beanie, a Corgi-Chihuahua mix came racing to the front door and skidded on the planked floor as she turned a corner. Her little face was lit up, eyes shining, and her mouth turned into what couldn't be anything other than a smile.

Mary's greeting was equally as enthusiastic, without the tail wagging and frantic kisses. She called up the staircase lined with three original Warhols.

Despite Beanie the place was as spotless as if it were a show house, not a place where someone really lived, especially with a four-year-old rescued dog. It was a stunning living room with Gio Ponte chairs and matching sofas in mushroom-colored Ultrasuede and handcrafted parchment end tables.

Beanie followed her into the kitchen with its Gaggenau appliances. As previously arranged with Corliss she found the dog's food and toys in a Tory Burch bag on the concrete countertop with a typewritten note as to feeding schedule and contact numbers for the vet and the groomer.

Mary scribbled a note: "I HAVE BEANIE," on a pad by the phone and gathered the food, toys, and small plush bed. "Come on Beanie, you're going on vacation too."

And indeed she was.

The ocean beach was empty except for another dog walker far enough away to look like the letter A in Morse code—a dot and a line. Mary Moody watched as Beanie happily ran circles around Otis and yapped as she darted under his legs when he stopped to sniff a particularly interesting piece of driftwood. That was the thing about dogs: Beanie didn't care if Otis peed on her and she would never take it personally. It was one of the points Mary made for why being a dog was better than being a person. No blame or guilt or self-castigation, no rent or bills. Of course Ellen would argue, "No thumbs," and Diane shuddered at the thought of lying on an ant hill, but Camille had the only valid counterpoint, "abusive owners."

Trying to empty her mind completely, Mary tested her memory as she walked. Each walk she did with Otis she would either go through the multiplication table, state capitals or, like today, the Morse code she learned as a child at her grandfather's side. Dot, dash is A. She had reached dash, dash dot, the letter G, when her phone rang.

She was halfway between Atlantic Beach and Indian Wells, about a half-mile walk with the ocean on one side and dunes on the other, when she noticed the dogs investigating a mound that looked like the sort of thing just meant for rolling in. She started to run toward them. "Hello? Oh! Wait." She screamed out to the dogs but only Beanie responded. Otis was too far gone, already halfway into his roll. "Damn it! Otis! Stop it!" She yanked him off the long-dead seagull and flinched away from the stench.

"Shoot!" Back into the phone she said, "Hello. Sorry about that." She had no idea who was on the other end.

"Are you okay?" It was Kate, a member of the Hamptons and Hollywood elite who unlike so many others was down-to-earth and unassuming. Just a regular gal worth a gazillion dollars.

"Ach, Otis rolled in the grossest thing."

"I hate when they do that."

Mary laughed. "And how are you today, Miss Kate?"

"I am in a bind and if anyone can help me it's you." Mary's clients, Kate and Steven, had her on a hefty retainer as a personal concierge, but in truth she would do anything for them, with or without a fee. Unlike many of her other clients—self-important, wealthy summer denizens who hire Mary and spend a small fortune to make an impression in the Hamptons—the Spielbergs were unpretentious and essentially uncomplicated. They knew East Hampton as home, not *The Hamptons* as others see it. While the eight towns that comprise the Hamptons have a plethora of celebrities, the truth is they create a billboard, like Chicago's beautiful Gold Coast hiding a large, plain city: behind the glitz of celebrity are the locals working three jobs servicing the billboard to afford the area where many of them were born.

"Okay. What can I do?" She tossed a stick into the ocean for

Otis to chase hoping a dip would wash off the seagull stench.

"I have to throw a party this Saturday at our house. Forty people. Cocktails. Dinner. Maybe live music. Something simple."

"Dance or background music?"

"I'm not sure," Kate said.

"What's the party for?"

"A Chinese developer named Zhang Xin and her family. We met them this past week and fell in love with the whole family. They're here on vacation so we invited them out for the weekend."

"Talk about a self-made powerhouse," Mary said, throwing a useless clamshell into the water. Otis was having none of it. The developer Kate mentioned was one of the most powerful women in the world, worth literally billions, but was known to be down-to-earth and devoted to her young family. "Did you know she was in Stone's movie *Wall Street*?"

"Are you serious?"

"Oh yeah. Small role. She played a business executive."

"How do you know so much about her? I'd never heard of her before," Kate asked.

"Oh, I retain all sorts of useless information. Or not so useless," she added at the same time Kate did.

By the time the call ended Mary had convinced Kate to do a clambake. "What is more Hamptons than that? Besides, it's something her kids would probably like too, and the weather is going to be beautiful." It would also make her life easier. "Trust me."

"I always do."

After the call Mary put the phone in her pocket where she discovered gold: a dog biscuit. Otis would do anything for a treat, no matter how small. She walked to the water's edge, held the treat under his nose to get him good and interested and heaved the little thing as far into the ocean as she could. It didn't go far but in his eagerness Otis threw himself into the water, soaking himself well over seagull contact point. He came out crunching.

Ah yes, the simple life of a well-loved dog.

CHAPTER THREE

Corliss's assistant Ruggiero sat on the bench outside Starbucks with his trenta caffè Americano and sighed with contentment after his first sip. It cost more than it should—more than he really had—but the indulgence was worth it for a short-term thinker such as him. He couldn't cogitate beyond the daily five dollars he put down for the coffee because if he did he would realize (as he had while doing his taxes) that the daily five became a monthly one fifty and the monthly one fifty became an astonishing eighteen hundred a year that he was spending on a simple cup of coffee a day. That was same amount he paid in rent for a small, shoddy mother-in-law apartment attached to the home of a woman known to the police and neighbors for drunken misbehavior.

Her random nude ritual dancing in the backyard might have been enough to make a lesser man leave, but utilities were included—cable, electric, phone and heat—so he shut the shades rather than look for another apartment.

His sister had pointed out that if he put the extra one-fifty toward rent he would likely find a better situation, but she might as well have been talking to a wall. Ruggiero would never consider amending his coffee indulgence. Instead, he blamed Corliss for his state of affairs: it was her fault that he was making so little money that even a cup of coffee was a hardship.

Because of her parsimony he lived in essential squalor and was unable to save for the future despite the fact that because Corliss's time was divided with two other galleries, the full weight of East Hampton fell to him. True, as his sister pointed out, Corliss covered his medical and dental insurance, but she should. And his sister's criticism that he dined out three or four nights a week? She just didn't understand. How could she? She was comfortable with her husband and their combined incomes.

All Ruggiero wanted was fair remuneration. After all it was not easy being the assistant to one of the most notorious art dealers in the country. He knew how much *she* made and how much *he* made and the divide between the two was simply not fair.

Why should he deny himself the modest indulgence of a cup of coffee because Corliss was so cheap she made her last assistant reimburse two weeks' pay when the poor girl was out for knee surgery?

"Hey," Agda Eck's bassa voice as she flopped herself next to him jolted him out of his reverie causing him to spill a drop of coffee on his Ralph Lauren chinos.

"Damn it, Agda, what's wrong with you?" He pressed a napkin to the spot on his crotch.

"Here. Let me fix it," she said as she aimed her water bottle at his lap.

"Stop it," Ruggiero slapped at her hand as he pulled a small tube of stain remover from his satchel.

"Touchy today, aren't we?" Agda laughed.

"Yeah, well you seem to be in a good mood. What's with *that?*" he asked, rubbing the stain effectively off his pants.

Agda stretched her forty-two-inch legs out and admired her worn leather work boots. She knew where each and every paint splatter and nick came from, making her shoes more like the history of her life in the last three years than a simple pair of custom-made Rufflanders.

"And you seem to be particularly cranky today." She took a long draught of her extra sweet chai latte and watched a blonde on a cellphone drag her Yorkie who was struggling to do his business while being yanked at the neck. "Hey!" she called out. "Hey! Give your dog a break!"

The woman scowled at Agda but stopped long enough so the dog could relieve himself. It was when she started off again without picking up the tiny turds that Ruggiero stepped in.

"Excuse me, Miss?" He stood up and politely pointed out that she had forgotten something.

When her response was a sigh he reached out to hand her several tissues he had plucked from his bag and said very softly, "If you don't pick that shit up and throw it away I promise you I will smear it in your pretty blonde hair." The doughy, curly-haired man held out the tissue. His smile was enchanting, the tone of his voice almost mesmerizing. How could she possibly refuse him?

"Pig," he muttered returning to his seat.

"I love when you do that," Agda said.

"You like conflict."

"Au contraire, mon ami. You avoid conflict by scaring the nuts off people. I love that."

"You like intimidation." He savored the last dregs of his coffee.

"I think I do. Especially the way you do it. With a few choice words you can turn a moment into a three-act play. Not many people can do that. Takes talent."

Ruggiero shrugged and made a face, but in truth he loved it when Agda complimented him. That this supremely talented, gorgeous, Finnish artist was his friend was one of those things that surprised and delighted him. Her name dropped in an art crowd was huge cachet but the fact that it was a real connection was testimony to his worth.

"Come on." He stood up. "Walk me to work."

She stood and towered above him. "So, the wicked witch is gone?"

"Yes," he hissed with a smile.

She nodded, draped her arm over his shoulders and stopped only to greet Eric Firestone, another local gallery owner whom they both liked.

Agda tuned out as the two men chatted. She was thinking instead about the week ahead and what needed to be done. Time was of the essence, but Ruggiero had planned well and now things were finally in motion. It was good.

CHAPTER FOUR

"It'll take twenty minutes," Henry promised knowing perfectly well that was malarkey.

"Man, I'm workin'," Tristan Cooper rarely said no to his old friend Henry Armstrong, one of the few local artists he admired and genuinely liked.

"I'll buy you lunch." Henry added some incentive. "The piece is just too big for me to install alone. I had Carlson lined up but he just bagged out."

"You haven't had a reliable assistant since Hope. I liked her."

"You did. All the more reason you should help me today," Henry sighed. There was no need to remind Tristan that he was the reason Hope, the most perfect assistant an artist could have, had left the Hamptons and moved to New Mexico.

"You ever hear from her?" Tristan asked.

"No," Henry lied. "Just meet me at eleven. You have a pen?"

"Oh, all right." He scribbled down the information. "Can you make it one o'clock? I'm in clay."

Henry paused and sighed. Finally he said, "Twelve but no later, okay? This is a quick in and out. I promise. I have a deadline tomorrow." Henry had learned long ago that making dates with Tristan always meant negotiation.

Tristan hung up without another word and stepped back from the table. While much of his work was metal and wood, he loved the sensuality of clay. He was almost ready to fire the kiln. Almost, but not quite.

CHAPTER FIVE

Diane Ajam, menopausal with twenty extra, impossible-to-shed pounds, had never imagined she would find love. True love. In her fifty-seven years she had had passion and disaster but over the past six months in reviewing her history she realized that she had never known real love. Until now.

Real love didn't catapult you into mind-numbing highs and lows; it was calming. It was solid terra firma, not sky walking. It was trust and respect. And it was still passionate. God was it passionate.

Shielding her eyes with her hand she looked out at the vista of a cloudless sky over azure waters and palm trees. Not a soul in sight. She held her breath to memorize the moment of peace and anticipation.

She slipped out of her robe, baring herself to the seductive elements, and with no disparaging thought to her form, slid into the endless pool and began treading water for thirty minutes during which time she planned for the glorious day ahead.

CHAPTER SIX

With Otis hosed down and both dogs snuggled side by side on a massive dog bed, Mary glanced at her schedule. Aside from her growing roster of clients, she was now wading through a list of gala gentry clamoring to hire her to help with their charity soirees. Of the eighty charity events scheduled for the summer, there were only two she had volunteered to work on—one for animals and another for the indigent elderly—and two she had been hired to help organize.

Coffee in hand she went to what had once been the main floor master bedroom and now functioned as her office. Five large white boards lined one side of the room: four for ongoing events since she never had more than four at a time, and one dedicated to smaller projects for her year-round clients for whom she functioned as a private concierge.

She stood at the doorway and sighed. Despite the fact that she worked with other event planners and local freelancers, there was getting to be more on her plate that she could manage.

It was, she knew, time to hire an assistant.

Finding the right person was a challenge in a job like this where the emphasis on discretion and privacy was an imperative, but in the Hamptons where one's greatest cachet was who you knew, or who people *thought* you knew: the temptation of bragging about being at Alec Baldwin's house was simply too great for most people.

She walked to the fifth white board, added the Spielberg clambake, then went to her desk where she jotted down a list of preparations for the party as she placed a call to London.

Now she would find out if her offer to the new singing

sensation, Gabby DuBois, was a crapshoot that had paid off or not. DuBois was far less likely to agree to sing at a wedding than Celine or Usher, both of whom she had helped procure in the last year, one for a Bar Mitzvah and the other an anniversary. Everyone has a price. But early in a new career DuBois's handlers were afraid of cheapening missteps, though half a million for forty-five minutes' work plus expenses was hardly cheap.

"'Lo love, how are you?" DuBois's manager answered.

Twenty minutes later Mary e-mailed the contract to England, copying Bob and Bob, the current lords of Manhattan nightlife at whose wedding DuBois had agreed to sing.

Four minutes later the phone rang and the older Bob was singing her praises. "You're like fucking Rumpelstiltskin weaving gold out of straw! Quit your day job and come work with us." He said this every time they spoke.

The other Bob was screaming in the background, "Tell her! Tell her!"

Even over the phone it was more energy than she could take before noon.

"Oh yeah," Bob said. "We were talking to Shaquille the other day and told him all about you. He has an eye on a place out there and we told him he *has* to hire you to be his guide."

"I'm not a broker," she said at the same time the other Bob called out, "Mentor!"

"Diva, whatever. We gave him your private number, was that okay?"

"Would it matter?" she asked.

"I suppose not since it's done. All right dear, we have to go boast and make plans."

The line was dead before she could say goodbye. She erased that task off the white board, stepped back and took stock.

Most daunting was the wedding for a bride brat who spent Daddy's money as if it were hers. Mary had been reluctant to take her on as a client from the very beginning, but the bride's mother, Lillian, was a friend of a friend and despite the net worth that placed them in the Forbes 500. Lillian was a good egg and funny. Funny was always good.

She wandered to the windows and watched the birds at the

feeders. Red-bellied woodpeckers, blue jays, cardinals, titmice, catbirds, wrens and chickadees all fed, circled or waited their turns at the feeders while the mourning doves ate whatever dropped to the ground and the robins splashed in their baths.

Transfixed by the birds and the lush colors of the peonies, freesia, and honeysuckle, she gave a silent thanks to her trio of friends, Ellen, Diane, and Camille.

It was because of Di and Camille that Mary had created a new life for herself in the Hamptons as the premiere concierge for the rich and famous. It had started so simply. One day Diane was complaining that she wanted her car detailed before she returned to the Hamptons from a shoot in Europe and Mary, having nothing to do at the time, had offered.

"Don't be ridiculous." Di had dismissed the offer.

"What's ridiculous? I have nothing to do. My house is finished. I might as well be useful."

"Mary, that's something I have staff do. It's demeaning."

"So pay me. Fifty bucks."

"Absolutely not."

"A hundred."

Here Diane paused and Camille had jumped in. "You can hire her at a rate of one-hundred and fifty dollars an hour and if you like we can put her on retainer as your house manager."

From that point on Mary simply listened to the two women negotiate what was to be the start of her new career.

Now she had a long list of clients and Diane had turned out to be her "charity case," as Camille put it. She did a range of services that assured the uninterrupted flow of her clients' lives while they were in the Hamptons. She was like a modern-day Dolly Gallagher Levi from *Hello Dolly*, who could arrange anything. But because of her connections *and* her legal acumen, she had created a much more lucrative niche and name for herself. Arranging to have Beyoncé perform at a wedding had started the ball rolling. As a result she had become the go-to girl when folks with too much money wanted a creative means of proving it to their friends and acquaintances.

She glanced at the clock. It was time to start arranging Kate and Steven's party.

She placed a call to Purdy, the king of clambakes. She knew it was early enough in the season for the short-notice business to be welcomed.

Within half an hour the menu was planned, the logistics sketched out, and they had agreed that at such short notice it would be best to do the event at the sprawling house with its enormous lawn rather than at the beach.

Next, the music. She called Nancy Atlas, a sexy local musician whose group The Nancy Atlas Project was nothing short of kickass. Nancy had opened for Suzanne Vega, Paul Simon, and Jimmy Buffet, just to name a few headliners, and she was open to doing private gigs. She would be perfect for the Spielbergs. However, it was likely that she was already booked for a Saturday three days away.

And she was. However, her gig didn't start until ten that night and Mary was asking for an early event. She sweetened the substantial pot of gold by inviting Nancy and her family to the party, since there would be children Nancy's kids could play with. With other local unpretentious luminaries with children, like the Seinfelds and the Stephanopouloses, sure to be in attendance, Mary knew it was a good mix.

After that she called a caterer she knew who wouldn't be offended that she was just asking for a bar set-up and four waiters. Everyone needed work and the added impetus that it was for a high-end client made it more likely that they would say yes. Which everyone did including the rental company, the florist, the valet and the babysitter.

Amazing. It was not yet ten thirty and she had arranged everything for the event. She would call Kate later in the day to give her an update. Considering what they were paying her it had to at least *look* as if it took time to arrange.

She heard the tapping of puppy nails on the wooden floor as Beanie entered the room following a big yawn. Mary couldn't help but smile and take a moment to give Beanie a good body scratch, after which the puppy contentedly went to the office dog bed and settled in.

After entering everything in her laptop Mary made notes on the fifth white board and studied her day ahead. Aside from meeting an artist at Diane's to receive a painting and a late lunch with a potential new client, she pretty much had the day to organize her summer schedule and maybe put an ad in the *East Hampton Star* for an assistant.

She was changing clothes for the workday when the phone rang.

"Hey." Diane's voice sounded as if she was next door and not in Alaska scouting a site for her next film.

"Hey to you. You sound chipper for what, six in the morning for you, is it?"

"Oh, yeah."

Mary thought it was odd that Diane was scouting sites herself and not leaving it to her usual location team, but when she had asked about it she had been reassured that Diane wanted to see it for herself.

"So," Mary paused. "How's Alaska?"

"Cold. Have you met Henry Armstrong yet?"

"No. We talked a little while ago and we're going to meet at noon. He's going to drop off the work at your house and hang it for me."

"I thought I arranged for you guys to meet at the Living Room," Diane said referring to a local Swedish restaurant where she knew Mary could take Otis.

"It's not a date, Di. Its business and it makes more sense to meet him at your place. This way he can hang it when he delivers it."

"Huh." A huge sigh filled Mary's ear. "He's a nice man, Mary. You should be nice to him."

"That's a nice idea," Mary said.

"It's time and you know it."

"Time for what?"

"You know perfectly well what it's time for."

Mary remained mute. Only she knew how far her distrust of others had gone. Marshal's betrayal had had an effect she never could have expected and she couldn't seem to shake it. For the last three years she had only offered the most superficial part of herself to newcomers, not allowing herself more than an arm's distance connection. It was easier that way.

"You should open yourself up to love, Mary."

Mary's silence was deafening thanks to the tinnitus she had developed since leaving the din of the city.

"Or at least to getting laid," Diane said with a laugh.

Mary rolled her eyes. In truth she missed lying beside someone in bed but couldn't imagine it. She knew she would recover. Someday.

"Have you found what you're looking for?" Mary changed the subject and put the focus back on Diane.

"What do you mean?" she asked.

"Locations."

"Oh, yeah. A few." Diane then countered with, "How's business?" They often played ping pong like this, neither one wanting their private lives to be the center of the other's attention despite their friendship which had seen them both through hard times.

Mary told her about the upcoming event.

"No pigs this week?"

Mary laughed. "The Royal Dandies! You have to admit they're cute."

"They were pigs!" Diane had razzed her about babysitting for three tiny piglets, to which Mary had grown much attached.

"Mo, Larry and Curly." Mary chuckled. "Did I tell you their owner had to build a separate little house on the property for them? It seems they were given a diet by the breeder that was meant to keep them small, but it would have killed them. So the vet told her what to feed them and now they range from one hundred and fifteen to one hundred and fifty pounds!" Mary laughed. "They're still adorable."

"Right. With their own little mansion on the ocean. And you think Corliss is odd."

"I never said that. Where did that come from?"

Diane was known to stir a pot just to get a rise out of people.

Corliss had come to Mary through Diane. Di and Corliss seemed to have forged an unlikely friendship, which baffled everyone since Diane was socially gregarious and Corliss sullen. Diane was corpulent and Corliss was a stick of gum with lips.

"When are you picking up Beanie?" Diane evaded answering.

"She's here. Look, I have to go."

"Call me after you meet Henry," Di yelled into the mouthpiece.

Beanie followed Mary into the kitchen where she opened the sliding door so the dogs could wander in and out at will while she was gone.

It was a beautiful day. The sky was perfectly clear. She lived in a place where she could leave the house unlocked and the back door open for the dog. She loved what she did, which changed every day. Yup. All in all, it was a great life.

She gave each dog a treat but as she got to the front door they were fast at her heels, as if to say, "There is no way you are leaving without us."

And they were right.

CHAPTER SEVEN

"Henry?" Mary said as she opened Diane's front door. Standing before her was a tall, lean handsome man with a mischievous twinkle in his dark eyes.

"Mary?" The lilt in his voice was most definitely English.

She nodded as she looked slightly up into his eyes, which meant that he was at least six-three, a good four inches taller than she.

"How very nice to meet you," he said. "I've heard a great deal about you. Diane is a real fan, I should say. And lord knows you have quite the reputation out here. Good, I might add."

Mary pursed her lips into a tense smile. If a fix up was Diane's intention, she thought, she could have done a lot worse. Henry was indeed a cut above the norm at a first glance.

"And you're the artist," she turned the focus on him.

"Guilty. I have the piece in my car."

"Right, and I'm the chump who offered to help him deliver it." The gravelly voice came from a man with a thick head of tousled grey hair who stepped into view. He had been standing off to the left of Henry on the expansive veranda.

Startled, Mary laughed and said, "Hello, Chump."

"Name's Tristan. Tristan Cooper." He nodded once, offered a crooked, endearing smile and extended his hand, which she shook.

"Please. Come in," she said, shaking off the thought that Tristan could have been a model for Frederick Remington. It was easy to imagine him in chaps, spurs and a worn Stetson.

"Thank you," Henry said. "I'm glad you changed our meeting place. This makes more sense."

"Yes, well, I think my old friend was trying to play matchmaker and thought the atmosphere at a restaurant would feel less work-like. I'm sorry."

"Don't be. I'd say she might have a knack for it."

When Mary didn't respond Tristan jumped to Henry's rescue and said, "Yeah, right. And I'm your chaperone, Angelica."

Mary looked confused until Henry quickly explained, "Juliette's nurse. Tris and I have an ongoing game of who can stump who with Shakespeare."

"Who's winning?" she asked.

"I am," they said in unison.

"So whose house is this?" Tristan asked as he followed the leader into the house.

As Mary led them through the foyer and down a hallway to the study she gave Tristan a quick overview of Di, whose films he knew, and her having been introduced to Henry's work at a mutual friend's house. "She's becoming an avid art collector, fell in love with his work and the rest is history."

When they entered the study, Otis struggled to get up to greet the newcomers and Beanie sat wiggling with delight.

The men divided, Henry greeting Otis and Tristan Beanie.

"Are they yours?" Henry asked.

"He is. I'm puppy sitting for her. That's Otis and she's Beanie."

"As in Redding?" The end of the sentence lilted upward.

She nodded. "When I first got him as a puppy the song 'Sitting on the Dock of the Bay' was playing so I named him after Otis Redding."

"One of my favorites." Henry glanced down at Otis. "Come to think of it they look a bit alike."

Mary laughed and asked if they wanted coffee.

Tristan accepted the offer and Henry asked, "Is tea too much trouble?" He looked up from where he squatted with both dogs.

"I'll only be a minute," she said, already headed out the door.

"Oh man, she's hot," Tristan said when they were alone. He flopped down on one of several club chairs and swung his legs over the arm of the chair.

"Yeah, well do me a favor *this* time, bugger off." Henry said and gestured to Tristan. "Come on, man, sit right."

"Fuck you," Tristan smiled as he complied.

After Henry had taken a tour of the room, surveying the books; an Oscar for directing an oddly funny film about dying; the artworks, and the gaping hole where obviously his piece was to hang, Mary returned with a tray that had a little something for everyone. Coffee. Tea. Dog biscuits.

"Have you worked with Diane long?" Henry asked.

With surprising ease Mary told Henry and Tristan how she had met Diane when she was an attorney and represented her in her divorce, how the friendship had grown and how Mary had come to live on the East End as a concierge. She surprised herself opening up so quickly, and chuckled to herself as she offered Henry more tea.

"Well personally, I am thrilled that Paris and Chicago remained in the hat." Henry's smile was beguiling.

"Well, *that* was a nice little fairy tale," Tristan said setting his empty mug on the tray.

"You think?" Mary asked, strangely attracted to his bluntness.

"I do. Classic pretty princess meets boy, loses boy, and strikes out on her own *but* with a touch of elegance. You could be played by, I don't know, maybe Julia Roberts, but she might be too old," he added as means of flirtation. "Now, as great as this has been I don't know about you guys but I don't have all day. Can we get this sucker hung?"

It was an easy installation and the abstract piece looked as if it had been on the study wall forever, the rich colors almost embracing the cozy space.

"This is her favorite room. She'll spend hours enjoying this," Mary said, studying the piece.

"Do you like it?" Henry asked, feeling a little anxious.

"I do," she said, not moving her eyes from the canvas. "I don't normally like abstract work, but this feels as if it has a soul. And passion."

He let out a silent sigh. Henry believed that at the core of every artist is an intricately woven pod of insecurity and hubris. He was among the lucky few who could say he made his living, and a good one at that, from his work, so he tried not to care if the occasional cretin didn't like his art. But every now and then it mattered. Apparently, it mattered with Mary.

"No question the boy has talent." Tristan had always admired Henry's work. It was what had initially brought them together as friends.

"Oh," she issued softly as she stared at the work.

"What?"

"There's someone I want you to meet. Do you have a minute?" She glanced from Henry to Tristan and back again.

"Sure," Henry said casually, knowing perfectly well he had a deadline looming for shipment tomorrow.

Tristan sighed and nodded.

Taking a side door from the kitchen Mary led Henry, Tristan and the dogs along a fragrant stone path lined with mature magnolia and hydrangea trees, under a bower of wisteria vines, and past a carpet of vibrant wildflowers. The path led to the first of two tiny guest houses Diane called the cabañas, always emphasizing *ya* at the end of the word.

Parked in front of the cabaña in a small, graveled drive was a battered blue 1980 Ford pickup truck.

Mary opened the door and stepped back, allowing Henry to enter first, wanting to see his reaction.

"Wow," Henry said when he entered and saw an armoire that covered the entire east wall. It was enormous and the first thing to which the eye was drawn. The exquisite workmanship was awe-inspiring. Despite the size of the crafted wooden piece it wasn't overwhelming.

Tristan practically bumped into Henry because he, too, couldn't take his eyes off the work.

Studying the piece from left to right it became immediately clear that the artisan had created a story with every line and detail in the carving.

"Beech wood?" was the first thing out of Tristan's mouth.

"Birch and beech," answered a man Henry had not noticed and still did not turn to because he was taking in the artwork before him.

After a long pause Henry said, "This is magnificent." He

finally turned to the unimposing man in cream-colored overalls and a hot pink tee-shirt. "Did you do this?" he asked.

"Yes."

Henry offered his hand. "I am in awe, sir, of your talent." Despite the formality of the words, Henry's humble sincerity was clear.

The carpenter, a compact man with wide cheeks and onyx-colored, almond-shaped eyes, had an easy smile.

"Henry, meet Paulo the master carpenter. Paulo, this is Henry, the painter I was telling you about. And this is Tristan."

Paulo's wide smile revealed large white teeth, one framed in gold. "Thank you," he said as he firmly gripped Henry's and then Tristan's hands. "You are Tristan Cooper?" he asked.

Tristan nodded.

Paulo brought his calloused, stained hands to his mouth and bent his head. "I follow your work," he said to Tristan. "And I am honored you both like this. Just a few more finishing touches and I will be done."

Mary watched as the three men fell into an easy conversation about the work and what had led Paulo to his art and East Hampton.

Three men so very different from one another and yet two of them—as different as night and day—intrigued her: the good man and the bad boy. One could actually be a relationship and the other a passing fling. Like they would both want her, she chided silently. It might be way too soon for a relationship, but a fling, now that was a distinct possibility. Oh for God's sake who was she kidding? She wasn't ready for any relationship other than work. She shook her thoughts away and reengaged.

The young carpenter had come to the States from Peru one summer to visit family. He met and married Lina, who had lived in East Hampton most of her life and was a citizen. Together they had a beautiful little girl, Paulina. "My wife made up the name by combining ours." He lifted a shoulder and tried to suppress a smile.

"I think it's beautiful," Mary said.

"Yeah. Right?" Tristan tucked his hands in his pockets. "I mean, what if your names were Harold and Sonia? Christ, she could have been named … *Sold.*"

"Or Hania, which is beautiful, too," Mary added.

"Speaking of family, I am sorry but I promised my daughter I would chaperone her class field trip to Long House," Paulo looked like a stump in a Sequoia forest, a full foot shorter than everyone else.

"Ah, from one art to another. The art of nature," Henry said offering his hand. He knew the Long House well as did every other artist on the East End. The sculpture garden and home of textile designer and crafts collector, Jack Lenor Larsen, is a hidden gem open to the public in East Hampton. "I look forward to following your career, Paulo."

"Thank you." Paulo beamed and nodded as he shook Henry's hand, then Tristan's. As he was hurrying out the door he told Mary he would come back after the field trip and clean up from his morning.

When he was gone Henry shook his head as he studied the armoire. There was artistry in every single stroke of the knife or chisel. "This man has been touched by God," Henry said, not taking his eyes off the work. "Not that I am what you would ever even remotely consider a religious man, but talent like this—even with formal training—doesn't just happen." Henry stood for the longest time his arms crossed over his chest and said nothing.

"Yuh, nice job," Tristan said threading an unlit cigarette between his fingers like a baton. "How'd you find this guy?" he asked Mary.

"He worked for a contractor I had hired to do some work on my house. One day he had brought lunch when all the others had gone out. We got to talking and I noticed he was carving a flute for his daughter. It was beautiful. So when Di talked about this project I immediately thought of Paulo. Then Diane's friend, Corliss Blines,—" Here she turned to Henry. "—the same woman who introduced your work to Diane, negotiated the contract."

The men shared a barely discernible glance.

Tristan grunted.

"She hasn't seen it yet," Mary added.

Tristan's cigarette snapped mid-twirl. "Damn it," he said as he picked up the pieces from the floor.

"I should like to be friends with him," Henry said glancing down at Tristan.

"I'll give you his number," Mary promised as she walked them to the main driveway.

She extracted an envelope from her back pocket, which contained Henry's sixty-thousand-dollar check for the artwork. "Sorry it's folded," she said as she handed it to him.

"Thank you." He slipped the envelope into his pocket. "You know my mother raised me to celebrate accomplishments large and small. And I should very much like to celebrate this, but alas," he shrugged and pushed his mouth into an exaggerated frown, "I can think of no one other than you with whom I would like to celebrate. Will you join me for dinner? If nothing else, we should do it for Diane."

She liked the way his eyes crinkled around the edges when he smiled.

"I'd like that," Mary said. "When?"

"Tomorrow?"

"Oh, I can't. What about Wednesday?"

Two long days away. "Wednesday," he repeated as if he didn't know. "Yeah, that should be good. Do you know Dockside in Sag Harbor?"

The very local Sag Harbor restaurant that occupied half of the American Legion Hall was one of her favorite spots.

"I can see you do. Good. Then Wednesday at seven. That way we can still catch the sunset." As he shook her hand it struck him that she was nearly as tall as he, a rarity among women. He could actually look her straight in the eyes without having to bend his head. And such beautiful brown- and gold-flecked eyes too, framed by a fringe of wispy bangs. All this went through his mind until it was obvious that he was holding her hand a moment too long. She gently slid her hand out from his and looked at Otis who was simply sitting beside her minding his own business.

"Nice meeting you, Tristan," she said shielding the sun out of her eyes with her hand.

He had the passenger door open and as he slid on a pair of Ray-Bans he said, "Oh I'll see you again, Miss Mary. You can count on it." With that he slipped out of sight into the car.

"Well then," Henry said, "Wednesday?"

"Wednesday." She stepped away from the car.

CHAPTER EIGHT

Justifiable homicide.

The phrase was in the back of the killer's mind all day like a calming mantra. Justifiable expunged culpability. Homicide was an end result that could be squarely placed at Corliss's feet.

At 4:28 that afternoon came the profound understanding that this justifiable homicide gave the killer some control of destiny.

Whatever doubts or fears that had arisen throughout the day in the aftermath were now quelled.

And it was good.

CHAPTER NINE

When Henry left, Mary called Diane to tell her the painting looked stunning. Diane's spirits were surprisingly high, considering she was alone in Alaska.

"So what did you think of Henry?" Diane asked.

"He's very nice," Mary said.

"And cute. And talented. *And* rich. Did I mention that? The man is the whole package. And he's *tall!*"

"We're going to have dinner together this week," Mary told her.

Diane squealed with excitement. "I knew it! I should hang out a shingle as a yenta. "

"It's just dinner," Mary cautioned.

"Yeah, yeah. A dinner *date*. When was the last time you had dinner with a man who wasn't a family relation, close friend, or a client?"

Mary covered with, "Don't be ridiculous," but in truth it had been years. Her first date with Marshal had been at Dovetail, which then became *their* place. He had even proposed to her there. She shook her head to clear the cobwebs where he was still an unwanted resident.

Mary easily flipped the conversation back to Diane, where it stayed until they ended the call a few minutes later.

She checked the time and knew she could either take Otis and Beanie for another walk before her next meeting or drop them off at home. Normally she would take Otis along with her. He was content to stay in the back of the car—a second bedroom to him where he was happy to snooze and wait for Mary.

But with Beanie along there were no guarantees that there

would be peace in the car. She would take them home.

This was a no-brainer.

Apparently so was her lunch date.

At Pierre's restaurant Mary sat across from her prospective client, a frail looking, neurotic clothing designer who had just bought a house in Sagaponack and was out for two days to close on the property; a three-acre spread on what was once part of a potato farm.

The woman seemed to have no mind of her own. How she could have created a multimillion-dollar enterprise was beyond Mary.

"What time do people have dinner out here?" the woman asked over espresso as her eyes scanned the empty Bridgehampton French bistro as if she might spy someone of import.

"When they get hungry," Mary answered, knowing perfectly well what the twit meant.

"No, darling, I mean people of *significance.*"

"Well, Jerry and his wife like to eat at six, Steven at seven, Jack insists on an eight o'clock seating and Betsy, well she doesn't eat at all. Loring, unlike everyone else, likes to wait until nine." She made it up as she went along, using generic names that could be someone famous in the area, but she had been thinking of Jerry Jacobs, her accountant, and Steven, a fabulous physical trainer in the area.

"Loring who?" The woman leaned imperceptibly closer.

Mary put an index finger to her lips, lowered her eyelids, and shook her head slowly.

The woman nodded contemplatively, as if she knew precisely who Mary was referring to. "Well then I think you ought to make me seven-thirty reservations. Here," she dug into her Judith Leiber bag and pulled out an envelope. "Here is a list of dinner reservations I will want in July. I'll get August to you in a week."

Mary stared at but did not reach for the paper. She had been very clear that this was a preliminary screening and the painful forty-five-minute lunch was about all the time she wanted to spend with this woman. She folded her hands in her lap and said, "Patricia, I don't think I am the right person for you. I can recommend someone in Montauk who might better serve your needs."

It was if she had been slapped in the face. "Montauk? Montauk is like ... like *tacky*! I don't understand."

"This is going to be a very exciting time for you and I think you need someone who can give you the time you deserve. I am afraid with my schedule I won't be able to do that."

"But I simply *have* to have you," the woman blurted, all semblance of composure lost. "If it's money, well, money is no object."

The waiter discreetly placed the check between the women. Patricia picked it up and glanced at the total, $57.56. She then tossed down three twenties, and dismissively told the waiter to keep the change.

Mary acted as if she had not seen the transaction, but she had, and she knew that in fact money was very much the issue for this woman. It defined her. She was like so many others Mary had once felt she had to work with. Now Mary was able to pick and choose her clients. This Botoxed, tightly wound, high-maintenance nightmare did not make the cut.

"I told *all* of my friends that you are working for me. You can't do this. We had an agreement." Her clipped words spat like little pellets.

"We had an agreement to meet, and we have." Mary slipped a card out of her bag and slid it over to Patricia. "I suggest you call this woman. Trust me; she's just what you are looking for." Mary stood, took some bills out of her wallet, and handed it to the waiter as he passed. "Thank you," she said to him, making up for the insult Patricia had left in lieu of a tip.

"Your reputation is *ruined* you, you ... giant," the woman hissed through gritted teeth.

Mary smiled and said, "It's a chance I am willing to take. I wish you the best, Patricia." Without a glance back she left the restaurant and a fuming Patricia, who she knew would call the woman on the card, a woman who would have ample warning from Mary of what to expect. However, the thick-skinned local Montauk connection was accustomed to nouveau riche divas and added a hefty sum for what she called the PITA—pain in the ass—fee. It would, Mary knew, work out for everyone.

She walked the length of Bridgehampton Main Street and passed storefronts that were mostly furniture and real estate, a few restaurants and a number of blonde, slender, already tanned clone-women wearing over-large sunglasses.

Paces from her car a voice called out, "Mary! Hey! Mary!"

She turned and saw Charlie, architect to the stars, standing in the middle of the sidewalk with a Cheshire Cat look on his handsome, if pudgy face.

Dear Charlie was bigger than life with an endless supply of stories that always left you laughing. They had met at a banker's bizarre dinner party in Shelter Island where the host was unveiling his new Charlie-designed home to two hundred guests. The banker's invite sent to his white guests said they must wear black, to his black guests that they wear white and to all others black and white. He wanted to create a visual image that would be nearly as striking as his new home.

Mary had worn lime green and Charlie pink. They immediately became fast friends.

"Whoa, girl. Where are you racing to?" Charlie asked, kissing the air next to her cheeks.

"I am racing *away* from a nightmare." She mentioned the designer.

"Oh my God, I met her!" he shrieked. "The woman is ca-razy. She actually thought she could get a landscape architect to redesign her property for under five. I mean *really*. What is she, a pahper?" He said pauper like the true boy from Boston that he was.

"Okay, what's with the ascot?" Mary asked fingering the silken scarf of gold and blue wrapped around his neck.

"Oh my God you should see this with the smoking jacket. To die for." He sighed. "I dunno. Felt like dressing up for the day."

Mary stepped back and took him in from head to toe, from the ascot to the wrinkled pink Oxford shirt designed with little blue whales, the baggy khaki shorts and flip flops. Charlie held out his hands and did a graceful pirouette.

"Lovely, yes?" he asked.

"It boggles the mind that a man who looks like this can create the most subdued and beautiful modern architecture I have ever seen. You look more like you'd create something akin to Gaudi on acid."

Charlie hooted. "Don'tcha love how deceptive a costume can be?"

After several minutes an elderly couple came up and swept Charlie away to their lunch date.

As she neared her car her phone rang.

It was Camille, who said, "You're not going to believe this, but I just signed on for a last-minute gig in the Hamptons. Can I stay with you for a few days?"

"Oh my God yes! When?"

"In a couple of days. It's just one afternoon at some estate. Haute couture. A designer is having a private show for one of her clients and select group of friends."

"Ew," Mary said.

"I know, but it brings me to you. Pick me up at the bus?"

"You bet." Mary was thrilled they'd have solo time with together.

"Okay now that that's settled, what's new?" Camille asked.

The response kept them on the line together long past Mary's arrival home.

CHAPTER TEN

The locals in the Hamptons have a quiet sense of ownership that excludes the weekenders or the summer renters whose sense of entitlement would be funny if it wasn't so often ugly.

Geography, history and wealth have combined to create the lure of the area and the impact of the breathtaking beauty one takes away with them, even the cynical. People talk about the natural light that has lured artists here since the 1800s, but unless you have seen it, especially in late October, you can't understand it. One hundred miles separate the Hamptons from Manhattan, but it is a different world; a place where at night the sky is a light show glutted with stars, the constant rolling of the sea creates natural background music and the towns, when not infested in the summer, are as quaint and slow as a Rockwell illustration.

Each group complains about the other but they are inextricably tethered. Extract one element and it would cease to be. The wealthy, the tourists, and the locals have a common investment.

However, at just about any deli in the morning you can find a gaggle of reps from all walks chatting amicably over coffee as they wait for their breakfasts with newspapers tucked under their arms.

Outside Brent's Deli a small clutch of people were smiling in the warm morning light stalling before their day ahead. Two splintered off to their cars parked on the side of the building.

"Hey, how you doin'? I haven't seen you in a while."

"Right, not since before Christmas. I have no complaints. You?"

"Come on, how do you complain on a day like this? Life is good."

They talked for a few minutes as they stood by their cars. Just before leaving, the driver of the Toyota said, "Saw you on Further Lane the other morning. Good for you." A knowing wink. A quick good-bye.

Both cars pulled out of the small parking area and headed in opposite directions.

But several miles later on Old Stone Highway as the blue truck pulled into Landing Lane, the killer punched the dashboard and let out a litany of loud expletives.

CHAPTER ELEVEN

As Mary pulled into a parking space in front of the Dockside Bar and Grill her phone rang. It was the second time during the day that Diane was calling, which was unusual when she was traveling.

"What are you doing?" Diane asked instead of saying "Hello."

Mary responded in kind. "Diane, are you okay?"

"Yeah, why?"

"Because you're calling a lot. What's up?"

There was a long pause.

"Di? You there?"

"I'm fine." But it was clear that she wasn't. "It's just … work."

"Is there anything I can help with?" Mary could see through the window that Henry was already at the bar talking and laughing with several people. She relaxed and studied him as she waited for Diane to address the real reason for her call.

"No."

Mary waited. Even from this distance, her eye would have been drawn to Henry, who stood out in a crowd.

"Is it the scouting?" she asked.

"No."

"Maybe you should come home early," Mary suggested gently.

"I dunno." Pause. "Say, I've been trying to reach Corliss. Do you know if she got off all right?"

Mary made a face at the phone. Really? "I don't know. I suppose so. She's on vacation, Di. She probably turned off her phone," she said tersely, wanting to be with Henry. "Look, honey, I have to go. Come home."

Diane finally said, "Yeah, you're right. Good-bye." And without waiting for Mary's response, she was gone.

Though she had met him when she was wearing jeans and a t-shirt, she was now in a black Calypso cotton and silk tank dress, her bare shoulders covered with a turquoise cashmere wrap. When Mary walked into the restaurant Henry's face lit up and she remembered her grandmother once telling her, "When I saw your grandpa's face light up on our first date I knew he was the one for me." Mary pushed aside the thought yet couldn't help but wonder what her own face revealed, because her smile was irrepressible.

The brightly lit eatery was a local gem that visitors in search of the Hamptons scene often discount because it is housed in the American Legion Hall across from the marina. Visitors expecting glitz around every corner are often disappointed with the casualness of the area, not realizing that a place like the Dockside is in some ways a more authentic gauge than the various nightclubs that change names and ownership from summer to summer.

Dinner with Henry wasn't like a date at all. The prerequisite scattered moments of silence in a first date were abandoned to laughter and sharing of food, an undisturbed flow of words back and forth and a bottle of wine.

She learned that he had settled in East Hampton years earlier and had once been in love with a fiery Portuguese woman named Deluca who lived with him for three months and when he was away on business had disappeared with three of his paintings, leaving only a note that simply read *Sorry*. He was the youngest of three siblings in a very close family, most of whom were still in England, but he saved the best for last. He handed her his phone.

"That's Gert," he said, beaming. "I'm adopting her from ARF. I've been walking her for a few weeks now but I had to wait until one of my deadlines passed, which it did this week."

You would have had to be dead not to melt at her soulful eyes looking up at the camera with a greying ginger-colored face.

"Oh Henry, she's lovely. She's a senior?"

"She is and she's mine. Or I'm hers. I pick her up tomorrow. I didn't want to take her today since I was going out tonight and, well as silly as it sounds I wouldn't want to leave her alone her first night, even though she would probably just sleep."

And that was the moment Mary melted.

Henry's moment had come much earlier when a friend and local interior decorator tried to horn in on their dinner when she recognized Mary Moody, a contact she could use. Mary knew a hundred women like the decorator—human kudzu in the Hamptons—the women who squeeze out sphincter smiles and wear unconvincing patinas of sincerity, all the while oozing false confidence.

When the woman pulled up a chair and poured from their bottle into her empty wine glass Mary said, "I don't mean to be rude but Henry and I are enjoying a private dinner. Perhaps we can all get together some other time."

The simple honesty left the decorator dumbfounded. Despite her rage at having been summarily dismissed, she recovered, knowing she would want to use Mary at some point in the future, and as graciously as she could she left them alone to return to her friend at the bar, another leaf in the kudzu.

"That was bloody brilliant," Henry whispered when the interloper was safely at the bar.

"You were telling me about the piece you sent out this week," she said, not missing a beat.

Henry was smitten.

After dinner they walked to the end of the wharf, where he kissed her.

They fit perfectly in one another's arms and while the sensation of being held made her heady Mary pulled away, took a deep breath and placed her hands gently on his chest to create a fabricated distance.

When neither of them spoke, she took his hand and they started back to their cars.

"Gert has asked specifically to meet Otis," he said.

"She did?" Mary linked her arm through Henry's.

"It was the last thing she said when I left today."

"Well then, they must meet." She considered suggesting dinner for the next night, but caution mushroomed like a monolith shooting up from nowhere and stopping her short. "I have a busy few days and then Camille comes out. Shall we all get together for a dog walk when she does?"

"I would like that." Henry said, trying to sound cool, feeling disappointed for the wait but giddy like a schoolboy that she wanted to see him again.

At her car Mary turned and said, "I had a very nice time tonight. Thank you for dinner."

He held her two graceful hands in his, brought them to his lips and said, "I like you very much, Mary Moody. And I am looking forward to getting to know you." That said, he released her hands, nodded and walked to his car.

As they each drove off they shared one thought. Maybe, just maybe this was the one.

CHAPTER TWELVE

June and Esther had been friends since the kids—now all in their fifties—were in diapers.

In the wake of the years there were three husbands, two divorces, three lovers (four if you include the weekend lesbian tryst—not with each other), one breast cancer, five weddings, too many funerals, one freak accident that cost June her sense of smell, and one hip and two knee replacements.

"Looks nice," June said indicating a new lighthouse folly in Esther's front garden by the hearty red knock-out roses.

"Peter put it in," Esther said striding toward her friend.

"He's a good kid." June had always favored Esther's eldest. "And the roses are amazing."

"I know. Even I'm impressed this year," Esther glanced at the vibrant wall of color.

"Which way?"

Esther upped her chin indicating the right where the houses thinned out exposing bay views.

The street was empty as the two old friends started on their daily neighborhood constitutional. They had gone about three blocks when Esther stopped and asked, "Jay, do you smell that?"

June sniffed and shook her head. "No. What?" Esther knew perfectly well that June had lost her sense of smell after a nasty spill in the blizzard of '96.

But Esther didn't answer. Instead she wrapped her arms around herself and slowed her pace walking another ten paces. She then stopped. "I want to go home," she said, making an about-face.

"Esther. We're just getting started. Come on, let's go." June didn't move.

"No. I don't like the way it smells," Esther said, continuing home.

"What does it smell like?" June had caught up with Esther and was again at her side. "You know I can't smell. What is it? Septic?"

"No."

"Fertilizer?" June kept up with Esther's increasing pace.

"No."

"Insecticide?"

Esther shook her head.

"Well what? What? My cooking?"

"Yeah, that's it. Your stuffed peppers." Esther kept her gaze straight ahead but managed a mirthless smile.

"Very funny."

"I know," Esther agreed, glad to change the subject. But it was too late; the smell had entered and was snaking its way through the cerebrum, into the cerebellum and squeezing the medial temporal lobe. She could already feel the headache starting.

A block from home it was clear to June that Esther was going into a spiral and there was nothing other than time that would stop it. Something had triggered the past. But what?

CHAPTER THIRTEEN

Had it not been for endangered eelgrass Corliss Blines might have rested undisturbed for months. But a tall, slight man with an enormous passion came upon her body just forty-eight hours after her submersion.

The Nature Conservancy member had been tracking the growth of the deliberately planted eelgrass for ten months, pleased that this crop seemed to be taking, unlike others in the past that had fallen to the warm water temperature.

It was all quite by accident. By horrible, horrible accident. The conservationist discovered what he first mistook to be a bag of garbage. Swearing under his breath at the carelessness, no, filthy ways of lazy pigs that use the bay shoreline as a dumping ground for their discarded lunch, condoms, beer bottles, and whatnot, he grabbed at a black plastic bag with two slender fingers and a surprisingly long thumb.

The heft stunned him. Good God, this could crush the life out of the tender grasses. What was wrong with people? Did they care so little about the planet that…

He let out a stifled scream when he realized what he had between his fingers. The plastic bag was barely covering something horrific. Jumping back, he tripped over his own feet and fell bottom down into the still, cold water onto the very grasses he was trying to protect. Flailing, his heart pounding, he stumbled with great difficulty out of the water, tearing out the grass beneath his waders.

Numb with fear he stomped in a circle, pounding his fists on his thighs, issuing expletives he knew but had never spoken before. Tears rolled down his gaunt cheeks in his rage. His rage was twofold. First he would never ever get that image out of his head, but more pressing was the fact that he was now placed in a situation in which he had no desire to be.

That dead person and the grass were secondary to the fact that he was now going to be the center of unwanted, unasked-for attention that would undoubtedly result in hives.

He had to think. *Think, think, think!* The word ricocheted inside his head as he slapped its shell with the heels of his palms.

Here was a man who relished anomynity. Given an option he would have probably chosen to be a piping plover and not a human at all. But in his self-defined role as steward to endangered plant life he had to make a decision; to inform the police, knowing they would destroy his beloved vulnerable grass, or leave the body and let someone else come upon it as he had.

His body felt as if its entire contents had turned to electrified mush. He grabbed a towel from the back of his car and set it on his seat before slipping behind the wheel as if the vehicle could protect him.

He needed time. Suddenly cold, he needed warmth. He needed to get out of here before someone else saw him and mistook him for the killer.

"Oh dear God!" he whispered as the heater warmed the already warm car. "That person was murdered. Of course they were murdered. There was no head," he hyperventilated and then repeated, "Oh my God," over and over as he put the car in gear and pulled out of the lot.

His feet and legs were itching from the water trapped in his waders and he panicked at the idea that bacteria was nibbling at his digits. The fear of losing one of his perfectly shaped, long, delicate toes made him speed through the lane to Old Stone without a thought of hitting a deer or squirrel or chipmunk.

"Dear sweet Jesus, this is not fair, not fair at all. How could this happen to me? You had to go and check on the grass today?" He derided himself. "Just ignore it. Pretend it never happened." He took a swipe at the windshield which was fogging from the moisture and his heavy breathing. "But what if they find your tire tracks? Or your footprints! What if you left evidence behind that would point to you having been there? Oh God, and what did I do to that sweet grass?"

Again tears streamed down his normally pale cheeks, now reddened with anxiety.

"Just calm down. Get home. Shower. Have a cup of tea and think about what to do. *You* didn't do anything wrong so stop acting … guilty. Because that's what you're doing you know, you're acting guilty."

And so for the next twelve minutes, the time it took to drive to his small but neat home which he owned outright since his mother's passing in September, he debated what to do and why God should see fit to have placed him in this situation.

If Mother was alive he'd talk to her about it, but now there was no one. He knew what she would say; she'd tell him to mind his own beeswax. *"Let someone else deal with it."* He could hear her voice as clear as a bell. *"The last thing you need is to be brought into someone else's business."*

But he was afraid.

"Son, there is nothing to be afraid of." Her familiar monotonic exasperation filled his head.

He couldn't get the sight of the headless body out of his mind. Eyes open or closed, it was all he could see. And then he realized … it was a woman!

"I told you son, a woman will be your undoing."

He pulled into his driveway and as he walked from the car onto the pristine grass lawn, to the safety of his house, he clamped his hands over his ears, trying desperately not to hear Mother's admonishments.

He couldn't know that old lady Mitchell who had lived across the street for the last thirty years was watching his odd behavior from her living room window. She shook her head and clucked softly. "Well, it's finally happened." She sighed. "Over the edge. Crazy as a loon." She took comfort in the fact that once again her prediction was spot on.

CHAPTER FOURTEEN

Corliss's assistant, Ruggiero, held the check in his hand, leaned back in the Aeron chair and smiled. So many pretty zeros. Even one-third, which was his share, still provided more than he had made in a single transaction ... ever. While Corliss cultivated clients and artists it was Ruggiero who did everything else from the paperwork to the crating and shipping of the artworks. When she opened the Florida gallery a year ago, making it the third gallery in her growing enterprise, she had finally given him the account books to keep with her oversight. From there it was a short step to finding a way to dip into the till without being noticed.

He pulled out the calculator for the fifth time and after tapping happily at the keyboard he again studied the display of his take. Nine years' worth of trenta caffè Americanos. He chuckled and lifted his gaze to the front door of the gallery that rang in a newcomer. It was Tristan Cooper, one of Corliss's original stable of artists. In fact, one of Tristan's pieces held the honorific place of display in the huge front window.

"Mr. Tristan," Ruggiero said, slipping the check into his pocket and the calculator into the table drawer. There was nothing as gauche as a desk at Gallery CB. It was stark white save for the antique English chestnut table, the black chair, a straight-backed guest chair and the displayed artworks: twelve canvases and four sculptures, two of which were Tristan's. "How are you?" he said, lifting his chin in greeting as he rose.

"Not bad, not bad," Tristan sauntered in as if he owned the place. He made it a point not to look at *his* work, but rather the canvases. "Nice," he said nodding to a work by another local artist, Jerry Schwabe, of purple trees sandwiched between green and blue landscape. Tristan studied the piece which was unlike Corliss's other more abstract pieces. "Very nice," he repeated rocking back on his heels.

"One of the nicest guys you'll ever meet," Ruggiero said as if he was friends with the artist whom he had met once briefly.

"Yuh, I know Jerry. We've known each other for years." It wasn't a lie exactly. They had both been a part of the Hampton's art scene for years and even hung at Ashawagh Hall in Springs several times together but there is knowing, and then there is *knowing*.

Ruggiero admired much about Tristan as an artist but didn't like the whole *I'm-a-Hemingway-manly-man-man* swagger. "So, what's up?" Ruggiero asked with hopes of getting this putz out of here so he could go to the bank. "Corliss isn't here," he added.

"Where is she?" Tristan asked now taking in the other artworks.

"She's on vacation." Ruggiero sighed, silently adding, "as if it's your business."

"Really?" He was surprised. "She never goes on vacation. Where'd she go?"

Ruggiero shrugged. "I have no idea."

"Come on man, that's bullshit," Tristan chuckled. "You're her right hand and you don't know where she went?" Tristan flopped onto the Aeron chair and leaned back hiking his clay caked heels onto the table. "I don't think so," Tristan sang the taunt sweetly.

"Well I don't. And get those nasty things off my desk."

The two men locked eyes and much to his credit Ruggiero did not look away.

Tristan scraped his heels off the desk and said, "Look, I'm here for my check. It's been three months, Ruggiero, and I know you be the keeper of the strongbox. Time to pay up, my friend." He crossed his muscular arms over his well-chiseled chest and straightened to his full height.

"You know only Corliss can sign checks, Tristan. She'll be back in a couple of days."

"When?"

Ruggiero flicked a piece of invisible lint off his sleeve and said, "Next week some time."

"I want my money," Tristan gave each word equal emphasis, as if veiling it as a threat would make any difference to Ruggier, who had absolutely no power whatsoever in the gallery.

"I'll let her know."

"You do that."

When the door closed Ruggiero exhaled.

"Asshole," he muttered as he locked the door. He needed to get to the bank before it closed. Should he go to the one across the street or the other branch on Pantigo where they didn't know him so well? It was a big check to be cashing but he knew it would clear.

He tucked his phone in his pocket and decided that considering the size of the check it would be best to go where they knew him. He figured a moment of flirting with the teller Iesha—who didn't seem to understand his orientation—would ensure a seamless transaction.

But he was wrong.

The discretion he had hoped for was not to be. Apparently banking laws regarding check cashing are very specific. The teller Iesha directed him to the assistant manager who pulled in the bank manager, which made him the center of attention he very much did not want. He could cash the check as long as his personal account could cover it—which was a joke. He could deposit it in his own account and withdraw the cash when it cleared, but that completely defeated the purpose. He could deposit it in the business account, which was out of the question. The more they discussed his options the more frustrated he grew until at the end of the confab he left the bank feeling like Lou Costello at the end of "Who's on First."

However, once out on the street with a few good gulps of fresh air he considered that what he learned in the bank might have been worth the annoyance.

He called Agda and explained the situation. "I'll pick you up and we can go to your bank," which is exactly what they did.

With the check deposited to her account and Ruggiero's cash commission safely in his satchel, he suggested she buy him lunch at the American Hotel to celebrate.

"Don't you have to go back?" she asked.

"She'll never know," he said as he opened the passenger door to his car.

A truer word was never spoken.

CHAPTER FIFTEEN

Dogs run up into the dunes all the time; it's what they do. And some dogs return with unearthed little treasures like a deer leg, or a feral kitten, fish parts or chicken bones left from sloppy partiers.

But Ernie, a four-year-old treeing cur, a breed known for their hunting skills, was the first to surprise his owner with a discovery so grotesque as to be riveting.

The famously unflappable doyenne of a local fishing dynasty and proud Ernie owner growing, ever frustrated at his refusal to come when called, followed the bad boy up into the dunes where he proudly pranced toward his owner with a peace offering: a human leg or, more precisely, calf.

Not one to relinquish such a tasty morsel without a fight, his owner took the moment, grabbed his collar, leashed him and continued into the dunes where she found Ernie's little heaven on earth and the reason he had dropped the leg for her. Sticking up like totem poles growing out of beach grass patches were two arms without hands, and one leg sans foot.

Ernie strained against the leash to get back to the land of limbs but his owner, for the very first time in her sixty-six years, let out a scream so visceral she scared not only the local wildlife but Ernie who broke free and made a mad dash back to the beach.

CHAPTER SIXTEEN

"I'm sorry it took so long to call but you are a genius," Kate exclaimed about the clambake as Mary waited outside the Huntting Inn on Main Street for Cam's bus to arrive. Originally owned by the Reverend Nathaniel Huntting and his wife, the place is a tired beauty that is home to the Palm Restaurant and an inn with twenty rooms.

The Spielberg party had been a huge success. Mary had been there at the start and the finish and knew that this was one of those parties people would always remember fondly because of its simplicity. Well, that and the fact that it was at a beachfront estate owned by one of the century's most brilliant directors and his talented wife, with a guest list of political and entertainment luminaries. Mustn't lose sight of reality, she reminded herself as Kate continued to praise her until Mary ended the call to field another from Annabelle.

Clients like Annabelle, inescapable in the concierge business, really need babysitters and not high-priced professionals to mediate their lives.

But Mary had time because Cam's bus was late.

Otis looked longingly out the window, eyeing the pachysandra that blanketed the brick walkway of the inn where he and every other dog liked to mark, but Mary was not swayed. She would not let him sully the beauty of the grounds where literally thousands of pink tulips that lined the path to the inn and the intricate, old cherry tree at the end of bloom, its base softly rimmed with fallen petals, created the very vision visitors expected from East Hampton. It was a breathtaking billboard for a tired building.

She listened to Annabelle Norton, whose father had bestowed upon his only child a fortune from scrap metal. The girl was in a snit. The initial call, which Mary ignored, had come in at six thirty that morning. The pressing matter that had driven the entitled heiress to tears was that she wanted a waiter at Nick and Toni's fired for rudeness.

"What did he do?" Mary asked, having fielded calls like this before from Annabelle.

"You *know* I can *only* drink Keurig coffee, right? And I am a *very* good client there, right? I spend a fuck load of money there, right? Well they don't have it! How is that possible? And the waiter was this snotty fat bastard I want fired. He actually had the audacity to suggest I have coffee at home!"

Mary rolled her eyes as she listened to Annabelle rant. Her first instinct was to remind the heiress that people were starving and she was a pathetic brat. She took a deep breath. Next would be to scratch Annabelle from her client list. But Annabelle was young enough to still learn that the world didn't really revolve around her, so she said, "Annabelle, think about it. I want you to take a deep breath and tell me do you really want to take this man's livelihood away from him because he suggested an alternative that made sense? He didn't have what you wanted. There was nothing he could do. He is simply a waiter there, not the owner. Do you really want him fired?"

She waited as Annabelle considered this.

"Yes," she mewled. "He made me look like an idiot in front of my friends."

Mary had known Annabelle since the young woman was ten during her parents' contentious divorce, in which Mary had represented her father. That was eleven years earlier and Mary had somehow fallen into the role of mentorship for the girl. Now the young billionairess had hired Mary to oversee the details in her life. Mary was one of the few people who could confront Annabelle without too much scarring.

She said nothing.

"I know what you're thinking and it's bullshit," Annabelle finally said, losing steam.

"What am I thinking?"

"You're thinking I made an idiot of myself, not him."

Mary smiled. If Annabelle could realize this there was hope that the spoiled rich brat could grow.

"Do *you* think that?" Mary asked.

"No." Annabelle whined.

"Really?" Mary laughed gently. "Annabelle, honey, you know it's not the waiter's fault. I'll talk to Toni and see if they can accommodate a machine there, which you will pay for and keep stocked. But no one out here has that in their restaurant. Why do you insist on repeating this same scenario? You're just calling bad attention to yourself."

"I am not."

"Yes you are. Think about it." The bus pulled in front of her. "Oops, I gotta go. Do something kind for someone today, Annabelle, it'll make you feel better."

"I hate you."

Mary's laughter ended the call.

Mary got out of the car to greet Camille. An old man with a cane and shoes too big for his feet was navigating the bus steps. Camille, who had once modeled in an Alexander McQueen fashion show where she made walking in six-inch heels on a flooded runway look easy, gently helped the old man steady himself. She wore Levi's and a white tee-shirt and her eyes were hidden behind sunglasses, but she still took Mary's breath away.

"Girl, I have missed you," Camille said as she embraced her old friend. Camille was Mary's only female friend who was even taller than she by an inch.

"You have no idea," Mary said as they hugged. "You look fabulous as always."

"I am exhausted. I might just stay here for a month!"

Mary grinned and knew if there were any of her friends she could live with for a month it would be Camille. They had lived together in college so the easy pattern was always there.

"You up for a dog walk?" Mary asked.

"Does the devil wear Prada?"

They went directly to the Springs dog park. It had once been a twenty-two-acre nursery and was now a fenced-in puppy playground with a path that looped the circumference.

It was like stepping into the eighth wonder of the world, with an assortment of beach grasses, wild thyme, wildflowers, holly, rhododendron, and Russian olive trees all creating pockets of fabulous sniffing spots. All of this was fenced in with a ten-foot cyclone fence to keep the deer out and the dogs in.

When Mary and Camille arrived they watched in wonder as a hawk taught its young how to hunt. Both women were stunned when after a dive into distant grasses the hawk rose into the clear sky with its prey struggling in its beak.

"Oh my God, that was a bunny!" Camille cried out.

"No, no it wasn't. It was a rat," Mary said, convinced it was a chipmunk, which would also upset the citified Camille. "Come on," Mary said threading her arm through Camille's. "Let's walk."

"I met Ellen's new beau," Camille said when they stopped in the back pasture, a mown green lawn, and threw a ball for Beanie, who Camille had fallen in love with at first sight. Otis was busy butt-sniffing other equally curious dogs as scattered dog owners sat on benches or milled about in small groups.

"She actually introduced you to him?" Mary feigned shock. Her childhood friend, who had been part of the felt hat quorum to decide Mary's fate, rarely introduced the men she was dating to Mary, Cam or Di. She had a myriad of excuses but it all boiled down to insecurity.

"I know. I think I was a stand-in for you. He's a really nice guy. The absolute yin to her yang. He's mellow...."

"She's not," Mary filled in.

"He's quiet...."

"She's not."

"He's chubby...."

"That's great!"

"I know. They're a really cute couple. They look like two little Weebles together. What about Diane? Have you heard from her?" Camille asked.

"A few times. She doesn't sound good."

Entering a second round on the loop after Mary had filled Camille in on Diane's whereabouts and calls and her dinner with Henry, her phone rang. She watched as Otis enthusiastically sniffed the bottom belonging to a sweet, goofy twelve-year-old Pug named Olive.

It was Henry.

"As much fun as I had with you the other night, I officially have myself a new best girl."

Mary stopped and smiled. "You got Gert!"

"Seems like eons ago already," he caught himself mid-chide. "I did and she has asked to meet you."

Mary pointed to the phone and mouthed "dinner?" to Camille, who nodded. "Why don't you come to my place for dinner and bring Gert. My friend Camille's here."

"Ah, a chaperone for Gertie and Otis. Good choice. I would love to."

Mary gave him her address and they agreed to meet at seven.

"Okay, update time," Camille said as they slowly rounded the final loop with Beanie in the lead and tired Otis a good twenty paces behind.

CHAPTER SEVENTEEN

The cigarette pack was nearly empty. She counted how many were left: four. "Three," she said aloud to no one as she slipped another into her hand. "Seventeen and it's not even dinnertime."

Diane shook her head in disgust as she tried to light the end of the cigarette, making it a moving target. Twenty years without so much as a puff, and poof, it all goes up in smoke. She chuckled sadly.

She studied the canvas of pink-and-golden sunset before her and poured herself the last dribbles of the champagne she had bought to celebrate love.

She took a hard drag and muttered, "Fucking bullshit." She polished off the bubbly and smoked. She had waited five days. Five long days. Either something bad had happened or she had been dumped again. Either way it wasn't good.

She tossed the cigarette into the bottom of the flute and clumsily rolled off the chaise. As much as she didn't want to do it, she knew she had to be straight with Mary since she was the only one who would be able to help her. Every time she had called her this week it was with the intention of asking for help and every time she had backed away.

After a long search she found her glasses, squinted at the display on her phone, forgot for a moment what she was doing and then remembered, which had an almost sobering effect.

"Mary. Mary. Mary," she repeated as the phone rang. She flopped down on the oversized, cream-colored sofa and held her breath. She would not cry. Pretend its business. Pretend it doesn't matter.

But even as a high priestess in the movie industry, an industry devoted to make-believe, she knew this was one time she couldn't pull the wool over anyone's eyes, especially her own.

CHAPTER EIGHTEEN

Gert was a seven-year-old golden-lab mix who had been brought to ARF six months earlier when her owner died.

Otis, Beanie, Mary and Camille were smitten at the first introduction. Mary fell for her soulful eyes and Camille for her goofy long face. Gert was obsessed with Henry but when Otis showed interest it was clear that a new friendship was about to blossom. Beanie seemed unaware that she was second fiddle and happily went about making rounds from dog to person to dog to person. Camille scooped her up and gave her a hug.

During dinner Otis shared his big bed with Gert and Beanie and the three cuddled together as if this was the most natural thing in the world. Mary envied dogs their ability to simply be.

But she wasn't doing too badly herself: it had been a long time since she had not only been attracted to a man but felt so at ease. Henry was comfortable with himself, which made this new attraction feel uncomplicated. No doubt she would impose that later. Ah, the human condition.

Over dessert the phone rang, disrupting the calm.

The answering machine kicked in and she heard Diane's voice. "Mary." Long pause. "Mary, please pick up." And then what sounded like a sob.

Mary raced to the phone and took the call in her office.

The look on her face when she returned said only that the evening had come to an end. Henry thanked them for a wonderful dinner and at the door said, "I don't know what's wrong, but if you need me, I'm here for you. Okay?"

"Thank you." There was the briefest moment of awkwardness when she considered kissing him good night, but instead she bent down and kissed the top of Gert's head.

"Lucky dog," Henry said as he pecked Mary's cheek with a fleeting kiss before leaving.

"What?" Camille asked before Mary could turn around from closing the door.

"Diane's not in Alaska."

Camille waited.

"She's in St. Croix. Seems that Corliss was supposed to meet her there but she never showed."

"Diane and Corliss?" Camille's brows arched into a question mark.

"Apparently so."

"And she waited this long to tell you?" Cam asked.

"She's convinced she was dumped but wants me to make some calls and see if I can find out whether Corliss made it to the flight or chose to go elsewhere." This meant calling in some stiff favors because the daunting task was not one easily accomplished.

"When does Di come back?" Camille asked, clearing the table.

"Tomorrow."

"Go on. Do what you have to do. I'll take care of this," Camille said loading up the last few things into the dishwasher.

Mary's first call was to Ruggiero to see if Corliss had been at work.

In his own inimitably snarky way he assured Mary that Corliss was on vacation.

Three hours later Mary learned that Corliss had never gotten on the plane.

"Now what?" Camille asked as she handed her friend a cognac.

"It's too late to call Di with bad news. Hopefully she's sleeping it off."

"She was bombed?"

"And smoking." Mary opened the back door and Beanie shot past her to the fenced-in yard, followed by Camille. Otis stretched slowly and finally joined them on the patio.

"Did you know they were a couple?" Camille finally asked.

Mary shrugged. "I think I might have suspected but honestly I didn't care so I didn't even think about it."

The two women sat in silence watching the dogs scout out the perfect place to do their business in the brilliant light of the full moon.

Camille looked up at the cloudless sky stippled with stars. "When I was a little girl I always thought stars were holes in the sky and that the light that shined through came from a whole other dimension."

"American Indians used to believe that the stars were portals through which the dead could watch the living."

"Is that true?"

"Who knows? I read it somewhere. It's a concept."

"A creepy one if you ask me. When I die I either want it to be over or to move on to the next adventure. The idea of watching life seems a little like torture."

"Right; like reality TV," Mary smiled.

"So, what do you think happened?" Camille asked.

"Got me. But it's an uncivilized way to break up with someone, don'tcha think?"

"Better than you and Marshal."

Mary laughed. "Yeah, but one day mine will make a funny story. This one would just hurt."

"What do you mean *one day*?" Camille laughed. "Baby, that story was hysterical from day one."

"Really?" Mary seemed genuinely surprised, which only made Camille laugh harder.

"Think about it. Liza Minelli?"

Despite herself Mary couldn't help but smile, then chuckle and nod. "I get it. Yeah, I suppose it is kind of funny."

But there was no stopping Camille's infectious laughter until finally the two of them were gasping for air with tears running down their cheeks.

When their laughter died out Mary said, "But not showing for a vacation? That's bad."

This, for no apparent reason at all, got them started again into a new fit of laughter and another round of cognac.

CHAPTER NINETEEN

The conservationist was deeply unhappy in his indecision. It had been days since he had discovered the body and still he had not called the police. Every time he reached for the phone his mother's cautions overwhelmed him.

"Someone else will find it. Busy yourself with something else."

She was right, he knew. Eventually someone else would find it and he could be done with it all. But his trip to the bay this morning had done nothing to allay his fears. It was still there, still looking like garbage. You would think the trash collectors would have noticed it but people are lazy. God forbid they should cast their eye beyond the radius of their designated pick-up.

What the hell was wrong with people? Were they so wrapped up in their own microscopic worlds they couldn't see what was right in front of them?

He was different, he knew. He was choosing not to engage in this because it was none of his business. Garbage collectors were in the business of removing trash and this was their job. Lazy fools.

Surely people walked their dogs along this stretch used mainly for launching boats and kayaks, of which there should be many this time of year. Local workmen often read papers in their trucks as they ate their lunches looking out onto the bay. Schoolchildren were brought in groups to study marine ecology. And apparently some used the location regularly for coitus given the disgusting used sexual debris littering what had to be a favorite spot.

It was not a place most vacationers would visit unless

brought there by a local company to kayak or paddle board. It was off the beaten track, but the conservationist thought a dog would have found the body by now.

Perhaps one had. Perhaps the body was being eaten by passing carnivores. Crows. Disgusting creatures they were, too. Or seagulls.

The thought made him shudder.

He rose so abruptly that his teacup went flying across the table and he broke down into racking sobs, as he did when his mother died when they had been watching *Chopped*. One minute she had been making fun of a finalist in the dessert round and right in the middle of her sentence, she simply died. He would never forget it. "That fatty girl's gonna—" and that was it.

He had looked over at her and saw that her chin was resting on her chest and the Fig Newton cookie she had been eating had fallen to the floor.

A small handful of his conservancy acquaintances, as he could call none of them friends, had gone to the funeral, along with old Mrs. Mitchell from across the street who was, he knew, only there for something to do in her otherwise boring life.

He staggered to the counter and grabbed a towel to mop up the spilled tea. The unabsorbency of the cheap towel exacerbated his frustration and he snatched up the teacup that had been his mother's favorite and threw it against the wall, shielding himself from the rebounding shards.

His body trembled with unaccustomed rage. Without thinking he reached for the salt and pepper shakers shaped like ducks that his mother had anthropomorphized to the point of giving them names: Pete and Sarah. Pete was the first to go, hurled through the air with a force the conservationist didn't know he had. Sarah's demise came when he slammed her to the floor.

He was just getting started. With absolutely no control over himself he went through the house, wreaking utter destruction on his mother's porcelain figurine collection, her velveteen images of Christ and Elvis, her eyeglasses, her entire bedroom from drapes to lamps shaped like colonists on horseback, her romance paperbacks, and her beloved collection of ersatz

Wedgewood boxes. At the end of the conservationist's frenzy he stood in the midst of the slaughter and took a deep breath.

He waited. After a moment he stood slightly taller. Nothing. His breathing slowly returned to normal and still he waited for her voice to belittle him, to shame him for his feelings and actions.

The realization that she was really gone had a profound effect. He actually smiled. Slowly at first, but it grew to the point that by the time he had broom in hand he was whistling. There were no regrets that she was finally, in his head, dead.

As he cleaned the aftermath, tossing other beloved items he had missed in his rampage, he wondered if the dead person in the bay had been like his mother, a stifling tyrant who sucked the life out of her son and replaced it with fear. What if the dead body had been hers and the hand that had caused the death had been his?

The more he cleaned the more he came to identify with the killer. What if they had been pushed to the point of no return? What if after years and years of trusting a selfish liar they had finally broken and lashed out with such force it ended in death? Might it be justified? A life taken for a life wasted?

By the time he had emptied her room of everything except the furniture he had come to a decision.

He loaded his car with the detritus of her life and went to the dump.

CHAPTER TWENTY

Cam had already left for the shoot by the time Mary returned from her early morning walk with Otis and Beanie. Barely in the house, she called the caterer with whom she was working on Missy, the brat bride's, wedding.

"I've been looking for an alternate space," Mary said as she gave each dog a treat. "Mulford Farm is just too small with the expanded guest list." The 1680 Farm is on East Hampton's Main Street and limits weddings to 200 people. At this point the wedding was now up to 300.

"I *need* a head count," the caterer said.

"I know. I looked at a house on Georgica Pond that would fit the bill. The interior is over ten thousand square feet and it sits on eleven acres. It's on the market—if you want to buy it—but they would be willing to rent it for an event."

"Oh sure, I'll think about it," he laughed. "Look, we know we're over occupancy at Mulford so tell the little cow if she doesn't move it I would have to be out. It's illegal. Let me know."

"Will do. But let's plan it for three hundred and assume I'll be able to reason with her." Mary made coffee and checked her e-mail before calling Diane. There was no answer.

An hour later Camille walked through the front door.

"What are you doing here?" Mary asked.

"Well, I got to the house over on West End, which I found no problem, thank you very much, and there was chaos. Everyone was there, the designer, dressers and models, but the woman who was hosting the show wasn't feeling *up to it* and wanted to do it tomorrow," Cam laughed. "Then when she realized how much that was going to cost her she blamed it on the event planner insisting that she got the date wrong! I mean what gall. Can you imagine?"

"Unfortunately, yes. What did they do?"

"Well after going back and forth with this red-hot mess of a woman, they finally agreed to move the show to next week and we all left." Cam led Mary to the kitchen where she poured herself a cup of coffee.

"So you're going to be here until next week?" Mary asked with a broad smile.

"Probably. But I doubt that I'll do the show. Show? It's nothing more than a rich woman's whim. Gross. I mean it was a nightmare. I say let the younger, hungrier girls deal with that."

"Oh la grande dame is beyond that, eh?"

"Hell yeah. I paid my dues and those days are gone. The only reason I agreed to it in the first place was to have an excuse to see you."

"You never need an excuse."

"I know that. My agent got the designer to agree to pay my day rate for today, thank you. Then I told him I thought I was booked next week and would get back to them."

"Well I'm glad you're here," Mary said.

"Me too. I can tell you right now it would not have been worth my day rate to do that. However, on the ride back I had a chance to think about this whole thing with Diane. Why would Corliss just not show up and not call? I mean she can't be so ugly she wouldn't at least let Di know she wasn't coming."

"I know. But Corliss has a horrible reputation. They say she's a bulldozer on two feet. I would be hard-pressed to find two people who have good things to say about her."

"Doesn't matter. Diane seems to be in love with the woman. Besides, we all have made questionable choices in love at some time or another in our lives. And who knows? Maybe Corliss was a very different person with Diane. Maybe Diane didn't give in to her every whim and they had a good relationship. Let's face it; Diane Ajam is not the most easygoing chick in the nest."

Mary nodded.

"I liked Henry." Camille smiled as she glided onto a kitchen stool.

"Gert's cute, isn't she?"

Camille grinned.

"No, really," Mary protested, "I like the fact that he adopted a senior dog."

"You know you just might owe Diane for this one."

"Yes, I live in fear of owing Diane," Mary laughed.

Several minutes later the doorbell rang, exciting Beanie into barking, which scared the hell out of Otis, who hadn't heard the bell but now had to prove he was as watchful over the house as he had always been.

Diane was standing at the front door looking as if she had just returned from the wars. Her hair was a ratted mess, her eyes were swollen, and there were stains on her shirt. When she saw Mary, she fell into her arms and burst into tears.

Mary held her silently, letting Diane spend herself. When she finally pulled away Mary saw that her old friend had aged considerably since they had last seen one another a few months earlier.

"How did you get here so fast?" Mary gently led Diane into the house, where Diane stopped dead in her tracks upon seeing Camille. The last thing she wanted was an audience. But what the hell? It was Cam and she was safe.

"I couldn't stand it. I took a private jet to East Hampton."

She smelled of stale cigarette smoke.

Diane let herself be led to the table and said, "I'm sorry. I didn't know where else to go," as she slouched onto the chair.

Neither Mary nor Camille had ever seen Diane so deflated, not even during her divorce when Mary first met and represented her.

Mary brought Diane a cup of coffee and Camille settled in across from her seemingly beaten friend.

"Did you learn anything?" Diane asked.

Camille and Mary shared a quick glance. "She never used the ticket. That's all I know."

"Did she trade it in?" Diane persisted, reaching into her bag for a cigarette.

"I don't know. Let's go outside so you can smoke."

Diane got up and led the way, not bothering to take anything but the cigarettes and her orange lighter. Camille grabbed Diane's coffee and followed. Mary set a tiny terra cotta planter upside down on a base in front of Diane to be used as an ashtray.

"I am such an idiot," Diane mumbled.

Mary leaned back and crossed her legs. "Start from the beginning."

"I made the fatal mistake of falling in love," she groaned. She couldn't meet their eyes. She knew she was the envy of all her friends. She had a great career, two great houses one in LA and one here and an apartment in the city overlooking Central Park. She had money, friends, relatively good health and a body of work most filmmakers would kill for with an Oscar and two Emmys to prove it, but she was a big fucking loser when it came to love. Maybe not as bad as Mary, and as far as she knew Camille hadn't been involved with anyone seriously since that asshole Jonathan from Chicago, but it clearly didn't bother them. Diane wasn't meant to be single. And she believed she had the real deal this time, but no. Who would want her?

Diane stared at her hands and the thinning skin that covered them. She made two fists, pulling the skin taut as if she could pretend the aging process hadn't started: the demise of her already compromised desirability. She knew that this fatal affair was the precursor to the rest of her life, which she would live alone. Single. Lonely. Never ever trusting anyone again.

"We were supposed to meet on Buck Island in St. Croix. I rented a private villa." Diane squeezed her swollen eyelids together. "I thought we were so happy." She burst into tears; heart-wrenching sobs so antithetical to her nature that Mary and Camille both sat frozen in place.

Camille's eyes begged Mary to do something and Mary's eyes in turn asked *what?*

It was Otis who finally did something. He let out a small cry and shoved his head between Diane's legs.

Diane hung her head and rubbed Otis. She knew she had to tell them; she couldn't hold it in any longer. And very slowly, as if telling Otis a bedtime story, she revealed her history with Corliss Blines.

"The first time we met was at a Spin benefit in October.

Well Christ, I don't spin, but I figured what the fuck, it's a good cause—breast cancer. I figured if I had a heart attack there would be plenty of granola heads who would be able to save me, right? So, I got in the back row hoping to disappear and who am I stuck between but Heidi Klum and Corliss Blines. I wanted to kill myself. All these people in the room were so happy and excited and *'pumped up!'* it was disgusting. I had never seen so many white teeth in my whole life. I swear to God I figured it out that there was at least one hundred and sixty thousand dollars' worth of dental whitening in that room."

Mary was transfixed because as Diane spoke, she continued crying.

"So I start the ride thinking I am not going to be competitive because, please, look at me, do I really think I am going to compete with Blines or Klum or Jessica Seinfeld who was spinning in front of me? Jerry, *maybe*, but not her—she's in fucking great shape. They all are! So I was going at my own pace when I realized that Heidi and I look a lot alike. Seriously, if you took me and pulled at either end, you would find that Heidi and I look exactly alike. I shared this insight as we pedaled and the only one who thought this was funny was not I'm-married-to-a-funny-man-Seinfeld, or even Miss Klum, who you *think* would have chuckled, but no, Corliss Blines. Everyone else was asking me to shut the fuck up but really, it's not like this was a serious class, right? I made a huge donation and we're supposed to have fun. Diane Sawyer's group was having fun. Me? I was schvitzing and getting hemorrhoids. It wasn't until after the event was over that it even occurred to me that I didn't have to participate at all, I could, I could, I could—" She tried to catch her breath in between sobs. "—I could have just given them a check and been done with it.

"But afterwards Corliss thanked me for making an otherwise boring time so memorable. We left the benefit together and went to the Tavern for a martini, even though it was noon. I figured out a month later that I went to that farcockt benefit to meet Corliss. I am telling you we always laughed," she cried inconsolably. "We even laughed at Sartre's play *No Exit*, which we both loved."

Not knowing what to say, Mary asked, "So how long have you two been seeing one another?"

"Seven, eight months."

"Why didn't you tell us?" Mary was baffled since they always told one another everything. It was the safe place—this quartet of friends.

"She didn't want anyone to know. It was all so new for her and...."

"It was new for you too, wasn't it?" Camille asked.

Diane nodded. "Yeah but it was somehow easier for me. I knew she was the one. She isn't like anyone else I've ever known." Diane told them how the relationship had started, taking them both completely by surprise, and how perfect it seemed to be. The clandestine element only added to the excitement in one way and made it feel like an oasis in another. "Where is she, Mary?" she asked as if her friend would know. She put out the cigarette and reached for the coffee with a shaky hand.

"I don't know, honey."

Diane's face slowly screwed into itself like a baby about to howl and when she took a breath she cried, "Am I so fucking unlovable?"

Mary pulled her chair next to Diane and hugged her friend who had never before, not even after her mother died, shown such depth of pain.

After several minutes, Diane held up her hands. "Okay. Thanks." She took the tissues Camille offered and said, "I should go home. Can you call me a cab?"

Mary didn't move. "I'm sure she has a very good reason for not being there, Diane. We'll find out. I promise." This was hardly a promise she could keep but it seemed to placate Diane.

"Oh, by the way," Mary said, "The armoire in the cabaña is magnificent. I can't wait for you to see it."

Diane put down her mug and looked at Mary. "Do you honestly think a piece of furniture will make me feel better?"

"Well, I...."

"Look, I think I want to be alone. I'm going home." She rose from the table and rubbed her face. She felt old, stupid, boring and ugly. She didn't need witnesses to how she would deal with it as she had for the last several days, drinking herself to sleep with a bottle of pinot noir.

"Okay, we'll drive you home." As they walked to the car Mary said, "Di, you are a wonderful woman, and I am sure there is a good explanation."

"Really. Name one."

"Cold feet," Mary said without hesitation.

None of them knew how true that was.

As a matter of fact at that very moment Corliss's legs (sans feet) had been uprooted from their planting in the dunes like totems surrounded by beach grass and were now in Hauppauge at the medical examiner's.

In the car Mary took a call from a client who had a problem with the color of her pool, a problem that would *ruin her life*. If ruination could come with the shade of grey being two shades darker than she had imagined, Mary wondered what the woman would do with poverty or shingles.

Another call came from Henry who thanked her for dinner and asked if everything was okay. His tone was so sweet and caring but Mary could only say, "Can I call you later?"

Once at the house Mary suggested again that they look at the armoire Paulo had created.

Despite Diane's objections, the two women and two dogs followed Mary as if she were the Pied Piper.

During the short walk between the house and the cabaña, a walk fragrant with wisteria and clematis, Mary went on and on about the fabulous job Paulo was doing in there and how he might even have finished it by now.

Paulo's truck was parked out front which meant Diane would get a chance to see him.

She opened the door, looking at Diane, wanting to see her expression when she saw the masterpiece, and stepped aside to let Diane have her first glimpse of his genius.

Diane's jaw dropped and a second later she let out a bloodcurdling scream. She ran in place, pumping her fisted hands as she shrieked and bounced from foot to foot, her flip flops slapping loudly on the slate.

All the birds in the surrounding trees responded by

screeching back and taking flight. Even Otis started to trot back to the house with Beanie in hot pursuit.

At the same moment Camille's hand flew to her mouth and her widened eyes revealed horror.

Just as Mary turned, her hand still on the doorknob, a putrid stench hit her hard and she saw what they were responding to: a lifeless body was dangling from a rafter.

She too let out a short scream as she reeled back and shut the door, pushing Diane.

Diane was panicked. Her generous figure jogged furiously in place, and it felt as if she would never stop screaming to take a breath. It was Camille who grabbed her by the arms and shook her.

"Stop it, Diane!" She repeated this several times, shaking Diane, but when it had no effect she slapped her across the face.

Otis barked from a safe distance.

Diane slapped back repeatedly at Camille with both hands, missing each time, but the world was suddenly quiet, if only for a brief moment.

Diane turned on Mary. *"Are you out of your fucking mind!? Did you really think that would cheer me up!?"*

"It's not as if I put him there!" Mary yelled back.

"Well who the fuck is it?" Diane screamed.

Mary opened her mouth to respond but wasn't absolutely certain since she had only had the briefest glimpse. She shut her mouth and opened the door a crack to look inside. It was Paulo. Dear, sweet, talented Paulo in his overalls. And he was grotesque.

She quickly shut the door, trying to keep back her breakfast, and whispered who it was.

Diane had stopped screaming. Now all that could be heard was their heavy breathing and the distant sounds of landscapers preparing estates for the gentry until one indignant blue jay let out a single cry.

"What the fuck is going on, Mary?" Diane asked through clenched teeth.

Mary shook her head.

"There is a dead man in my cabaña."

"Really Diane? I thought it was a piñata." Her hands shot to her mouth and she raced to the side of the building to be sick.

"Christ. I need a cigarette." Diane turned and stormed back to the house, yanking off her sandals in the process and swearing the whole way back, with Beanie following close behind.

Camille waited for Mary. When she saw her rounding the corner, Mary's face was ashen, but she seemed okay, all things considered. "You all right?" Camille asked as she put a protective arm around Mary's shoulders. Otis joined them and nuzzled Mary's leg. She patted Otis's head and assured him everything was okay.

Mary shook her head. "No. I'm not okay. He was a great guy, Cammie. There's no way he would have killed himself. He was in love with his wife and daughter and life. I'm telling you this is insane. It doesn't make any sense. He was a good, good man."

"We have to call the police," Camille said, taking control.

"Yeah. But first we have to calm Diane down."

"She'll be okay." They started toward the house. "At least this will take her mind off Corliss." They walked back to the big house in silence.

CHAPTER TWENTY-ONE

"I thought you stopped smoking," Camille said when they entered the house.

"I started again in St. Croix." She took a deep drag and seemed to hold it forever.

Mary took the phone off its base.

"What are you doing?" Diane barked.

"Calling the police."

"Wait!" She held out her hand and hurtled toward Mary, who threw her arms defensively in front of her to ward off a tackle.

Di, who had wrangled the phone from Mary, asked with surprising calm, "What are you going to tell them?"

"That there is a dead man hanging in your cabaña."

Di thought about this for a long moment.

Camille gently pried the phone from Di's hand and said, "Di, you are understandably overwhelmed right now, but we have to call the police." She handed the phone to Mary and said, "Mare, call them. Diane, sit down." She pulled out a stool at the island and though her eyes were kind her voice was firm.

Camille and Diane listened as Mary reported the death. When she hung up they were all silent.

The fact that a man was dead only feet away seemed to have settled in like a shipwreck on the ocean floor.

Before anyone could speak the intercom for the front gate buzzed. A man indentified himself as Detective Nick Petrucci.

"That was fast," Diane said.

Mary released the lock and went to the front door to await his arrival. By the time the man with short, dark spiky hair, a

smattering of freckles and a *Mr. Incredible* jawline walked up
the steps Diane was standing beside Mary when he identified
himself.

"How did you get here so fast?" Diane asked without
identifying herself.

"I'm sorry?" Nick Petrucci looked like he had just stepped
out of *GQ*, not a police car. He was just under six feet tall,
wearing dark grey slacks and a pristine white shirt that was
open at the collar, revealing a strong neck and a tuft of dark
hair. His smile was crooked.

"We just called the police literally minutes ago," Mary
explained, stepping aside to let him in.

Nick wiped his feet before entering and looked from woman
to woman. It was a study in opposites. One was round, dark and
mature. The other, Mary, reminded him of Gwyneth Paltrow ...
a stick figure with blonde hair and moving parts.

"I wasn't aware that you had called." He waited for them to
say something.

Finally the older woman said, "We did. I'm Diane Ajam and
this is Mary Moody. Come in." With this she turned and headed
into the kitchen, a place that felt somehow safe for her despite
this insanity. It was the place she had spent the most time with
Corliss, here or in the bedroom. She shook her head, trying to
dislodge the painful thought of her lover. Lover. How could she
have been so wrong about her?

Nick Petrucci walked into the kitchen and all he saw was
Camille. She was mesmerizing with light chocolate skin, high
cheekbones and the greenest eyes he had ever seen.

After introductions all around Nick asked, "You called the
police because?"

All three women spoke at once, making it impossible to
discern any words other than "dead" and "cabaña."

He held out his hands and pointed to Diane. "This is your
house, right?" He knew that Ajam owned the property where
Paulo Vargas had been working. He was here in fact because
Paulo's wife had called the police when her husband didn't
return from work two days earlier. Nick knew that people
go missing all the time, usually because they want to. The

twenty-four-hour wait time passed and the police put out a
BOLO, be on the lookout for, and questions were asked, but they
had no leads. This morning Paulo's wife Lina showed up at the
police station in a rage and insisted they look where he was
working.

Diane said yes as she lit another cigarette.

"What happened?"

She opened the back door and said, "Follow me."

They all did, with Mary and Camille lagging behind. Otis
trotted ahead of Diane, his tail wagging high above him, the
grand marshal of the parade. Beanie made a detour into the
flower bed looking for a marrow bone she had hidden the last
time she was here with Corliss.

Diane opened the door without looking inside. She was
watching the detective, whose face changed not one iota as he
assessed the scene from afar.

"Did you enter this room?" he asked them, taking out his
cell phone.

All three women murmured no.

Mary reached down and grabbed Otis's collar to keep him
from entering the now putrid-smelling space.

As the detective spoke to the dispatcher, he carefully
studied the area around where they stood. He shut the cabaña
door, ushered everyone back into the kitchen and started asking
questions.

He started with Mary who seemed more in control than the
house owner.

"Was Mr. Vargas working there unattended?"

"Paulo was making an armoire in there. I trusted him
implicitly. There was no reason for me to be present when he
was working."

"So he had the code to the security system?"

"To the areas that he needed to access."

"The entire property?"

"The house and other outbuildings have their own security.
When he was working he would usually close the gate. I can't
say that he did that all the time. He was here a lot. It was a big
project."

What had started as a difficult day ended many hours later. The local police had to wait for the Suffolk County police and medical examiner who oversee all suspicious deaths in the county, though Detective Petrucci, who seemed accustomed to such events, thought it was clearly a suicide.

The county detective, Gabe Lasworth, was leading the investigation and obviously knew what he was doing. He had spoken to each woman individually and ultimately asked for the security tapes from the cameras.

Mary was still sickened from viewing Paulo up close. As she was the only one who actually knew Paulo, she had been asked to ID the body to save his wife the pain.

It was hideous. The once energetic, cute man was nothing more than a memory. His face had been drained of all blood and was white and grotesquely swollen. His lips were blue and the tip of his now-black swollen tongue pressed against his teeth. A deep ligature mark surrounded his neck and one eye remained open.

She pressed the heels of her hands against her eyes but it was no use. The image was burned into her memory. She was tucked into the corner of a sofa trying to find comfort in the soft embrace of the cushions.

Diane paced. Beanie followed her this way and that and back again, over and over.

Camille sat on the floor rubbing Otis behind the ears.

"Petrucci's an idiot," Mary said as she massaged her forehead.

"Why?" Camille asked.

"There is no way Paulo killed himself. The more I think about it the more convinced I am."

"That would mean that he was killed—murdered—on my property. Well, that's comforting," Diane said, still pacing.

"Maybe not, but I know in my gut it's true."

"Who would have killed him?" Camille asked.

"I don't know. I didn't know him outside of here."

"Then how can you be so sure he was murdered?" Diane asked. "I mean I live here alone for God's sake, Mary. Think about what you're saying. Oh it doesn't even matter. You've planted the seed and I'll never sleep here again. I hope you're happy." She flopped down on her armchair and let out a long, raspy sigh as she glanced at Henry's painting. Nice.

"For all you know, Mare, he could have had a very dark side." Camille, always the voice of reason, thought it prudent to try and give Diane some peace. She knew her friend well enough to know that if she got an idea in her head, she would worry it until it was in tatters. Diane's neurosis was what made her such a good filmmaker.

"Yeah." Diane took to the idea immediately. "For all you know he was bipolar. Or maybe he had a drug problem and owed someone money."

"Stop it," Mary warned. "You saw how beautiful his work was. That doesn't come from a frayed soul. That piece is delicate, almost angelic."

"Oh puleese, think Van Gogh. I know artists, Mary. They're all troubled."

"Everyone is troubled, Di. And while artists may be more in touch with their personal torments, it doesn't mean they could all kill themselves."

"I don't care about *all* of them, Mary. I care about the dead one on my property." She lit another cigarette. "If nothing else, where do you think his soul is?" When no one answered, she did. "Right here, that's where. Oh dear God!"

"No it isn't," Mary said calmly. "He's with his family."

"How do you know that?" Di challenged.

"How do you know he's not?" Mary countered. "Look, I'm exhausted and the dogs need to be fed." She got up and started for the door.

Camille followed behind, willing herself to keep quiet.

"You're going home?" Diane whimpered.

"I'm exhausted, Di. I have a headache and the dogs need dinner. It's nearly dark, they haven't been walked and while you didn't know Paulo, I did, and I am very, very sad for his loss."

"I'm afraid to be alone here."

The last thing Mary wanted was a sleepover with Diane, but there seemed to be no avoiding it. "Well let's go then. But no smoking in my house. It stinks."

"Camille, will you stay here?" Diane sounded pathetic.

"No, baby. You come back to Mary's. Go on up, pack your toothbrush and come on over when you're ready, okay?"

It was said as a fait accompli; Diane could not argue. She watched the four of them walk to the car. She shut the door and leaned against it. It wasn't fair. Damn it, life was not fair.

She opened her eyes and took in her expansive entryway where she could see into the living room and kitchen. "Listen, Paulo. If you're here I think you should go home now. We found you. It's done. Go to your family." She stepped slowly toward the staircase absolutely certain his eyes were on her. With her heart beating she raced up the carpeted steps, into the master bedroom en suite where she slammed the door. One glance in the mirror annihilated all thoughts of Paulo. She was a mess. She needed to shower. She stank of smoke. Her hair was greasy. Her make-up had long ago smeared off leaving darkened mascara shadows under her swollen eyes. "Who would want you?" She sobbed as she turned on the four shower heads.

CHAPTER TWENTY-TWO

The next morning came too soon.

Having left Otis, Beanie, Diane and Camille, Mary drove to Corliss's house, at Diane's insistence.

She found the inside of the house exactly as she had left it. Corliss's Escalade was still in the driveway, the hood cold to the touch, and her cell phone was still on the kitchen counter along with Mary's untouched note.

A chill went up her spine.

She ignored a call from home, not wanting to deal with Diane, and instead drove to Corliss's gallery.

Ruggiero was just coming up the street, coffee in one hand and his cellphone pressed to his ear in the other. He stopped in his tracks when he saw the woman in front of the gallery. "I'll call you later." He ended the call abruptly.

Though they had never met Mary was pretty sure this was Corliss's assistant so as he neared, she smiled and asked, "Ruggiero?"

The corner of his mouth twitched in lieu of a smile and his hands felt clammy as he reached into a pocket of his satchel for the keys.

"Yes?" He avoided direct eye contact.

"Hi. I'm Mary Moody. We've talked on the phone a few times ..."

He slowly released his breath and allowed himself a genuine smile though she didn't see it because his back was to her as he opened the door. "Come on in. I have to turn off the alarm," he said hurrying to the back of the space.

Mary watched as he scurried delicately across the gallery in

Alden tasseled loafers. When he disappeared behind the back wall she focused on the artwork. Jerry Schwabe's work was always eye-catching and she made a mental note to introduce him to Bob and Bob, but as she turned she nearly bumped into a metal sculpture on a pedestal. The power of the piece, however, nearly bowled her over. The base was a rough bronze cube from which several sets of arms and hands were trying to push through the box for escape, stretching so taut the fingertips appeared to be exploding. At once she was assaulted by an intensity of feelings; panic fused with grief and terror. The work was at once both compelling and repelling. She stepped back, studied it and glanced at the artist's name.

"Talented guy," Ruggiero said, startling her.

"I just met him the other day," Mary said.

"I'm surprised you don't already know Tristan's work. He's been out here forever. Even does some of his own forging on the smaller pieces. He works in all mediums and is equally facile in everything from canvas to wood crafting to stone, but I think I like his ceramics and metal work best."

"Does he sell?" she asked.

Ruggiero paused. "Tristan's work isn't for everyone," he started diplomatically. While he didn't like Tristan, he would sell cow dung for a commission. And in truth, Tristan—apart from being an asshole—was a gifted artist. "It is a very discerning collector who chooses such commanding creations. Are you interested?" He asked.

"I could be. I actually have several clients who might be interested. Do you have a catalog of his work?"

Ruggiero slipped on his kindly smile and tipped his head to one side. "Oh, I'm afraid not. Or if we do it's quite dated. Between us, while Tristan's work is undeniably powerful, the artist, I am afraid, is difficult to represent. Most recently Corliss has been selling his work in Eastern Europe."

Mary shook her head. "Well at least he's selling. Not all artists can say that."

"True, how true," Ruggiero sang. "So, what brings you here, Mary? Not that I'm not thrilled to finally put a face to the voice, but what can I do for you?"

"Actually, I was wondering if you had seen Corliss." She asked casually.

"When? Since we last spoke?" He asked. "She's on vacation. You know that. You have Beanie." Here his eyes widened and he asked, "You do have Beanie, don't you?"

"Yes. Of course."

"Good, because I'd hate to think of that poor dog alone in the house all this time." Ruggiero liked the dog almost as much as he liked Corliss, but he knew it was right to be concerned. "So if you have Beanie why are you asking about Corliss?" he asked.

Mary debated for only a moment. "I don't think she went away." She went on to explain what she had found at the house and alluded to the fact that Corliss had never made it to her destination. "She's been gone six days, Ruggiero. I think that's cause for concern." When he didn't respond she said, "I think you need to call the police and file a missing person complaint."

He laughed out loud, a sudden gust of sound that fell flat between them. "Are you *crazy*? I don't mean to be rude, but if you're concerned about Corliss and you've been poking around her house, I suggest *you* call the police."

Mary set her face to reveal nothing. Of course it was stupid of her to blurt out that *he* should call the police, she could have eased into that, but his reaction, his laughter, was vexing. "You're absolutely right, Ruggiero. I should go to the police. I'm sorry I bothered you."

As she turned toward the front door he followed after her and continued his defense. "It's just that I have no cause to call the police, Mary. You do. You seem to have what you believe is proof. Of what, I don't know. Look, not for nothing, she's an adult and worth a bloody fortune. She could have told you she was going in one direction, went the other and bought everything she needed when she arrived. I mean I'd love to help you, but honestly I'd feel like a fool calling the police because she didn't come home from vacation on time."

He was right. And Mary told him so. But despite that she couldn't let go of the feeling that Ruggiero was a snake and likely a poisonous one at that.

CHAPTER TWENTY-THREE

There are times when facing the inevitable is the last thing you want to do. Sure, you can put it off an hour or a day, perhaps even years, but there always comes the point when you are looking it squarely in the face.

It had taken time to muster up the courage, but the conservationist knew there was no avoiding it any longer. He had stopped by Landing Lane to check that the corpse was where it had been all week, like he was expecting it to get up and walk away.

White knuckling the steering wheel down Springs Fireplace Road he made a right on Cedar and pulled into the police station ready to do his civic duty. There were no more voices in his head cautioning him to mind his own beeswax. He had thought this through carefully and decided that though his grasses would in fact suffer at the activity he was about to trigger, it was only right that this woman be found and given a decent burial.

Unfolding his long body from the car he entered the station and looked about. A voice from above said, "Can I help you?"

The conservationist was a tall man, topping out at six-three when he was standing straight, which rarely. What felt like a good three feet over his head was a window cut out from a wall where a round woman leaned forward and repeated her question. His favorite movie, *Grosse Point Blank*, had a scene where John Cusack was in his therapist's (Alan Arkin's) office. Arkin sat behind his big, impressive desk and Cusack sat across from him in an armchair so subtly diminutive that the top of his head barely reached the desktop. The conservationist had actually laughed aloud at the movie's restrained, easy-to-miss humor, but now, in a similar situation it wasn't so funny.

He swallowed. His mouth had been dry as sawdust when he first entered the building but now he was fighting back the sudden onslaught of saliva. He stared up at the great Oz looming above him.

"Sir? Are you all right?" she asked blandly.

He was burdened with the choice of whether to stay or go. His straight back slowly bent with his indecision.

He opened his mouth, releasing the single word "I" several times before sealing his lips and shaking his head. He looked down at his perfect, bare toes poking out through the leather straps of his Birkenstocks and took a deep breath.

He heard her mumble something, knowing it wasn't for him, and he turned to leave.

Before he made it the five paces to the front door he felt a hand on his arm.

He turned abruptly, saw nothing, then looked down and there she was, all five feet of her, the woman from the window. Her name tag read Winnow.

Her face was kind as she peered up at him. "You okay?" She seemed to really care.

He shook his head. "I found a body at Landing Lane." It came out in one quick breath. The one sentence he had practiced over and over in front of the bathroom mirror was exhaled and no longer his responsibility.

He figured they didn't need to know how long ago he had first discovered the body, nor how close he had come to keeping it to himself. Just that it was there.

And so, as he stood there with his heart pounding, began the first real event in the otherwise dreary life of the conservationist.

The officer gently led him back to the steps and into the offices behind a door. Surprisingly, what ought to have been a tragic moment, a moment of great solemnity, had the virginal conservationist nearly heady with excitement. He would, he knew, follow the round officer anywhere she led him.

CHAPTER TWENTY-FOUR

Mary pulled into the long driveway at the Lily Pond estate of the brat bride's parents and took a deep breath before approaching the six-bedroom, seven-bath house.

Lillian opened the door before Mary could ring.

Lillian was almost as tall as Mary, but her life seemed etched on her face. It was a kind face with humor, intelligence, and unlike most other women in her circle, without surgical assistance to alter the reality of her sixty-odd years. Perhaps because of that she came across as a woman you could trust to mean what she said.

"You have no idea how glad I am that you're here," Lillian said as she embraced Mary.

The brat bride Missy appeared in the foyer, her stubby hands resting on her stubby hips sporting a carrot-hued, store-bought tan. She was not happy. In the fifteen times Mary had seen Missy she had seemed truly happy on three occasions. Other than that the girl inevitably left one with the impression that they had just spent time with an angry old soul.

Missy flipped her expensive hair out of her eyes and sighed, "It's about time."

"And hello to you, Missy," Mary countered.

"Jack said you're looking for a new venue," she said referring to her father. "You couldn't talk to *me* about this? Do I need to remind you that this is *my* wedding?"

"Missy," Lillian said firmly as she physically stepped between them. "Stop it."

"I *have* talked to you, Missy. You haven't listened. My job is to make sure you have the most glorious wedding—"

"Your job is to do as I say!" She actually stamped her stubby foot as she said this.

Both Lillian and Mary looked at her in disbelief.

Finally Lillian broke the silence and said, "Okay, we're going to sit down and go over things like civilized people. Do you understand?" she asked both women.

"Yes," Mary responded.

"Fine," Missy huffed as she turned on her heels and stomped into the enormous yet cozy living room.

Mary and Lillian shared a glance and followed.

With Mary seated in an armchair and Missy pacing, Lillian settled on the sofa and like a referee issued the rules of engagement. "Missy, I want you to listen to Mary, who has done this a thousand times before and knows what she's talking about. It is why we hired her, do you understand?"

Missy's response was a sigh.

Mary couldn't understand how Lillian could have raised such a nasty mess. Brides could always be a little anxious, but she had never come across one so very unlikeable.

Mary laid out the situation. "We're out of time, Missy. You have continued to invite people knowing perfectly well that as charming as Mulford Farm is, it could never hold more than two hundred people. Considering the number of guests now it's imperative we change the venue. I've met with a broker who has a perfect place just up the road on Briar Patch that she's holding for us." Here she pulled out her iPad and scrolled through images of the estate for mother and daughter to see. "I'd like to take you there now, but as you can see in these pictures there's ample space to accommodate more than three hundred guests. Look, we always knew we were pushing the envelope there but now it's out of the realm of possibility. If we change the location right now—today—we have enough time to make whatever modifications we need and we can make the changes seamless. As it is we're very lucky because the buyer backed out and the owner needs the money. I've also spoken with the caterer who has the rental company, waiters, purveys all at the ready to make the change. But we have to do it now."

"I actually know that house. Oh my, it's stunning," Lillian said.

"I don't see why we can't have it here," Missy insisted barely glancing at the images.

"It's not big enough," Mary said. "For three hundred guests at a sit-down dinner with a dance floor and a band, and no outdoor space, it's just not possible."

"Don't be stupid. It's only fifty extra people and this place is huge," Missy dismissed Mary.

Mary paused. She closed the computer, composed herself and said, very calmly, "Fifty or a hundred—which it actually is—is a huge number for a sit-down dinner and Mulford won't allow it. But Missy, since you know better than everyone else, I am going to suggest that you finalize the arrangements for your wedding. You have a week and the caterer's number, and he will accommodate you as best as he can, but I can assure you that the original venue will not work now. I have done everything within my power to make certain that on your wedding day the only thing you have to concern yourself with is you—which is clearly not a problem—but I am done fighting you." She stood and looked at a stunned Lillian, to whom she handed a card. "This is the broker for the house. Leah's a good woman and you should have the agreement in your e-mail since I sent a copy to both you and Jack. I'm sorry it's worked out this way but your daughter is impossible." Here she looked at Missy who stood leaning against the grand piano no one played. "I don't know what your problem is, but you have been rude to me just about every step of the way. I am trying to help you and you act as if I were the enemy. You need a venue that can accommodate you, Missy. That's it. So good luck to you, my dear. I'm done."

Without another word Mary walked to the front door and let herself out.

As she opened the car door she heard Lillian call out behind her, "Mary! Mary, wait."

Mary held out her hands. "Lillian, I'm sorry. I would do just about anything for you and Jack, but she has pressed my last button."

"I know, I know. And I don't get it. She's really a good kid but this has been a nightmare, and I know it. I don't get it, but I know it."

"Maybe she doesn't want to get married," Mary said.

Lillian looked helpless. "I don't know. She and Patrick have been inseparable since grade school. Who knows what's really going on in anyone else's mind? I mean I try to talk with her, but she just shuts me out. And it was never like that. Only since this stupid wedding." She covered her mouth with her long fingers. "Oh God, I can't believe I just said that."

Mary grasped Lillian gently by the arms and said, "Look, my job was to orchestrate and be the middleman. Right now you have the best caterer on the East Coast. His team does everything. He knows what to do."

Lillian interrupted, "But we *need* the middleman. I can't do it. Missy certainly can't do it. Look, she's a pain in the ass and I know it, but just hang in there. Just a few more days, that's all. I promise you she'll behave."

Mary chuckled.

"Okay, so I can't promise that, but we do have enough time to set up both locations, right? I mean she has her heart set on that stupid farm."

Mary stared at her. "Lillian, that's insane. Do you have any idea how expensive that is? You'd be throwing two separate weddings. As it is you'll lose your deposit when you cancel Mulford and the rental of the estate alone is *sixteen times* the cost of Mulford. *Sixteen.* That's huge. Also I don't even think we could get a second tent at this point. But we do have time to change the location for the tent we have. I'm telling you, renting both spaces doesn't make sense."

"I want her to be happy and I'm tired of fighting."

"Talk to her, Lillian. Find out what's really going on."

"Are you really quitting? You don't seem like a quitter," Lillian added.

Mary sighed. "It's a good thing I like you," she said with a half-smile. "I'm here. Removed, but here. Right now everything is in place: the rentals, florist, and musicians. Most of that is easy enough to up the numbers for, but the caterer has to order more rentals, food, plan prep time, get extra kitchen staff and waiters, and that takes time. As far as the flowers and whatever, we can always have them deliver to the final destination, whether it's Mulford or the house. Call me after you two have talked, okay?"

"Thank you."

Mary nodded and got into her car dreading her next meeting almost as much as the last: home and Diane.

CHAPTER TWENTY-FIVE

Back at Mary's home Diane sat in silence after Mary delivered the news of what she had found at Corliss's house and her meeting with Ruggiero.

"What does it mean?" Diane finally asked

"I don't know. Ruggiero said—"

"Ruggiero has no spine," Diane cut her off.

"That may be, but that means we have to file a missing persons complaint. And that would bring you into the fray. With Paulo...."

"Do it," Diane said in a deadened voice. "I don't care about my reputation anymore. Something's wrong with Corliss and I know it. I *feel* it. She wouldn't just disappear, Mary. This was the real thing." She paused. When she finally spoke her voice was calm and her pronouncement incontestable. "You have to find out what happened. Please."

"The police ..." she started to say, but Diane held up a hand.

"Are ineffective out here and you know it. They're overpaid and underintelligent. I want to hire you to look into this and I will not take no for an answer. Please." All the air seemed to leave Diane with her one final word.

Mary and Camille shared a glance.

"I don't know how," Mary said softly.

"You're the brightest woman I know. You'll figure it out." She stood stiffly and shut her eyes. "I don't care what it costs or what you have to do to make this right, but if Corliss is missing, it's not because she chose it. I have to know what's happened. I couldn't trust anyone else but you with this, do you understand?" She took a deep breath and stared at Mary before saying, "I am asking you to try. That's all. Try."

Mary's nod was barely discernable, but it sealed her agreement to do just that, try.

Diane then walked to the foyer, picked up her $15,000 Prada handbag and when Camille protested her leaving, Di promised that she was fine and ready to be alone.

"Wow," Camille said when they were alone.

"Well this sucks," Mary said.

"Well yeah, but shit, this is bizarre."

"Which part?"

Camille's eyes grew wide and her mouth drew into an exaggerated frown as she stared and shook her head. "All of it, baby. All of it. It doesn't make sense. Two people you know in two days? One dead and the other, who knows?"

"Yeah. And she wants me to solve it. As if that's possible." Mary flopped down into a soft chair and let her long legs splay out in front of her.

"Anything's possible," Camille said unconvincingly.

"Corliss could be anywhere, right?"

Camille nodded.

"But we know Paulo's dead. Right?"

"Yeah." Camille wasn't following.

"We also know that idiot officer Petrucci, you have a crush on, thinks it was suicide. But how much does he know anyway?"

"Seems to know a lot if you ask me. You are asking me, right?"

"In a theoretical way. I don't trust him. I think he acts like he knows everything and doesn't know squat. The good thing is he's only a town officer and not Suffolk County, which means he has limited say. However, that being said, I don't know anything about the Suffolk police."

"Their lead detective seems to know what he's doing," Camille offered.

"Gabe Lasworth? Yeah, I suppose," Mary sighed.

"You know you gotta do it, girl." When Mary looked at her blankly she added, "Call the police about Corliss."

Mary nodded but didn't move. Finally she said, "Don't you think it's sad that Corliss is not missed by one person other than Diane?"

"Honey, the woman is on vacation!" Camille laughed. "How many times do you hear from me when I'm on holiday?"

"But she's not."

"But nobody knows that for sure. Not even you. *Or* Diane. She can assume, but that don't mean shit and you know it. It's possible that Ruggiero was right when he said she could have gone anywhere she wanted without packing more than her credit card."

"Will you call Petrucci?" Mary asked with a whine.

"Why? I am not gonna tell him this girl is missing if that's what you're thinking. It's none of my business." She crossed her arms over her chest underscoring her refusal with body language.

"No, I just want you to find out if they still think Paulo killed himself, that's all. You can do that, can't you?"

"What difference will it make?" Camille asked

"I just want to make sure his death is really investigated and not swept under the rug."

"Would they do that?"

Mary shrugged. "Come on, Cam, his name was Paulo Vargas not Brad Pitt or even John Smith."

Camille nodded. "You could hire a professional. I know a detective in the city who's got a great reputation."

"I was thinking of a reward. Five thousand dollars for information. What do you think?"

"I think if the police have deemed it a suicide you might have some resistance. I don't even know if it's legal."

"I'm just asking for information, that's all. How could they object to that?" Without even thinking about it she picked up the phone and dialed a number by heart. In less than seven minutes she had arranged to have an ad placed in the *East Hampton Star*. She worded it very carefully, offering a reward for information leading to an arrest in the possible murder of Paulo Vargas.

After she hung up Camille said, "I think that was just plain stupid. You didn't even wait for me to call the detective. What if he had said, 'It was murder and we have the killer right here'?"

"Then I threw away a little money on a useless ad."

"Uh huh. Now what?" Camille asked.

"I *should* call the police about Corliss."

"But?"

"But I want to deal with one thing at a time. I know Paulo is dead and that his family will need help. Diane owes him money for the work, so I can give them a check without it seeming like charity. I have to offer my condolences."

"And see what you can find out?"

Mary nodded. But she abruptly stood up and yelled, "This is insane!"

"You want me to go with you?"

"Yes, please."

"You need to get a check from Di?"

"I can write it and she can pay me back."

"You sure?"

Mary nodded. "I have the money."

"Think like a lawyer. Is it better to have it come from the employer or you?"

"I don't know. But I'm not going to ask her. Jeez, Camille, she has enough to think about. She'd chew my head off."

"Okay," she said holding out her elegant hands.

While Camille went to change out of her jeans Mary called Henry.

"I've been so concerned. Is everything all right?" He asked.

Mary gave him a Cliff Notes version of her day thus far.

"Good God. Is there anything I can do?"

"I don't think so, but I appreciate the offer," she said with a smile.

"I know we're new friends, but please know I'm here for you."

"I know," she said after a short pause.

"Good. Then also know I would love to see you whenever you can. No pressure."

No pressure: it sounded lovely.

CHAPTER TWENTY-SIX

Within forty-five minutes they were en route to the Vargas house, which was just off Gardiners Lane in Springs, not far from where Jackson Pollock, Lee Krasner, DeKooning and a host of other art world luminaries had once lived in a simpler time when the real estate in the area was affordable. Springs is the home of the local working class, but what had once been $1400 for four acres was now $500,000 plus for a small house on a quarter acre.

Paulo's simple, small house was tucked tightly between two others that mirrored it but stood out from the others in the care it was obviously given. Four cars were parked in the driveway and in front of the house.

Wind chimes hung from the eaves on the tiny front porch where Paulo had hung a small swing large enough for two. Affixed to the front of the house over the doorway were four delicate yet magnificent wood carvings: a bird, a lizard, a fish, and an ear of corn.

Mary took a deep breath before ringing the doorbell.

A small, wide man opened the door and looked up at the two Amazonian women. His head thrust forward from his neck and he seemed to understand, though not a word had been spoken.

"My name is Mary. I knew Paulo. I was hoping to talk to Lina."

He nodded, still saying nothing, and left them standing at the now-closed door.

The two friends shared a look.

Several moments later the door opened again and a graceful woman with long black hair pinned up, loose strands cascading down her elegant neck, stood on the threshold.

"Yes?" Despite the fact that dark circles underscored her swollen, red eyes she was still as beautiful as Paulo had said.

"Lina, my name is Mary Moody. I was a friend of Paulo's."

Lina's face melted as soon as she saw Mary. She nodded and tried to catch her breath. When she did speak it was nearly a whisper. "He was very fond of you. Very fond." She pressed her hand to her mouth. "Please, come in." She stepped aside to let the women enter and ushered them into the living room whose central focus was an enormous plasma screen TV hanging above the fireplace.

The man who had initially opened the door was now in the dining room, his left hand cradling half a sandwich as he stared at the interlopers with distrust. Three women sat on various sofas and chairs, the eldest dressed in black, with a wide mouth that looked like a seam tightly sewn. One woman got up to offer her seat on the sofa and the third woman tried to smile, thought again, and slipped out of the room.

Standing at the archway between the living room and dining room was Eduardo, a man in his thirties whose eyes were as dark as his hair and his mood.

Lina spoke first in Spanish and then English, making the introductions. Now Mary knew that the woman in black was Paulo's mother, the two other women were Lina's sisters, the hungry man was Paulo's uncle and the angry man was Paulo's best friend, Eduardo.

They now knew that Mary had been Paulo's boss, and oddly enough no one seemed to care about Camille, who clutched a large Citarella bag filled with store-bought casseroles, soups, sweets and fruit. One of Lina's sisters took it and thanked them, despite the mother's evil gaze.

"Please, sit," Lina said gesturing to the sofa. Camille did.

Mary stood in front of Lina and said, "Lina, I am so sorry. He was such a good man."

As if friends for a lifetime both women opened their arms and fell into one another's embrace. The mother issued an indignant sigh but did not move from her upholstered throne.

As the women released their hug Mary asked, "Have you

heard anything from the police?"

Lina shook her head. "They don't care. I had to force them to look for him."

Mary nodded. "I know."

"He did not kill himself," Lina stated emphatically, with no trace of an accent.

"I don't think he did either. But can you think of anyone who would want to hurt him?"

"No! He was a man full of love and life! He had only friends."

Paulo's mother spat something in Spanish and Lina responded. "I told her you are a friend. She thinks because Paulo is gone they will try to deport her, which is just crazy talk."

"Please tell her you can trust me. I will do nothing to jeopardize your family's safety."

Lina translated, the mother and she argued, and finally the mother held up her hand and hissed, "*Suficiente*." Then the old woman clasped her hands in her lap and bent her head, as if in prayer.

Lina took Mary into the dining room where they sat and spoke in hushed tones.

"Was there anyone Paulo had had any kind of run-in with?" Mary asked.

When Lina shook her she said, "I have been going through this over and over and over trying to think of everyone in our life, like maybe someone insulted me or Paulina, but nothing."

"Sometimes people envy men like Paulo," Mary suggested.

She nodded. "Yes. But no." She shook her head back and forth slowly.

"Look, I want you to know I just put an ad in the paper, a reward asking for information to find out what happened to Paulo."

Lina stared at her as if she was crazy.

"Can you do that?" Lina finally asked.

Mary shrugged. "I did."

"But the police. I don't think this is such a good idea."

"Right now I don't think we have any other choice. Bottom line is it's done." She took Lina's hands. "Tell everyone you know that I am offering a five-thousand-dollar reward for information leading to the killer's arrest."

Lina nodded. It was a huge sum of money. "Thank you," she whispered.

They joined everyone back in the living room and the girls told stories about Paulo that had them all laughing until they cried again. Most importantly, Lina knew Mary and Camille were on their side.

A short while later Lina walked Mary and Camille out to their car.

Mary took an envelope out of her pocket and pressed it into Lina's small hand. "This is from Diane, the woman who Paulo was working for. It's the final payment plus some to help with whatever you need. Lina, we're here for you and your daughter."

Lina could not speak and simply nodded. She noticed Camille studying the four carvings hanging on the house. "Paulo carved those. It is to honor the God Gukumatz, a hero of the Mayans. It represents the four elements of fire, earth, air, and water. The vulture is air, the maize earth, the lizard fire, and the fish, well ... water. For Paulo it was about civilization and the arts, but civilization in harmony, not this."

"It's beautiful," Camille said.

"It came from his heart. He carved them when I was pregnant with Paulina."

"Lina!" They turned and saw Eduardo filling up the doorway. "Come inside," he seemed to order.

She waved a dismissive hand.

"Who is that?" Mary asked.

"Eduardo is Paulo's best friend. Mama loves him."

"He seems...." Mary let the words trail off discreetly.

"He is what you call brooding." Lina glanced at the house and saw he was still standing there, like a sentinel hungry for battle. "His bark is worse than his bite. He is a sad man."

"Lina!" he called out again.

She ignored him. "Thank you for coming here, both of you. And please thank Mrs. Diane for this." She slipped the envelope into her pocket.

"Here is my card. You can call me any time, day or night. Okay? And remember, tell everyone."

She nodded, hugged the two women, and returned to the house, slipping past Eduardo, who remained at the doorway staring at Mary and Camille until they got into the Mercedes.

"Tell everyone what?" Camille asked.

"About the reward. You learn anything from what they were saying in Spanish?"

"Mama thinks you've got something up your sleeve. Otherwise, we won everyone over. I've been thinking about this reward," Camille finally said calmly. "A few things to consider: One, we don't know that Paulo was killed."

"He was killed."

"Two, this is why we have police. They're trained in this field."

Mary talked over Camille. "They don't care about a Spanish guy...."

"*Three*," Camille plowed over her, "There has got to be a better way to attract a killer other than with money."

"Well I don't know how!"

"Baby, you are getting involved in something you know nothing about, something that could be stupidly dangerous."

"It's done, Cam. Look, I've been thinking about this. Paulo was small but he was a powerful man. Whoever killed him had to be bigger and stronger—"

"Or it could have been more than one person," Camille added despite herself.

"Possible. But you would think the police would have found evidence. Think about what we know...."

"Right! What *we* know. We don't know anything!"

Mary continued undaunted. "Crimes like this are committed for a limited number of reasons."

"I can't believe we're having this conversation."

"Passion. Greed. Jealousy. Self-defense. Fear. Rage. Right? I mean I know there's some sort of list but I can't remember it, can you?"

"No."

"And in our crazy society nowadays people kill just for the kick of killing, but I think that's more likely to be a schmuck with a gun, you know what I mean?"

Camille said nothing.

"There are some things I am convinced of. First, Paulo knew his killer."

"You don't know that he was killed, Mary."

"Second, I think this was a premeditated murder, because it was so clean. That makes sense. I would think a crime of passion is usually messy, you know. Like I knew a woman once who was stabbed two hundred and twenty-two times and though the killer *tried* to make it look like a random robbery gone bad, the very nature of the murder was too passionate for that to be so."

"So?" Camille was slowly being drawn in despite herself.

"So I think Paulo knew his killer and it had to be a man."

"Why?"

"Because there was no sign of struggle. Now he might have been drugged, but the coroner would know that and then the police would know it was murder, but your idiot Petrucci seemed convinced it was a suicide."

"You don't know what he thinks," Camille said. "You barreled on ahead without waiting for me to call him, remember?"

Mary drove in momentary silence. "Okay, so call him," she suggested.

"Nu-uh," Camille said shaking her head. "You set the ball in motion. Live with it." A long pause ensued. Finally she sighed, "All right, did Paulo let people visit him at Diane's?"

"I don't think so. I mean every time I would just show up he was alone. He didn't strike me as the kind of guy who would think it his place to have someone over. He was an old-world gentleman kind of guy. Very respectful. I'm telling you, losing someone like him is a blow for the universe, in a cosmic way. You know? I did tell him he could bring clients to see his work if he needed to, so there's a possibility of that."

"What about my detective friend in the city? It might be a good idea to bring her in on this," Camille suggested, knowing that she was in for the long haul.

Mary nodded thoughtfully. "You know, I hate to say it, but this is kind of exciting," Mary said. "I mean I haven't felt this wired since I snagged Celine Dion to perform on a yacht for a lesbian wedding."

"That's just an ugly thought," Camille said, never a big Celine fan.

"Hey, the brides were thrilled, and Celine made a high six figures for forty minutes' work." Mary giggled.

"What did *you* make?" Camille asked.

"That's irrelevant." Mary asked if Camille wanted to join her on a dog walk. "Just in the neighborhood."

"No baby, I've got some calls to make. Besides someone should man the phones now for all the leads that will come in with your stupid SOS." She laughed.

CHAPTER TWENTY-SEVEN

The conservationist took the police to Corliss's body and now he stood by one of the police cars watching the trampling of his vulnerable eel grass. Landing Lane had been cordoned off with yellow tape and it seemed that the local police were in a holding pattern.

Having answered the same questions over and over the conservationist finally asked a plainclothes officer if someone would take him back to his car at the village police station where he had gone to report the crime, when in fact it was a town police matter.

Nick Petrucci felt for the poor schmuck, who clearly cared more about plant life than human. He figured given a choice the man would have fared better in life as beach grass than as a man, but there you have it. Life in a nutshell; you can't always get what you want. He certainly hadn't. In a perfect world he would be living out his days with Honey, but no. She left him for an overweight marine biologist named Cookie. *Cookie.* Only a putz or a chef would go by that name and Honey's new boyfriend was no chef.

The conservationist whined that he had things to do and they could have access to him later.

Have access. Nick figured the man spent his lonely nights watching crime TV. "I'm sorry sir, but if you could be patient just a little while longer...."

The conservationist knew this was going to happen. His whole life was going to be put on hold to accommodate these, these careless people whose nearly gleeful excitement at the discovery of a body was sickeningly palpable.

He crossed his arms over his sunken chest and watched the three-ring circus as he leaned against the patrol car. Only Officer Carla Winnow had shown him any respect. Carla. It's a nice name, he thought. And she had been so kind. She had brought him to a room and supplied him with a cup of tea as he waited for the detective to join them. They let her stay in the room as he was questioned because it was obvious that she had a calming effect on him.

But now she was nowhere in sight. Just like him she had been treated as a tool to be discarded when the job was done. Town, not village jurisdiction.

The men and women around him were like children play-acting. Every one of them seemed so excited to be there, already preparing to tell the story of the time they were present when.

If Carla were here she wouldn't be acting so childishly. She would have compassion both for the woman and the grass. He knew that.

And so as the minutes turned into hours the conservationist answered the same questions again for another detective, this one a kinder and seasoned professional from the Suffolk County force who treated him with the respect he knew he was due.

When he was finally directed into the back of a cruiser to be reunited with his car, a big stir came up from those gathered around the finally extracted torso, The conservationist watched, disgusted that he understood their excitement at viewing something so grotesque.

CHAPTER TWENTY-EIGHT

Mary, Beanie and Otis walked the quiet streets of her neighborhood in absolute harmony since both dogs could be walked off leash without fear of traffic. The house was two blocks from Gardiners Bay in an old neighborhood mixed with working class locals and weekenders' second homes. It is an area with no sidewalks, and one is likely to see more deer than people on the quiet streets. A few houses away from home Mary's cell phone rang.

"Mare? It's Oprah. Did I catch you at a good time?"

Mary smiled. "It's always good to talk to you. How are you doing?"

The two fell into an easy conversation wherein Oprah asked for a favor for a friend. Mary was able to supply the information and ended the call with, "Let me know when you're out here."

"Will do."

When she entered the house Otis and Beanie made a beeline to the kitchen where habit necessitated an after-walk treat.

Camille complied as she greeted the dogs effusively and asked how their walk was.

"Uneventful," Mary answered for them.

"Di called."

"And?"

"She wants to know how things went with the police when you reported Corliss missing, which, oh by the way, you haven't."

"Christ."

"Mm hm," Camille sang softly with a raised brow. "Might

as well get yourself a shovel 'cause you're gonna need it to dig yourself out of this one."

"Don't be silly. I am a respected member of the community who is simply—"

"A pain in the ass busybody as far as the police are concerned. First you don't trust they'll issue a proper cause of death for someone who died on Diane's property so you offer a reward without even telling them you did it. Now you're going to call them about a missing Corliss Blines. That puts you on the hot seat, girl, whether you like it or not."

Mary sat at the kitchen table and took a deep breath. "I know. But I promised her I would call the detective."

"Honestly? I think you should. This whole situation doesn't feel right," Camille said, taking a seat next to Mary.

"You know what I think? I think *you* should call him," Mary said as she held the phone and business card out to Camille.

"I already told you no way. She hired you. You do it."

"But he likes you."

"You think so?"

"See. You like him. Go ahead, call him. I'll give you a dollar," she smiled and batted her eyelashes.

Camille hesitated and Mary knew she had her.

"I'll even make a fresh pot of coffee," Mary said, quickly leaving the table.

She listened as Camille left a message for the detective revealing nothing about her reason for calling. Not so surprisingly he returned her call by the time the coffee was brewed.

"Oh hey, thanks for getting back to me so quickly," Camille said, unable to suppress a smile at his response. "Well I hate to bother you, and I know this is going to sound crazy, but I'm calling because a woman we know who was supposed to go on vacation never made it to her destination and we think maybe something happened to her." She listened. "Oh yeah, she's local." Again she paused. "Her name?" Here she glanced at Mary who nodded. "Corliss Blines. Uh-huh. Well, not me, no. Yes." She flapped Mary's whispered questions away with the back of her free hand. "Okay. We will. All right. Thanks."

"What?" Mary asked.

"I know you think he's an idiot, but that man is even sexy on the phone."

Mary stared. "Really? That's what you have to say?"

"Oh, no. He's coming over with Detective Lasworth. He asked us to stay put."

"Did he really say that? Stay put?"

"Yeah. I think it's kind of sexy in an old-fashioned sort of way." Camille got up and started out of the room.

"What are you doing?"

"Girl, I don't care if he's a certifiable moron, I am going to prettify myself."

"Pearls before swine," Mary mumbled as she grabbed her coffee, a notepad, and a pen and headed out to the back deck. The air was mild and the backyard was awash in sunlight. Beanie and Otis followed her, Otis to his own little sofa on the deck and Beanie to explore the garden.

Mary studied Beanie. What on earth would happen to this sweet dog if Corliss never returned? Whereas some dogs would mope around after having been left behind, Beanie didn't seem to miss Corliss.

Mary drew her attention to the blank page before her. On the top left side of the page she wrote PAULO and just under that the number one.

When no thoughts were forthcoming she drank her coffee and watched Otis sleep and Beanie chase squirrels. What on earth did she think she was going to do?

Finally she picked up her pen and wrote next to the number one:

1. Where—the cabaña

2. Who—would want Paulo dead? Did Paulo know his murderer?

3. What—did he do to evoke rage? Could he have been hiding something from us? Drugs? Gambling?

4. How—did someone get into the cabaña?

5. Why? Theft? Was anything missing?

6. When—did he die? Was his death designed? Was it premeditated or did it just happen?

A hanging didn't just happen. "Right," she muttered as she scratched it out. "That's just stupid."

Otis looked up as if he might agree given the ability to speak.

"Oh come on, I've never done this before," she told Otis. "You come up with a better way to start."

"Okay, I'm thinking maybe you've lived alone too long," Camille said from the doorway.

Mary looked up at Camille and cat whistled. "Wow."

"Mascara, base and blush, that's all," Camille dismissed Mary's inspection with a smile.

"You know you're wasting it on this fool."

"Baby, this old lady could use a fling right about now. It's been a long time."

"Oh please. The congressman would have married you in a second."

Camille made a face. "The congressman was fun but had no soul. He was a politician, not a statesman. But maybe we should really be talking about that fine artist of yours."

Fortunately the doorbell rang and Mary didn't have to respond. Instead she handed the reins over to Camille, who let Detective Petrucci in and offered him coffee, which he took light and sweet.

"I thought there would be two of you," Mary said.

"Detective Lasworth is tied up right now." He paused and turned to Camille, "You said your friend Corliss Blines is missing?"

"I didn't actually know her, but she is a client of Mary's."

He set his dark eyes on Mary and nodded once in lieu of posing an actual question.

She explained the nature of their relationship and all relevant events concerning Corliss during the past week, deftly leaving Diane's name out of the configuration.

He took notes as she spoke. When she had finished he asked, "Who was this *friend* Ms. Blines was to meet?"

"I'd rather not say." She knew this wouldn't play well.

Nick Petrucci nodded thoughtfully. "Ms. Moody, circumstances require that I get all the facts, not just those you are comfortable with or deem necessary."

Camille's eyes shot to Mary, who revealed nothing.

"What circumstances would those be?" Mary asked, impervious to intimidation.

Nick had discussed this with the lead detective, Gabe Lasworth, before leaving Landing Lane and they had agreed he could tell Mary that there was an unidentified body, but not about the torso or arms and legs at the ocean.

When the call came to Lasworth that a torso had been found he assumed the arms and legs would match the torso DNA, but matching that DNA to an unknown entity would have been the proverbial needle in the haystack. Now they had a possible link.

Lasworth was not a man who put much stock by coincidence. And while it was feasibly coincidental that the missing person call came in at the precise moment that the torso was being removed it bothered him that the call came from the same women who had been at the house where the hanging took place.

Given the nature of the Landing Lane find it would be impossible to keep it out of the news for more than a day anyway. That they had managed to keep the limbs quiet for so long was amazing, but the torso would be impossible to keep out of the news. In fact, by the time Nick had left the scene there were already a handful of local reporters converging on the site.

"A body has been found at the bay," he started.

"Is it Corliss?" Mary asked cutting him off.

"I don't know," he said, which was true. Without teeth or fingerprints the challenge of identifying the pieces had presented a challenge but with this new information the likelihood of identification was practically a foregone conclusion. However, this busybody didn't need to know that.

He took a deep breath and stared at her until an uncomfortable silence descended. "Okay, now I have questions for you. You think you can manage that?"

Mary shrugged one shoulder. "I just thought we were having a conversation."

"We're not." He stood to gather his thoughts and asked Mary about the last time she saw Corliss. It took twenty minutes of questioning to get to that morning when Mary went to Corliss's house at a client's behest. Here she explained that she had found nothing changed since her last visit when she picked up Beanie and went on to describe her visit with Corliss's assistant Ruggiero.

"How well do you know Corliss?"

"Not very. She's a recently acquired client."

"Did she have any enemies? Someone who would benefit from her death? Perhaps a family member? Children?"

As far as Mary knew the public list of people in conflict with Corliss was relatively long since she had apparently alienated almost everyone she knew.

Mary explained how Corliss's assistant Ruggiero was creepy, which wasn't a crime, but he did seem to have a sinister underbelly.

Nick looked at Mary and repeated, "Sinister underbelly?"

"Yes. That's the best way to describe it." She nodded.

"Okay. Did *you* ever witness a disagreement or friction between them?"

"No," Mary answered. "But I wouldn't expect to. That's not how it's done. Also there is bad blood between her and Robert Sarcoff. Everyone knows that. Oh! And Marcus Schulman. I heard they *hated* each other."

"Schulman the restaurateur?" Nick asked.

Mary nodded.

"And Sarcoff, who's he?"

"A local patron of the arts."

"What do you know about him and Corliss?"

Mary shook her head. "Nothing, just that there has been hostility between them for a very long time."

"Huh." He scribbled. "And Schulman?" he asked, barely looking up.

"A friend of mine was at the Palm this past winter when Marcus threw a drink at Corliss." Anticipating his, "Why?" Mary shook her head and shrugged. "I don't know why. Can I ask you a question?"

He nodded once.

"Was it Corliss you found?"

"Don't know yet. We have to wait for the coroner's report."

Unquestionably this was the most exciting thing that had ever happened in his life and part of him wanted to tell them about the torso and arms and legs at the beach but he didn't dare. While the lead Detective Lasworth seemed to think Mary was harmless enough, Nick wasn't so sure. And if he could help solve this case, instead of just being another local lackey detective to the Suffolk County squad, man oh man it could change things. What, he didn't know, but he needed a change and this was it.

"Who was Corliss supposed to meet last week?" he asked.

"I can't say just yet," Mary answered.

"Really? Perhaps it would be easier to answer it at the station," he countered.

"You can't do that."

"Of course I can. You're hindering an investigation."

Mary knew how bad it would sound that Diane was somehow connected to both Paulo's and Corliss's deaths but there would be little Mary could do to help if she was in the pokey, so she told him. More than anything it disturbed her that she could see a gleam in his eye at hearing this. That could only mean trouble.

CHAPTER TWENTY-NINE

The long line of traffic along Old Stone Highway had been a dead giveaway that the plan was not proceeding as planned. Secured across the entrance to Landing Lane there was yellow police tape. Fuck.

"Say officer, what's going on?"

The young, uniformed rookie merely waved the car on, not even looking at the driver.

The knot on the rope holding the concrete must have come undone; it was the only possible thing that would have sent her aloft so soon.

Fuck.

CHAPTER THIRTY

It was Detective Lasworth who went back to the estate and questioned Diane. A quick glance at the situation would have any investigator taking a good hard look at her: a seemingly happy man ostensibly hangs himself in her cabaña and her girlfriend disappears when they are supposed to be on vacation together, a clandestine vacation together.

His first impression of Ms. Ajam was that of a forceful, direct, high-strung and depressed woman likely suffering from menopause given her age, mood shifts in a single conversation and changing complexion. Since his wife was an arts critic for their local newspaper and loved Ajam's work, Gabe was aware of her as an Oscar-winning filmmaker.

It was curious that she was in the middle of what was turning out to be a potentially complex case—that is if all things were connected, but it was too soon to tell. It was likely, however, that the torso and recovered arms and legs belonged to the same person. In Gabe's mind that was a foregone conclusion.

The disappearance of Corliss Blines made it difficult not to assume that the body parts belonged to her, but many a false step had been made in a jump to a convenient conclusion.

Detective Lasworth gently questioned Diane, seamlessly turning the line of questioning in Mary's direction. "She seems like a good friend," he said.

"I don't know what I'd do without her," Diane agreed, glad to have the focus anywhere but on Corliss.

He smoothly brought the conversation around to how Diane had met Paulo: through Mary. It turned out too that Mary had arranged for his comings and goings. As a sidebar Diane told him that Mary hadn't wanted Corliss as a client, but that she couldn't say no to Beanie.

"So, Mary doesn't really like Corliss?" he asked.

"Well, they don't really know each other ..." Diane trailed off and then quickly added, "Mary has a lot of clients."

"But you and Mary are such good friends."

"Yes, but it was new with Corliss. It's not like Mary knew about Corliss and me. We kept it very quiet. You know how it is; everything is so new and in the beginning you see less of your friends as you get to know each other."

Gabe jotted *jealous* in his notebook followed by a big question mark.

"Were you aware that Ms. Moody has offered a reward for any news relating to Paulo's death?" A reporter at the *Star* had given Gabe a heads-up.

"Yes," she lied.

"Did you ask her to do that?" he asked.

"No, why would I?" Diane heard the way it sounded and quickly added, "But I'm glad she did. He was a very talented artist. Did you see the armoire?"

"I did. It's beautiful."

They spent the next forty-five minutes talking about Corliss, where he gathered what information Diane could provide about her family, friends, and business relations. Gabe's strength was that he could, as he had with Diane, make his line of questioning feel like a conversation all the while gathering information and giving away nothing. Not a whisper of what had been found at Landing Lane.

Before leaving Gabe asked Diane about the estate video cameras.

In the time that the police had gone over her property the only questionable thing they found was one security camera shifted just enough to video one small patch of ground directly beneath it rather than the expanse of path leading to the cabaña. Diane provided the names of those who might have had access: the landscaper, the maintenance man (who was on vacation), Paulo, and Mary.

CHAPTER THIRTY-ONE

Eight hamlets or villages comprise the Hamptons: Southampton, Water Mill, Bridgehampton, Wainscott, East Hampton, Amagansett, Sag Harbor and Montauk. Some folks like to toss Westhampton into the mix but whatever the boundaries, the *East Hampton Star* is distributed in all of these towns.

Mary's offer of a reward for information was figured prominently as she had taken out a half-page ad so no one would miss it, and she was right.

There was an article about Paulo's death—big news but relatively small coverage overshadowed by the town board's childish debates over roosters crowing and lights disturbing the night sky. It was the reward that had a thousand tongues wagging.

But from Southampton to Montauk there were only a small handful of people who read about the reward and considered it as something more than interesting. Some thought it curious, several entertaining, more than a few meddlesome, and one a threat.

It only takes one spoon to stir a pot to empty.

CHAPTER THIRTY-TWO

Mary slept in later than she had in years and it felt revitalizing after all the emotions from the day before.

After their time with Petrucci, she and Camille had gone to Diane, who seemed surprisingly calm after being interviewed by Detective Lasworth. Of course she was calm; he hadn't told her about the body found at Landing Lane. When Mary told her what she knew, Diane went into a tailspin.

It had been a long, difficult night. How does one soften such details? Diane's rage and grief was only quelled after she took two sleeping pills and fell into a deadened sleep well after midnight.

But that morning, Camille took Otis and Beanie to the ocean so Mary could work.

First, with her coffee in hand, Mary called Henry and told him everything that had happened the day before.

"My God!" he exclaimed and then after a short pause softly asked, "Was it Corliss?"

"I don't know. I don't think they know. But it stands to reason, doesn't it?"

"Look," he said, "I have to see you. I just want to touch base and see for my own eyes that you're okay."

"Paulo's wake is today. Do you want to go?"

"I do."

After several minutes more they ended the call with Mary extracting a promise that Henry wouldn't tell anyone what they had discussed.

Mary was anxious to deal with all the business she had put on hold.

She checked in with a local event planner who was both assisting in organizing final hotel arrangements for the brat bride and putting together the gift bags. At the end of the call Mary asked her to email the full list of guests and where they were staying. When that was done she hunkered down to work.

In less than an hour she had caught up on the imperatives and went to the basement where she had a makeshift gym.

After half an hour on the elliptical her phone rang.

"Hello, I'm looking for Miss Mary Moody." It was a woman's voice.

"Speaking."

"Hold please for Lady Regina Hollingsworth."

Before Mary could respond she was put on hold.

"Miss Moody?"

"Yes," Mary said cautiously.

"I'm terribly sorry to bother you but Alexandra Christina, Countess of Frederiksborg, insisted that you are the *only* person in the Hamptons who can help me."

Mary knew neither woman.

"My husband, Lord Hollingsworth, and I will be arriving in Southampton in two weeks and staying at the estate of Rachel Ray, whom we absolutely *adore*. Do you know her?"

"I know who she is."

"Simon and I thought it would be a *splendid* idea if we were to surprise Rachel with a catered champagne and caviar party as a thank you for her generosity for having us as her houseguests."

Red warning lights went off in Mary's head.

"Miss Moody? Are you there?"

"Yes. Do you know where you would like to have this party? And for how many? You say a surprise party, but as her guests she may have plans already in place for you."

There was a lengthy pause during which time Mary ended her workout.

"I think it best to arrange it at her house, and Simon and I have a guest list of sixty. Once the preparations are confirmed we will send out e-mail invitations. Simon is *smitten* with the idea of it being a surprise. Is this something you can do? I understand that you are both capable of such a task and the very definition of discretion. *Is* that correct?"

"It is." But this sort of proposition had disaster written all over it. "I'm in the middle of a meeting right now. Let me talk to my staff and get back to you within twenty-four hours."

"Time is ticking away, Miss Moody."

"I understand." She collected the Lady's e-mail and phone numbers and promised to be in touch.

Knowing the next few days were going to be challenging she decided to deal with this problem then and there. In less than half an hour, through several connections, Mary was able to contact Rachel Ray, and explained the delicate position she had been placed in with the Hollingsworths' request.

"Oh my God, are you serious?" Rachel exclaimed.

Mary assured her that she was and while she normally wouldn't tattle on a surprise party, she had a feeling this was something Rachel needed a heads-up on.

"*Sixty people? Are you serious?*"

"Yes."

"No way! I don't even know these people. I'm doing this as a favor for a close friend. First, I was just going to have dinner with them and somehow it got stretched into an overnight stay at my house, then two and now three, and it's not just the two of them but another couple. Oh my God, I can't believe this. What are these people, nuts?"

"I wouldn't want to be in your shoes. You know, it might be worth your sanity to find another place for them to stay while they're here."

"Well yeah. Jeeze, now I'm thinking they'll take little souvenirs from my house as proof they were there. What am I going to do?"

"I suggest you make room reservations for them at the Baker House for their stay. Tell them you've had an infestation of some sort of bug—which is really them—and you don't want them to experience any discomfort."

"A bug. That's great. I owe you."

Camille was back by the time she got out of the shower.

Over coffee Mary planned for the day. "Since Diane's hired

me to look into Corliss's whereabouts, I figured I'd focus on that today."

"Honey, I'm willing to bet everything I own that that body they found yesterday was her," Camille said hoisting Beanie onto her lap.

"I agree. So I figure I'll start with her assistant again and then talk to the other two people who I know didn't like her: Robert Sarcoff and Marcus Schulman."

"You know them? Camille asked.

"I've met Marcus a few times, but it's a relatively small town. I'll see what I can dig up. You okay alone?"

"I'm not alone," she said resting her chin on Beanie's head and giving the pup a squeeze. "Besides, I'll probably head over to Diane's in a little while. I don't think it's good that she's alone."

"I agree. Car's yours," she said referring to the second car.

Between the art gallery and her home she fielded two calls from clients; one who needed to rent a yacht for a party in two weeks—easy, and the other the Royal Dandies' mother who wanted her to stop by and see the new pig playhouse.

Though summer was not yet into full tilt parking in town was already a nightmare and she finally found a space in the large town parking lot.

About to get out of the car Mary's phone rang displaying a "private" number.

"Hello."

"I know who you're looking for," the caller whispered like Darth Vader, but still audible as they cupped their hand over the mouthpiece.

"Who is this?"

The caller hissed, "Never mind. Be at Citta tonight at ten." The always busy restaurant was in the heart of East Hampton on Newtown Lane.

"How will I know you?"

"I will know you," Darth Vader said, and the line went dead.

Mary froze with fear and excitement not knowing which direction to turn. She called Cam but there was no answer at home or on her cell. Damn. Damn. Damn.

On Newtown Lane Mary heard her name and turned to see

Henry, Tristan and Gert who was off-leash yet practically glued to Henry's heels. Mary greeted the old dog first with a big kiss between the eyes.

When she stood her first impulse was to kiss Henry hello, but she was suddenly awkward in front of Tristan and they did an odd birdlike dance that resulted in cheek pecks and made them both laugh.

"This is a most perfect surprise," Henry said beaming at her. "We were just going to grab a coffee and sit on a bench. Care to join us?"

Mary shook her head. "Thanks, but I'm headed to Corliss's gallery."

"She back?" Tristan asked.

"I don't know," Mary said gesturing toward the crosswalk, anxious to keep moving.

"Let's walk her to Core's. I need to get a check from her," Tristan said.

"Oh, Tristan I saw your work and I might have a client who would be interested. He's a collector, quite well-known I think." She told him the collector's name—someone who could definitely turn his ailing sales around.

"I could always use a buyer," he said. "Which piece did you see?"

"The one at the gallery. It's haunting."

"Have Mary over to your studio," Henry suggested to Tristan. "You even live near each other."

"What are you gonna sell my work too?" Tristan teased.

"You never know," Mary said.

The gallery was closed so they stood outside waiting for Ruggiero. Eventually the conversation came around to the reward in the paper.

"Oh man, that's right. I heard about Paulo. That's fucked up," Tristan said. "He seemed like such a happy little dude."

"That's why she put up a reward," Henry said.

"That was *you*?"

"Yes. And I've already had a nibble." She couldn't suppress her smile but didn't elucidate when they questioned further.

Half an hour later Ruggiero had still not arrived. Tristan

went off to get coffee, leaving Henry and Mary alone.

"I've missed you," Henry said. "You look marvelous." He squeezed her shoulder and smiled like a giddy schoolboy.

"Then I wear stress well," she laughed.

"Oh that's not good. Maybe we can grab a drink or a walk after the wake?"

She confided that she was meeting the reward caller at Citta that night.

"What time?" he asked.

"Ten."

"Fine, so we have dinner at Citta, then you go sit at the bar alone and that way if he's ill-intentioned I'll be there for you."

"I didn't even think about him being ... ill-intentioned," she said.

"See, you need me."

"Should I bring Cam?"

"Absolutely. There's strength in numbers. For all you know this person could be a freak."

Tristan returned with the coffee and Mary told him that Paulo's wake was that afternoon.

"Cool," Tristan said. "I might even go. I mean the guy had talent."

"Speaking of talent, I really would like to see your work," Mary said.

"Any time," Tristan said with a slow smile.

"Do you have time to go now?" Henry asked.

"No, I have a crazy day. Oh, but that reminds me, do you know Robert Sarcoff?"

Apparently both men did but it was Tristan who laughed and said, "That crazy fruit? Everyone knows him."

"Can you introduce me?" Mary asked Henry who said he would.

He then leaned forward and kissed her cheek as if to push her off. "I'll see you at the wake."

With that she left them on a bench with their coffees in hand and Gert at Henry's side.

CHAPTER THIRTY-THREE

The house was wrong. The conservationist paced the two-bedroom ranch eyeing the new, clutter-free look of the place, pleased with the change since he had gone from room to room to room tossing out everything extraneous until there remained only books on shelves, lamps on tables and overly large pieces of furniture to circumnavigate.

He cast a critical eye over every blank space and wondered how to fill it.

When he had returned from Landing Lane and the police station, he tried to calm himself by going online and found himself not at the nature sites, but rather looking at furniture warehouses filled with sofas and tables and chairs, all calling out to him. But this was crazy. His furniture was still perfectly functional and for crying out loud it wasn't as if furnishings had ever been of particular interest to him. Why now?

Each time he was lulled into examining a piece of furniture and drifting inexorably into calm, he quickly jarred himself free and clicked on the favorites bar where he chose a familiar eco-informative website. But inevitably, after only a few moments he would click on the back arrow and find himself considering the applicable difference between an L-shaped sofa and a sofa loveseat match. He was drawn to soft leather. Expensive, yes, but so inviting. He could imagine himself wrapped in the seat of an armchair that was meant only for him, not his father, whose chair he had inherited yet never really came to think of as his own.

And then, without really thinking about it, he placed a call to Anselmo, the handyman he used for fall and spring clean-ups and asked if he wanted a truck full of furniture. Anselmo would have to pick it up and the conservationist made it clear he would not pay to have it hauled, but if the little Ecuadorian wanted it, it was his.

Anselmo agreed. Even if he didn't want the furniture, he knew good homes it could go to. As reliable as the rising sun, Anselmo promised he would be there in the morning, nine o'clock sharp.

Having left himself no choice, the conservationist happily returned to his computer where he selected a leather reclining chair, a sofa and ottoman, two end tables, a dining table with four chairs and stopped just short of purchasing furniture to convert his mother's room into an office. He would leave that empty for the time being.

Before hitting the purchase button he measured and re-measured the room to be certain the furniture would fit precisely.

It would fit.

He was going to do this.

He had the money.

You only live once.

He slipped his hand into his back pocket to retrieve his credit card and a piece of paper fluttered to the floor. In neat, tight blue letters she had written her name and number. "I know this has got to be a shock. Here's my number if you need to talk." He studied her name: Carla. Carla Winnow. It was a beautiful name. As he was interested in the etymology of names he knew Carla came from Carl, which was born from Charles which meant warrior, and speculated as to whether Winnow had anything to do with the verb which meant to be free of unwanted elements. How fitting that she was a police officer.

He could still see her little fingers as she held out the scrap of paper to him, looking up with her warm eyes trained on his. "Seriously," she had added before he turned to go.

Without hesitation he clicked the purchase button.

When it was done he leaned back and exhaled, unaware that he had been holding his breath.

He looked around the soon-to-be altered room. Gaping

blank holes filled the bookshelves, holes he could fill with his things now, not his mother's ridiculous garbage. He stood slowly, like a man tired but wired after battle, and took each and every book off the shelves to replace them in an order he saw fitting.

The conservationist was reclaiming a life he had never really lived.

CHAPTER THIRTY-FOUR

Back in her car Mary called Marcus Schulman, the restaurateur who publicly hated Corliss. He told her he'd be at the restaurant in an hour and she could drop by.

Pulling out of the parking lot onto Main Street, she studied a cadre of news vehicles all gathered in front of the Huntting Inn where Detective Lasworth, a compact man with kind eyes, was staying. He stood in the middle of a tight knot of reporters and seemed to handle the onslaught of questions with ease.

With time to spare Mary decided to stop by the Royal Dandies' estate south of the highway in the exclusive area called Georgica. Mary could understand why Margaret, the owner of Moe, Larry, and Curly, was so devoted to her three little pigs; they were mellow, affectionate, clean, and surprisingly obedient. The small home she had created for them was amazing, with radiant heat floors, natural light from a wall of tempered windows with a view of the ocean, a seating area for visitors, a stereo, and beds covered in William Morris fabric, one red, one blue and one green since, "Pigs can discern color," Margaret said happily. "But now the kids are bitching that I love my little pigs more than them. They want a separate house on the property for when they visit!" She laughed. Curly sidled up to Margaret for affection, which she gave easily.

"So, what do *you* think?" Margaret asked.

"I love the house. It's perfect for them."

"No, should I start another construction site here?"

"What do *you* want to do?"

"Well, it's not as if I can't do it or we don't have the money or space."

"But?" Mary prompted.

"Honestly?"

Mary nodded.

"It bothers me that my adult children are still whining that they want more." Margaret let out a sigh. "Marty doesn't care either way, but...."

"But you've made up your mind. God knows you have more than enough room in the house for when your kids and grandchildren visit. Let it go and enjoy *this*, which I think you built just as much for you as these big guys." Moe pushed between Mary's feet and let out a soft snort.

Revitalized from her pig stop at Margaret's, Mary headed to Marcus's new venture off the beaten track in Noyack, a part of Southampton close to Sag Harbor.

This was Marcus's third stab in ten years at fulfilling his Mr. Hamptons Bon Vivant dream. The idea was to prove that he was more than just an entitled trust fund baby, but sadly he wasn't.

Mary, however, liked the fact that he kept trying. Others made fun that he always fell off the horse, but Mary admired his jumping back onto the saddle again and again and again.

He hired accomplished people who could create and run a great restaurant with their eyes closed, but each time Marcus blew the profit up his nose with the help of his loser hanger-on friends whose disruptive presence ultimately undid every success he had.

The new place, a very pretty hundred-seater, was called Lola's, after Marcus's cockatiel, and was already creating a name for itself.

Directed to the back of the building she stood at the threshold of the office and saw that Marcus was leaning back in his chair, eyes closed, and snoring softly.

Before she could announce herself he opened his eyes and said, "Yes?"

"Good morning, Marcus."

"Ah, Mary."

"Thanks for seeing me," she said.

"How could I not?" he asked as he stood and offered

an awkward hug, the kind often bestowed on peripheral acquaintances. "So, what can I do you for?" he asked, gesturing for her to have a seat in the chaotic office.

Mary didn't know exactly what she hoped to gain from Marcus so she went fishing with a harpoon instead of a hook to get things moving. "I understand you and Corliss are friends," she started.

He let out a hard, "Ha!" and sank onto his chair where he puckered his flaccid lips, not unlike Alfred Hitchcock's. "No, no, you know better than that. Did you just come here to make me laugh?" His glassy-eyed smile made her cringe.

"Not just." Odd how two words could sound flirtatious and stomach turning at the same time. Even if she could simply ask, *"Marcus did you kill Corliss?"* she figured true or not he would say *"No."* "Honestly I was hoping you could help me." This had popped out without any thought but when she saw the shift in his demeanor, she knew it had been the perfect thing to say.

Marcus sat up as he cracked open a can of Dad's root beer, apparently the breakfast drink of champions. "How?"

"I'm looking for Corliss and I figured you of all people might know where she is."

"Me?" He spit out an ugly laugh. "Why me? We hate each other."

"Exactly. You've heard the saying *keep your friends close and your enemies closer.*"

"Well, that's true enough but I haven't seen her in a long time. And I hope I never see her again." He ran his tongue along the corner of his mouth then took a swig of root beer.

"Why the bad blood?" Mary asked.

"Why do you care?" His pupils were the size of his usually green irises.

Mary shrugged. "I don't, really. But I do care that I can't find her."

He paused and then nodded slowly as he said, "Oh, I get it. You and her?" He smiled with delight and wobbled his head. "That comes as a surprise."

Mary said, "No," as she raised a single brow and shrugged one shoulder.

"Right. Then you should know I tried to do business with her but she fucked me over and made me look real bad with some heavy hitters. Your little friend didn't do right by me and honestly I think you could do a lot better than her. She's a viper." He snorted and seemed to like the description so much he repeated it. "Viper. Yeah. That's exactly what she is." He downed more sugar and, with a heavy hand put down the soda can releasing a splash of the root beer onto the desktop. He ignored it.

"Look," he said now clearly agitated, "I'm sorry you can't find your friend but I really don't care. There's nothin' I can do to help you." He stood up and sniffed.

"What did she do, Marcus?"

He rubbed a palm over his jaw and finally pinched his mouth in his hand and shook his head. "Nope. I'm not gonna go there." He kept shaking his head. "I'm gonna let that sleeping dog lie."

Mary quickly debated whether to tell him Corliss was probably dead just to see his reaction, but then what? He was outspoken about his feelings for Corliss. Could he have killed her? Maybe. *Let that sleeping dog lie* could have been taken any number of ways but Mary didn't get a sense that Marcus was the kind of man who would kill someone, let alone dismember them. Then again, anything was possible. At least now he knew that Mary was looking, and maybe that was enough.

She thanked him and promised, at his insistence, to come back for dinner soon.

But she wasn't going anywhere. When she returned to her car she discovered four flat tires. Three cars were in the relatively large parking lot and hers was the only one vandalized.

AAA said that a tow truck would be there within the hour, time she didn't have. She called Cam to pick her up and then, feeling uneasy in her vulnerability out there alone, she went back into the restaurant and told Marcus what had happened.

"Oh man, that sucks," he said.

"Do you have video cameras back there?" she asked holding her hands to keep them from shaking.

"Not yet. Look, what can I do? You want me to call a garage or something?" He sniffed.

"I did. They're sending a tow truck to take it to the dealer. Can I just stay here until my friend picks me up?"

"Well yeah," he chuckled. "Ain't nothing else around here." He paused. "You want a drink?" He figured it always calmed his nerves.

Mary shook her head. "Look, I'll just wait in the restaurant if that's okay. This way you can get back to work." "Or whatever," she thought.

By the time Cam arrived the tow truck was just pulling in. Mary showed the driver why she had called.

"Well, whoever did this really doesn't like you," the driver said as he examined the four flattened tires. "One tire could be a kid screwing around. Two is usually some asshole with a gripe. But *four*? Four is seriously premeditated. Three would have done it because you're stuck, but four is gonna cost you real dough. Plus, they punctured the tire on the rim so they knew a patch wouldn't fix it. Rims can't be patched. No siree, this is someone who has something on their mind," he said, shaking his head.

Mary tipped him and once in the car with Cam, grasped the steering wheel firmly to stop shaking.

"You want me to drive?" Cam asked.

"No."

A long silence ensued finally broken by Mary's admission, "Okay, that scared me. And he acted like it was nothing."

"Who?" Cam asked.

"Marcus."

"You think he did it?"

"No, but it could have been one of the kitchen guys doing his bidding."

Cam knew this was getting out of control and Mary should back off, but she also knew her friend too well to know that wouldn't happen. Despite Mary's obvious fright, perhaps because of it, Mary would only be more tenacious and Cam knew she would stay by her side.

CHAPTER THIRTY-FIVE

Diane was still in her pajamas and the kitchen reeked of smoke when Mary and Cam arrived. She sat at the table with a cup of coffee, an ashtray filled to overflowing.

Her high anxiety seemed to have been spent and there was a deadened calm about her. Normally a fastidious woman, Diane looked like a mess, the same mess Mary had been when her friends had come to her rescue.

Mary poured herself a coffee and sat across from Diane without saying a word. She glanced at Cam who was busying herself by emptying the dishwasher. To ask Diane, "Are you okay?" would have been ridiculous; obviously she wasn't, but she did anyway.

"No."

Diane's face slowly screwed into a tight canvas of pain and she cried. "I can't stop thinking that that was her in the water. Her *torso*. All night long that's all I could think about. I know. I know she's gone now and she doesn't have any pain, but I keep focusing on what her last moments were like and it rips me apart."

"Did you know her family?" Mary asked when Di had calmed down.

"I know she had a sister. They hadn't talked in years. She never really told me why but I think it was some stupid little argument that started when they were in their twenties, got out of control and finally became a wedge. Maybe a guy, but I'm not sure. She and I had talked about her taking the first step toward reconciliation." She reached for a cigarette and Mary grabbed the ashtray, emptied and washed it and returned to the table.

"Core was softening with me. Not just me, but with everything. She wasn't taking everything as seriously as she had."

"Do you know how to contact her?" Cam asked.

"Her sister? Why? You think she was involved?" Diane squinted smoke out of her eye and shook her head. "No way."

"She might know something," Mary said.

"Like what?"

"Well, if she was the beneficiary to Corliss's estate and let's say she was in financial straits, then she might have had a very good motive. Not to be the actual killer, but to have hired someone."

"I think its Ruggiero," Diane stated emphatically.

"Why?"

"You've met him. He thinks the world owes him something. Crazy thing is Corliss has him in her will."

"She does?" Mary and Cam shared a look and the same thought: motive.

"Does he know it?" Cam asked.

"Well, he *thinks* he's getting the business, but he's not."

"Explain."

"About a year ago Corliss had her attorney draw up a will. In it she gave the East Hampton gallery to Ruggiero because he's the only person who would run it properly. The other two galleries, the ones in Manhattan and Florida, likewise went to their managers. The stipulation was they keep the name CB Gallery aka Corliss Blines in all business transactions. When we met she started rethinking things. I think I convinced her that the best way to live on was through charity."

"So what did she do?" Mary asked.

"I don't know. Diane shrugged. "I know she changed it but we never discussed how except that she's added a few charities. I think it was all really a placeholder."

"How is that possible?" Mary asked.

"That we didn't discuss it?"

Mary nodded.

"It was none of my fucking business that's how. We had other things to talk about. I don't know how." Diane burst into tears and left the room.

"Well that went smoothly," Camille said.

"I can't imagine Ruggiero dismembering anyone. He's prissy."

"Wait," Cam said holding up her index finger. "Do you actually know someone you *could* imagine doing that?"

Mary gave this some thought and finally said, "Di."

The two friends gaped at one another before saying, "Naa," at the same time.

"He could have hired someone," Cam suggested.

"Oh my God I forgot … I got a response to the reward." Diane returned as she was telling Cam the details.

"But what about Corliss?" Diane asked when Mary was done.

"What do you mean?" Mary asked.

"I'm sorry about your friend Paulo, Mary, but I need to know what happened to Corliss."

"I'm working on it." Mary then told her what she had learned from her morning activities. "It's all about motive," she concluded. "If that was Corliss they found, then someone killed her for a reason. You want me to find out who that was. In order to *try* and do that I have to figure out what there was to gain from killing her. People murder for a short list of reasons. Jealousy. Greed. Revenge. Passion. Rage."

"Jealousy is passion," Diane cut her off.

"Okay but you get the point, right?"

Diane nodded.

"For all we know it could have been one of the other managers. I'm guessing she had an equally contentious relationship with each of them."

"Not really," Diane said. She gave Mary the names of the other two managers.

"So it's fair to say that you knew her better than anyone. Right?"

Diane thought about this and nodded.

"Tell me about the people in her life and her relationships. Good, bad, and indifferent. I have to know her life if I'm going to go wading through it."

And so for the next half hour Diane talked about Corliss,

and Mary took notes. It was clear, though, that Diane had lost something quite special. Diane was in her fifties and Corliss in her forties. Both had had relationships in the past, but it wasn't until they found each other that something seemed to click. They had experienced enough to know what they *didn't* want when they found each other.

Finally Mary said, "You know the police might focus on you. They know about your relationship, and Paulo died here. They may think there's a connection."

"They're idiots." Diane dismissed the thought as she stumped out her cigarette.

"Don't kid yourself. Lasworth is no idiot. Trust me."

Diane shrugged.

Mary paused. "Di, I think you also have to prepare yourself for unwanted news coverage. I am willing to bet that once they get a hold of your relationship with Corliss it's going to become the number-one focus for the news media. You're already in the news because of Paulo."

Diane nodded slowly. "I really loved her. I know the reputation she had for being difficult, but she had no time for fools. And yes, she was painfully direct, but she was honest and honorable. And surprisingly empathetic. Tell me how many people you know who can boast that." She shook her head for a long time, not talking, and finally said, "Last night I came to the realization that I don't care who knows she and I were lovers. Fuck 'em. I'm proud of what we had." She got off the stool slowly and reached for a bottle of wine, raising her brows at her friends to offer a glass. Mary shook her head, not voicing her concern that Di hadn't yet had breakfast and was hitting the wine. "You know the media. If I answer directly, don't play cat and mouse, respectfully ask for my space—chances are they'll leave me alone. I present no challenge or drama."

"Only to us," Cam said, adding, "Baby, you have to stop smoking."

"I know. It's disgusting," Di admitted.

Cam nodded.

"You're going to get through this," Mary said softly. "I promise you." She stood up and took the coffee mugs to the sink. "I want you to shower, Di. And just so you know, Paulo's wake is today. Do you want to go?"

"Yes."

"It's at the Yardley & Pino Funeral Home in East Hampton. Do you want me to pick you up?"

"No, I'll drive. And Mary," she said as Mary was leaving. "Thanks."

"I love you, Di." Without waiting for a response, Mary and Cam left.

CHAPTER THIRTY-SIX

No one likes to be backed into a corner.
Corners are where you get trapped like beetles and dust.

And dunces.

Unless you use the corner like a racer's starting block.

Focus. Brace yourself. *BAM*!

"You fuck with me I'll fuck with you," the killer thought, reading the reward for the tenth time.

Mary Moody.

Mary Moody.

What to do?

What to do?

What to do?

CHAPTER THIRTY-SEVEN

Mary was stunned by the turnout for Paulo's wake. The funeral parlor was so crowded people had to park up and down Rt. 27, some as far away as a quarter of a mile.

"Latino communities are very close-knit," Camille said as she sat back into the U-shaped booth at Cittanuova that night.

"True, but that crowd went way beyond the Latino community. I mean did you see the people there?" Mary asked. "Not only the number of people but the cross section?"

"Yes, Mary," Camille said, confident that her friend heard the implied ancient complaint of Mary's penchant for pointing out the obvious.

"There were over two hundred visitors while we were there," Diane said, bringing a martini to her lips. She had asked to join them knowing she needed to get out of the house and out of her head.

Three sets of eyes stared at her.

"How could you possibly know that?" Henry asked.

Diane shrugged. "I count people. It's my little OCD."

Over drinks they compared their individual experiences at the wake. Camille actually spoke with Eduardo, Paulo's angry best friend they had met at Lina's house. "I think he's in love with Lina. But you know he's really broken up about Paulo."

"That doesn't mean he couldn't kill him. Desire can make a person crazy." Henry spoke with authority.

"You mean jealousy," Cam said.

"No. No, *desire* It's a very different thing."

"That's true," Diane said. "Think of *Fatal Attraction, Play Misty for Me, Obsessed, Sleeping with the Enemy*. There are a zillion films like that. And as far as being broken up about killing someone you love, I bet Cain felt awful about Abel."

"I wouldn't bet on that one," Cam said. "But if what you're saying is the case, that the motive was desire and not jealousy, wouldn't he have killed Lina?"

"No. Think about it. *If* Eduardo desired Lina, killing Paulo would give him not only clear access, but—" Mary stopped midsentence as she watched Nick Petrucci approach their table. Her tablemates followed her gaze.

Nick nodded by way of greeting and apologized for interrupting their dinner. "Mary, Detective Lasworth would like to talk to you. It won't take long."

"Now?" She asked.

"Please."

"How did you know I was here?" she asked.

Petrucci just offered a shrug as response.

Mary knew that if she didn't go now it would look bad for her. Knowing she had time before her meeting with the reward seeker, she excused herself and went with the detective.

"I'll be right back," she told her friends over her shoulder.

CHAPTER THIRTY-EIGHT

Petrucci drove Mary one block to the back of the Huntting Inn parking lot where the Suffolk County Police mobile command trailer was parked.

Petrucci stayed in the car and told Mary that Gabe was inside the trailer waiting for her.

"I saw you this morning surrounded by the press," she said upon entering.

He frowned. "Bad news sells papers. Come on in," he said as he led her into an amazing feat of modern technology.

A fairly round man, Gabe Lasworth waddled like Batman's nemesis the Penguin, the inseam of his suit riding up with every step he took on his delicately petite feet.

The cramped but efficient trailer was crammed with computers and screens along two rows of tables with half a dozen office chairs. Empty coffee containers were scattered along all of the surfaces but otherwise it was a bastion of order. With Detective Lasworth was his technician, Donald, a young man with a pale complexion and a nervous tic that had his relatively small head twitching to the left every ten seconds or so.

"So how are you, Mary? You okay? This has got to be hard on you," Gabe said when they were both seated.

"Thank you. It is. Have you learned anything new?" she asked, taking in the portable police station.

He studied her with his impish blue eyes and assumed that she, like so many others, saw him as a paternal nice guy, not the faultless detective he was, or the once-sexy officer who could have easily attracted the likes of Mary Moody, but would have never done anything because he had Gail at home. Nonetheless he wondered when he had segued from Mel Gibson to Mel Blanc.

"Any nibbles on the reward?" he asked before taking a sip of cold coffee.

Could he have known? She had a feeling anything was possible with Lasworth and the bottom line was that they both had the same objective: to find out what happened to Paulo and Corliss.

"As a matter of fact I received a call today." She told him everything and waited for the real reason she had been called in for this visit.

"Huh," he grunted, glad he had arranged for the tail to follow her.

"I didn't see you at the wake today," Mary said. "But I was surprised you released the body."

"His family needed closure."

"So you do think it was a suicide."

Gabe sighed and debated what to tell this young woman who had just lost two people in her life. It's not as if she could cause any trouble. She was an attorney, a professional who knew the importance of keeping her own counsel. By the same token she was a busybody who had interjected herself in the investigation with this reward. Then again, she might have gotten a nibble.

"The autopsy revealed that your friend Paulo died from asphyxia and venous congestion, a result of hanging. There was no bruising, nothing to suggest forensically that he was, in fact, murdered."

Mary started to say something but Gabe held up a hand and continued.

"There is absolutely no physical evidence in the cabaña that there was even another person there. But I believe there was."

Mary froze. "Why?"

"Someone deliberately repositioned the one camera that could show us who entered the cabaña. The last useful evidence from the surveillance tape from Diane's shows you with two men going into the cabaña." He pointed to the screen where Donald was running the tape, which he froze with Mary, Henry and Tristan in frame. "That's Henry Armstrong, I know, but who's this?" Gabe asked pointing to Tristan with his pinkie.

Mary told him.

He wrote it down. "Okay, now Paulo leaves, then you three leave … and now here, a couple of hours later, Paulo returns and stays an hour, locks up and leaves." He hangs onto the last few syllables staring at the screen and then finished his thought when the camera jolts once and points to the ground. "And there, someone changes the angle." He sat back and glanced at Mary.

"Could it have been a loose screw or a squirrel?" She asked, suddenly feeling cold in the air-conditioned trailer. She wrapped her arms around herself.

He shook his head. "No. It required force. And here, it's not much, but that's the palm." She stared at the hand when he froze the frame and circled the area with a pointer. "Can you think of anyone who might have had access other than the people on this list?" He gave her a piece of paper with the typed names Diane had provided him with the day before.

Mary shook her head. "Any prints?"

Gabe frowned. "Wiped clean."

"I know this goes without saying," Mary said, "but I have often been accused of stating the obvious. I just want you to know that I didn't have anything to do with any of this."

Gabe chuckled. Plain and simple, he liked Mary. "Listen, I hardly think you could lift Paulo into a noose and I think it's unlikely that you could or would perform evisceration and dismemberment, though I might be wrong. But I promise you, if there is the slightest hint that your involvement is anything more than bad luck, I will bring you down as fast as a cheetah on a gazelle," he said obviously influenced by the BBC nature show he had watched with Gail the week before. Here he smiled with a friendly twinkle in his blue eyes and asked if she had any questions.

"Diane told me something today about Corliss's will and the galleries." She told him everything she knew, including the names of the other managers, not knowing he already knew about them but not yet about the will. He shot a glance at his assistant who nodded.

"Thank you," he said.

"Detective? Do you know more about Corliss?"

"I know the recovered body parts belonged to her. We're working on it. Have faith in the system, Mary. If nothing else, have faith in me. I'm very good at what I do."

"Amen," said the technician softly, with a left tic.

Gabe stood and gestured to the door.

Mary rose and as she started to exit said, "Detective—"

"Call me Gabe," he prompted.

"Gabe. Are you married?"

His laugh was like a tickle. "Very happily for the last thirty-eight years. I'm too old for you." He winked.

"Perhaps, but not for a friend of mine."

Before she made it halfway to Petrucci's car someone called out her name and when she looked up she saw a reporter from the *East Hampton Star*.

She liked Patty, a smart, gutsy woman whose articles you could always trust to be accurate.

"Don't tell me you're staking out this place," Mary said, jabbing her thumb in the direction of the investigative trailer.

Patty laughed and shook her head. "No. I was getting a gift certificate at the Palm. Any nibbles on the reward?"

"Mary?" Petrucci had pulled up.

"Oh, I'll walk back, thanks," she said.

"Your ad caused quite a stir," Patty continued with the reward.

"Really?"

"Oh yeah. Come on, how often have we printed a half-page ad for a reward? Apart from the debate of legalities, it's fabulous gossip."

"Lucky for me you don't do the crime reporting," Mary said with a mischievous grin.

"Don't trust anyone, Mary. Anyone." All cheer was gone in a flash and Patty added, "Well, I mean you can trust *me*, of course, but reporters, from the *Times* to the *Star*, all want the story and you know it."

"Of Paulo?"

"Paulo. Corliss. Two murders in the Hamptons in less than

a week? You betcha. That's news. *Big* news. Especially the gruesome way in which Corliss was killed." Patty shivered. "I mean it's sad because everyone's talking about how she died but not about her." Patty shook her head and changed the subject. "By the way, I bumped into Beth yesterday," she said, referring to the Montauk concierge to whom Mary had sent the nasty designer. Patty laughed again. "She asked more than double her normal salary and the woman didn't flinch, but holy cow, she sounds like a nightmare."

"She is. But Beth was forewarned."

"I have a feeling this summer is going to be full of them. You know what they say, summer people, some are not." She smiled. "Only thing that concerns me is the traffic."

They spent several minutes more on idle chat and as they parted, Patty said, "Remember, you be careful, Mary. You're one of the few I like."

CHAPTER THIRTY-NINE

Ruggiero had spent the better part of an absolutely miserable yet somehow stimulating day answering an unending and often repeated list of questions about Corliss.

He had been with three cops holed up in an airless trailer behind the Palm for six fucking hours. Like he didn't have better things to do?

He was at Agda's secluded cottage with its sliver view of Noyack Bay and well into his second scotch when he starting repeating himself. "I mean I think he thinks I killed her!" He issued a laugh with the single word "HA."

"Did they say that?"

"Not in so many words. But they kept asking me about the business and how she conducted herself in business and was I aware of anyone who might feel hostile toward her—*that* one nearly made me choke."

"So what did you say?"

"What *could* I say? I *had* to tell them the truth."

"Oh puleese."

"No, really, this is the po-lice we are talking about."

"You have nothing but contempt for the po-lice and you know it," she mimicked him. "Did they ask about—"

"No."

She topped off his glass.

"Oh, not too much. I haven't eaten all day. And by the way that's *traffic* cops I don't like, which is really all we have out here. *These* cops were detectives, the real deal. I mean we are talking about hardened men with hair on their knuckles that use machetes to shave." He set a hand on his chest and sighed.

"Sounds like heaven," she said, well aware of Ruggiero's type—another temptation they shared.

"You have no idea." It was, he knew stretching the truth, but he preferred this version and it would, with time, become his unimpeachable memory.

The more they drank the further they diverged from the interrogation and Corliss's ugly death and Agda got a complete description of all three plainclothes officers, imagining she might have fancied the one with a twitch, which reminded her of a lover she once had with Tourette's and an outrageous sexual encounter between them at a church in Brussels which ought to have been embarrassing but was only hysterical in the retelling.

When their laughter died down and a short silence followed, Agda raised her glass and toasted, "Poor Corliss."

For some reason this only made them laugh harder and harder until Ruggiero got sick over the side of the deck and onto his Alden tasseled loafers.

"Poor Ruggiero," Agda chuckled as she refilled her own glass.

CHAPTER FORTY

There is nothing quite as calming as a long walk. Jogging can be jarring and damaging; biking often requires too much focus or creates stress, but a good long walk at a leisurely pace can be beneficial for everything within the human frame from strengthening muscles to supporting good mental health.

The norm is twenty minutes for a mile, give or take a minute or two. At that pace an individual in fine fettle would clock three miles in an hour. With 5,280 feet in a mile and dividing it by the walker's average stride length in feet it was easy to calculate that 6,669 steps would be taken between point A and B and that again between B and A totaling 13,338 unobserved, untraceable steps.

Black sweats. Black hoodie. Black sneakers.

No street lights.

No moon glow.

No problem.

CHAPTER FORTY-ONE

By the time Mary returned to Citta, Diane had gone and Mary's dinner had been packed up in a to-go container. Surprisingly the bar was almost empty and it was nearing Mary's meet time, so she took a seat at the bar keeping a stool's distance between her and Henry and Cam, and ordered a burger because she was starving. Citta's burgers were as close as she would get to the 1770 House, their sister property.

Ten o'clock came and went without any newcomer entering the bar.

At ten twenty-five Mary's phone rang and she naturally expected it was the reward seeker, but she was mistaken. She couldn't have been more mistaken.

On the other end of the line a celebrity client noted for hyperbole and brashness was whimpering that something was wrong, terribly wrong. The banshee-like noise in the background and the client's story indicated that there was, indeed, a legitimate problem.

She begged Mary to come immediately and bring reinforcements.

Without a moment's hesitation Mary paid the bill and told Henry and Cam they had to come with her.

"Should I at least stay in case you know who comes?" Cam asked.

"No." As much as she wanted to meet Darth Vader, she knew she had to get to her client and would need help.

On the drive over to the very exclusive address, Mary explained the background.

The caller was one of Hollywood's elite who once upon a

time lived a storybook romance with her politico husband of six years.

Things changed, they divorced, all very amicably. Then tonight after a few martinis she had stopped by the house simply to say good-bye to the well-loved property that she had put her heart and soul into. It was all fair: she got the Fifth Avenue apartment and the Bel Air house and he got this and the Aspen houses, but she needed closure nonetheless.

He wasn't there.

He had changed the lock but kept the same security code and hid the extra key in the same place they had.

After she broke in it became clear that someone else had taken her place and was living with the Noguchi and David Smith sculptures, the Murano chandeliers, and original furniture by Eero Saarinen and Adrian Pearsall, in a house designed by Patrick Jouin and Sanjit Manku, whom she commissioned—not him. It was her love and sweat and creativity that made this house the showcase property it was—not his. Once there she knew it was stupid to come back for a final farewell alone, so she called two good friends. They called another two and before she knew it the place was a swarming with people she didn't know, partying like they belonged there. That's when she called Mary.

It was no easy feat but once the thirty rowdy revelers were corralled by Mary, Cam and Henry (posing as police officers) and the client's two friends and escorted off the property, Mary assessed the damage and called the celebrity's maid, Sheryl, who may have a big mouth but was efficient, fast and easily bought for the right amount. Mary left a message for Sheryl but didn't have the luxury of time, so she called her own housekeeper who brought another two women and they got the place spotless in relatively no time at all. It was amazing; it looked absolutely pristine down to glasses returned to the cabinets and a red wine stain completely removed.

The celebrity sat with her legs dangling in the pool and her mascara down her cheeks as she smoked a cigarette, tapping the ashes sloppily into the mouth of a water bottle.

"Wow, that was a drag," she said to no one in particular,

though Cam, Henry and Mary were sitting with her.

"I would say this is the finest example of being hoisted by one's own petard as I have ever seen," Henry chuckled.

"What's that supposed to mean?" the actress asked.

"You only hurt yourself," Mary explained.

"You did a nice job on the house though," Cam said and added, "That Murano chandelier in the foyer? Uh, uh, uh, it's magnificent."

"Thanks. I know. I have really good taste. You think he'll find out?" she asked Mary.

"Anything's possible, but I wasn't here. Were you?" she asked Cam.

"Not me."

"I was with Gert," Henry said.

Soon after the housekeepers were paid a very tidy sum and the key was replaced in its secret hiding place, Mary drove back to Newtown Lane and Henry's car.

"It's never a dull moment with you, Mary Moody." He leaned through her window and kissed her good night.

CHAPTER FORTY-TWO

Once a month Adam Strickland would play poker with four buddies—low stakes, junk food, good times.

He was a cheater and a good one. It was a rare night of poker that he didn't come home with a couple of extra bucks; enough to make it easier on date night with Sheryl, but not enough to make anyone suspicious.

"Share? Hey honey, I'm home." He tossed his keys on the hallway table and called out, "Hey beautiful, take a deep breath, can you smell da money?" He laughed as he cha-chaed up the hallway toward the bedroom.

She wasn't there. Nor in the bathroom, the laundry room, the kitchen or the den. But her car was outside. This didn't make sense.

He called Mindy next door thinking Sheryl'd be visiting, but there was no answer.

Grabbing a beer from the fridge he called her cell phone.

Nothing.

Damn. Where the hell was she? Now he was bouncing from being concerned, to pissed off and back again and ultimately scared but angry with himself because he knew he was overreacting.

He wasn't. But he didn't learn that until well after midnight when she was found at the bottom of their pool, her fingers and toes puckered prune-like, and her body bent in a fetal position.

Nothing in life had prepared him for her death.

CHAPTER FORTY-THREE

Before most people had had their morning coffee, Anselmo the handyman had packed up everything from the conservationist's house except for one reclining chair. The living room, dining room and master bedroom were now empty. When he was gone the conservationist swept and polished the wood floor.

Sun poured into the blank space. Light he had never seemed to notice before illuminated the floorboards, bounced off the blank walls and hummed with potential. For what, he was uncertain, but potential nonetheless. Hope. Just the word took his breath away.

Once he would have felt frightened by the empty space in which he stood. The prospect of change would have overwhelmed him into inactivity. The old conservationist would have sat at the table with his mother, teacup in hand, and listened to her alternately blast caveats for maintaining the status quo and wheeze as he did nothing but sip weak tea and nod.

But the new conservationist picked up the phone book and dialed the first-floor finisher he found. The house was empty; the furniture would be at least a day before arrival, and the floors needed to be sanded and stained. He hired the first company that agreed to come that day and do the job. He didn't care about the quality of the work nearly as much as getting it done.

With arrangements made he left the house, got in his car, and drove to Landing Lane to check on his eelgrass. It was time to see what damage the police, the press, and the curiosity seekers had done.

The damage was considerable. At one time this would have brought him to rage or tears but he surprised himself when he gently fondled a broken blade and said, "You will heal."

He honestly believed he was talking to the grass.

CHAPTER FORTY-FOUR

The day was unseasonably cool; enough to require a sweater for most folks, especially with the breeze coming up from the ocean. The predicted storm that had been moving up from the tropics had petered out over the cold ocean waters but that didn't stop the winds from churning.

Mary, Cam and the dogs walked in the neighborhood to avoid the wind.

Likewise with Henry and Gert, who only rose early to accommodate her new dad who liked to work in the studio in the morning. She would quickly do her business and tug the leash for home, breakfast, and a nap.

Tristan had been working since dawn.

Ruggiero was drooling on Agda's sofa.

Agda was in a fitful sleep dreaming she was a deaf mute.

Diane, who had been up half the night at the computer getting down an outline for a new film idea, was just falling asleep.

Richard Sarcoff, the moneyed collector and one of Corliss's nemeses, was excitedly preparing his home for his morning meeting with Mary Moody that Henry Armstrong had arranged.

Over coffee and a bagel Detective Lasworth was mulling over Corliss's will that he had finally received from her attorney.

Soon he would meet Agda Eck, a painter who that weasel from the day before had mentioned as one of Corliss's disgruntled artists.

Lasworth didn't like Ruggiero the minute he met him, and the document in his hand didn't improve his opinion any.

He sighed.

It was going to be one long day.

CHAPTER FORTY-FIVE

When Mary, Cam and the pups returned from their walk they noticed a note under the windshield wipers on the loaner car the dealer had delivered.

"Oh my God," Cam whispered after she read the note Mary handed her. She felt sick.

An ordinary piece of typing paper torn to a four-by-four-inch piece had the message YOUR NEXT. The cutout letters like a kidnap note were affixed around a generic picture of a pair of hands. Hands only.

Mary set her hands on the hood of the car and braced herself. Before going inside she took out her phone and called the police. "Shit. I think it's time you went home," she told Cam as the phone rang.

"And leave you here alone? Girl, are you out of your mind?"

The police picked up and Mary thought, "*Here we go again.*"

An hour and a half later, after a police tow truck had taken the car to check for prints and any tampering the car might have sustained, Nick Petrucci ordered one police cruiser of the three that had arrived to stay visible in front of the house.

"You okay?" he asked.

Both women mumbled something like "Yeah, sure," but it was obvious they weren't. "Call me if you need me. I'm serious. I just want to get this to Gabe," he said, holding up the note in its protective pouch.

When he was gone Cam thought a shower might calm her and Mary went to work because she had to.

Her first order of business was Lillian, who hadn't returned her other calls. Lillian told her they had arranged to rent the house on Briar Patch Road. The wedding, scheduled to take place in three days, would have thrust any other planner into panic mode and Mary was just at the tipping line.

"Honestly Mary, I am so embarrassed about this whole thing. I mean I know weddings are never easy but this has been …" Here Lillian paused.

"A nightmare," Mary finished her thought as she slipped onto her desk chair and pulled up the event on her computer. "So, this is good. I have spoken with all of the vendors and they all knew there would likely be a change. You've lost the full cost of the Mulford rental."

"Not a problem. It's only, what, twelve—five?"

Twelve thousand five hundred dollars could actually feed two hundred fifty people for a year in Kenya, Mary thought, but nothing like what they were entering into, which could feed four thousand people for a year.

"You saw the rental cost," Mary said.

"Yes. But what are we going to do? The place is gorgeous, close by and she's agreed," Lillian sighed. "Jack doesn't care about the money. He just wants it done and I have to agree with him. The question is, is it possible to get everything done?"

"Yes, but I have to get on it right now. Can you contact Leah about the house and email me an update?"

"Sure. As a matter of fact we're doing a walk-through today and signing the contract."

"Great. Listen, as soon as you sign the papers can you call Joe at the tent company? I'll give him a heads up to expect your call, but they need to start today and I can't be there. Tell him that the only thing changing is the location. I can get there later but he needs a call for when they can get in."

"Of course," Lillian said, taking down the information.

Having an immediate focus of work was keeping her nerves at bay.

The first and easiest call was to the caterer. Real professionals may cost more but are well worth the expense because they understand changes and don't get thrown—at least not in front of the client. Change of venue with several days' notice is a pain but he had been forewarned: more food, extra rentals, more staff, and perhaps another rental van if needed to transport everything and everyone from the city since they are not local.

The caterer now had only one day to make the alterations. Since he had known for some time that the numbers were going to be higher he had already accounted for that with the food, but the rentals and staff would have to be upped. However, he was also prepared for this and had put the rental company on hold and the additional waiters and kitchen assistants as well. Mary knew that for him, like herself, it was just a matter of a few phone calls, but the clients believed they were geniuses.

Mary had already arranged for him to be in East Hampton tomorrow with his stylist and two waiters to set the space, and the rest of the crew would come out the morning of the wedding. Since it was an early-evening event and the food was already being prepped, it would be as if there had never been an issue. She sent him pictures of the space so he could see the interior was so beautiful that candles and flowers would be enough to make it work.

The local florist was next and despite her whining about ten additional table centerpieces and a few large vases, which Mary knew could be a problem, Mary assured her that the arrangements needn't be identical if she couldn't get an order from the purveyor on time and finally reminded her that the compensation would alleviate her headache.

After going over the venue change with the valet company, musicians (the most easy-going group), and leaving a message for Joe at the tent company that Lillian would be in touch as soon as they could start, she poured herself another cup of coffee before preparing to call the local planner she had hired to assist with guest accommodations and gift bags. It was the first time she had worked with this particular local who had come highly recommended, but Mary had early on discovered that the woman had her limitations. Mary regretted not having called the Montauk concierge who was a little bull with a sense of humor and always got the job done without complaint. This one, despite her roster of past events, was innately anxious—not a helpful trait for a planner of any sort.

After one ring the planner picked up the phone and scolded,

"Where have you been? I haven't heard from you in *forever*."

In fact they had spoken a few days earlier when Mary had asked for the complete guest list and where each individual was staying but had never received it. Naturally this was cause for concern. Again Mary asked for the list.

"My assistant sent it to you."

"Well, I never received it. Can you email it now while we're on the phone and we can go over it together?"

Big sigh. "Well, I was just going out. Can this wait?"

"No. We have no time and I need to know where we stand."

Long pause. "Fine. Hang on." The planner put the phone down and deliberately took her time. Great. Now she was going to miss yoga class. She knew she should have asked for more money.

As the planner finally sent Mary the information Mary explained that the venue had been changed.

You would have thought that this was done intentionally to make the planner's life impossible, though in fact it had nothing to do with her part of the event.

Mary eyed the list as she half listened to the idiot on the other end of the line. "Do you know if everyone who needed a room has one?" Mary asked, seeing about a dozen names without hotel assignments.

"No."

"Do we still have empty rooms available?"

"I think so."

Mary could hear the planner's anxiety level rising.

"How many and which ones?" Mary asked. It was like pulling teeth and Mary understood why: the woman had no real organizational skills. People like this can easily turn even simple events into nightmares. Mary spent the next half hour helping the planner structure the list cohesively and asked her to first contact the hotels with availability and then the guests not yet allotted a room to find if they needed one. In a normal world this would have been a moot point but when dealing with the uber wealthy who have no concept or consideration for the work behind the scenes there were usually last-minute changes.

"Why should we call them?" she asked. "It's their responsibility, isn't it?"

"Well, it's our job to make certain everything flows seamlessly. It's just a courtesy call. You simply explain who you are and ask if they are set with accommodations and transportation. Chances are by this point they should all be covered, but touching base is what sets you apart from others who do this job and it is something people remember." Mary sounded calm but was seething.

The planner rolled her eyes. "Okay. So I will call ..." She listed the guests and as per Mary's suggestion highlighted their names.

"Okay, now about the gift bags," Mary started but was cut off.

"I don't know that I will be able to get the same bags," the planner said.

"It doesn't matter. Just make sure Lynn has the new names and that she makes a card for each new bag." Lynn Stefanelli was a brilliant calligrapher Mary had been using from the start not only because of her expertise and professionalism, but she had become one of the few friends Mary had made since moving to the East End.

After what felt like forever Mary had a shaky level of confidence that the planner wouldn't screw things up too much. The final concern was getting revised directions to the venue into the gift bags and Mary told Miss Lazy that she would email her the directions from each hotel. "It's imperative the right directions go to the correct people, right? Just remember, this will all be over in a few days."

When she emerged from her office Cam, who was finishing the newspaper, looked up. "I hate to say this but we're running a little late."

Mary glanced at her watch. "Gimme two seconds and I'll be ready."

"Thank God you have an extra car," Cam said as she fastened her seatbelt.

As the garage door opened and Mary backed into the driveway, they were silent, both holding their breath fearing the worst.

Three blocks from the house Mary took a deep breath. "I think we're okay," she said.

"As my old neighbor Mrs. Scheinfeld would say, *'From your mouth to God's ears,'*" Cam said with as close to a Yiddish accent as she could.

CHAPTER FORTY-SIX

All Mary knew about Richard Sarcoff were the rumors that his money came from a now-deceased partner who had kept Richard comfortably on the East Coast while he maintained a conservative family in Oklahoma; that Richard fancied himself an artist, and that he often opened his classic home and expansive property for charity events.

Sagaponack, a Southampton village between Bridgehampton and East Hampton, had been home for Richard Sarcoff since 1974, when at twenty-seven he fell hopelessly in love with Ed, a married Oklahoma oil man of great wealth, distinction, taste, intellect, and a family of five who knew nothing about his first and only real love for the young man with brilliant blue eyes.

Ed had purchased the 1925 estate which the two men shared for twenty years, when Ed would leave his wife and four children in Oklahoma to travel east four times a year for business.

Richard had tried to break it off any number of times, frustrated that he never had enough of Ed, but the truth is Ed gave so fully of himself when they were together that Richard couldn't let go. They both knew the love they shared, while fraught with the obstruction of distance, was a once-in-a-lifetime experience for the very few and fortunate.

When Ed died unexpectedly in 1995 at the age of fifty-eight it was his lawyer who informed Richard both of Ed's death and Richard's newfound wealth that included among other things the Hamptons House and all the contents, the Park Avenue apartment, the title to several very active oil wells, an excellent portfolio Ed had cultivated over the years, and a savings account

Richard had known nothing about. Though Ed's attorney and old friend made it clear that he thought Richard was a manipulative miscreant who had led Edward to sin, the terms protecting Mr. Sarcoff were rock solid and unimpugnable.

The family never knew.

The attorney never told.

Richard attended the funeral, a stranger at the back of the church no one noticed.

The Hedges Lane estate hidden behind twelve-foot-high privet hedges and Cypress trees was at the end of a long formal driveway. That one man occupied a six-thousand-square-foot house with a pool, formal garden, and tennis court no longer had Mary shaking her head in judgmental wonder as it once did. She had organized too many parties at estates larger than this to be impressed or appalled. It was just sad that a single man lived alone like this and one billion people worldwide—200,000 children—go hungry every day.

Richard was curious. What would Mary Moody want with him? Yes, yes, he was a force to be reckoned with out here, but simply *everyone* knew *her*. Maybe one of her rich clients had heard about his wire sculptures and wanted to buy one. He knew if he stuck with it, it was only a matter of time.

By the time Mary arrived, with a lovely black woman in tow, he was as convinced of his fantasy as if she had stated that as being the purpose for her visit.

A uniformed maid answered the door and led Mary and Camille into an enormous room filled with furniture. There were four separate seating areas, each with a sofa, coffee table, end tables and chairs, all covered in different flowered chintz, and at the far end of the room was a fireplace large enough to stand in. By the doors leading to the backyard were two velvet-covered card tables, one square with four chairs and one round with six. It was like stepping into Frank Wiborg's Hamptons of the early twentieth century where at any moment F. Scott and Gerald Murphy would enter a room arguing good naturedly, drinks in hand.

Richard finally entered with a Loretta Young flourish. "I am so sorry to keep you waiting. Did Hilde offer you coffee or tea?"

he asked, leading them toward the seating arrangement closest to the fireplace where he had carefully placed four sculptures on display: a dog, a mermaid, a chair and a toadstool, all examples of his finest wire work.

"She did, thank you," Mary said and then introduced Camille.

"So." He straightened his back, pressed his knees together and flattened his hands on his thighs. "How can I help you?" He was a slight man with rosy cheeks and a full head of once-red hair now dulled by time. He waited for the offer.

"Mr. Sarcoff—"

"Please call me Richard."

"Thank you. Richard, I was hoping I could ask you a few questions."

He manufactured a smile and nodded once, wondering which piece she wanted to know about.

"I understand you knew Corliss Blines."

His face froze. His thin lips fixed into an uneasy smile and his papery, yet greasy, pale skin lost what little elasticity it had and appeared as if it could chip right off his face. But it was his eyes that were most compelling; one second they were soft blue and in a flash they became two unblinking rounds of fury.

The split second had the impact of a lightning strike, but Richard recovered quickly, huffed an ineffective laugh and said, "I'm sorry. I was under the impression you were here for an altogether different reason. I believe you threw me for a loop, as my father would say." The tip of his dry tongue poked between his lips. "I am a great benefactor of the arts out here, you know. I had assumed you were here to discuss a project." He leaned forward and touched the dog sculpture, turning it half a centimeter to the left.

That Richard had taken up art when he was fifty-eight to fill his time after Ed's death, or that he never took a class because a true artist needs no training, was irrelevant. His friends encouraged him at the onset because it pulled him out of his depression, but the more he did, the less they encouraged. True to his narcissism he didn't notice that. All he knew was that he would not live a life ultimately defined as someone's son or brother or lover. With his art he had the chance to leave his own mark.

His art was why he had hated Corliss.

Five years earlier he had opened his house and gardens as a pop-up gallery for a gallerist with the only stipulation that his own work be included in the show with greater and lesser-known artists. That his art was shown with the early works of Sydney Butchkes, the contemporary James Kennedy and Eric Fischl, the sculpture of William King and the compelling ceramics of Bob Bachler, was the most exquisite accomplishment of his life.

Simply *everyone* attended, including Corliss Blines, who was a growing powerhouse in the arts. This was the first time they were to meet and Richard was beside himself with excitement.

Escorting her through the artwork scattered over his property he lingered at his own unmarked piece and asked what she thought.

Corliss studied the two-foot wire mess that vaguely resembled a chair and finally said, "It's a bit of a mess, don't you think? Should be called *Child's Play* or something like that. But, apart from this piece Donna's done a very nice job curating the show. And every single piece, even this one, shows so beautifully on your magnificent property. You should be so proud."

But he wasn't. He was mortified. It was impossible not to read the devastation on his face if one were looking, which Corliss was not as she had moved on to another big name in the crowd.

All pretense of civilized courtesy ended in that moment. From then on Richard loathed Corliss and was able to help stop several big sales for her over the intervening years and had initiated many a fly paper rumor.

Camille sensed his anger and jumped in, asking, "I realize you're a patron of the arts, but are you also an artist, Richard?"

He jerked his head toward her and nodded sharply.

"I'd *love* to see some of your work."

Whoever this pretty woman was, she was with Mary Moody, which meant she no doubt had the same ties. It would be foolish, downright selfish not to share.

"Well, as a matter of fact these," he gestured with a delicate hand to the coffee table, "are my most recent works. I call them my miniatures."

Camille placed a hand on her chest and said, "Oh my goodness, I have been admiring these since we sat down. They're so whimsical and yet the use of copper wire brings to it a dimension of complexity whose impact speaks to both the sociological as well as the emotional."

Richard nodded. "I can see you are an art enthusiast."

"Oh yes. May I?" she asked reaching to pick one up. "Are you familiar with Alexander Calder's *Cow*? Amazing. And my God, Naomi Grossman's work in wire? Fabulous." She gently lifted the dog off the table, thinking it was a cat.

"Corliss is dead," he said to Mary. "Who cares? Why are you here?"

"I have been hired to try and ascertain what happened and—"

He cut her off. "I'll tell you what happened. She went a step too far and didn't get away with it this time. My dear, I may have disliked the cretin but I am not so deluded as to think anything more than my bruised ego was at the foundation, which is hardly a reason to kill someone, even someone as loathsome as she. However, there's not an artist in twenty miles she hasn't cheated, manipulated, denigrated, misrepresented, or fucked. Your little friend Henry who introduced us knows exactly what I'm talking about. I believe you would glean more from Mr. Armstrong than you ever could from me." He struck a demure, almost saintly pose and asked, "Tell me, Miss Moody, do you have a legitimate client, are you here on behalf of the Suffolk County police or are you just a busybody trawling for gossip?"

His intended slap had the unexpected reaction of making her laugh, which confused him, especially because it was clearly a good-natured, honest laugh.

"I was friends with Paulo, the artist who was recently found hanged to death, and employed by Corliss. As an attorney I have been retained to look into their deaths."

"Who retained you?" Now it was getting interesting.

"That I'm not at liberty to discuss."

Richard looked at Camille, who offered nothing, not even a glance.

"But I am well aware that you are a man in the know out here. I thought you would be the best person to help me. I am sorry if I have been awkward." She cringed at her blatant flattery but it was out and she figured that at any minute she and Cam would be thrown out.

He held up a pale hand and waved it lethargically. Mary Moody needed *him*. Mary Moody had known about him without his ever having met her. To help her would be to ingratiate her to him.

He pursed his lips. "Well why didn't you just say so? I am more than happy to help you." He was already preparing what he would say to his friends. "Mary Moody and I are working *together* to...." This was fabulous.

And so the questioning began without resistance.

CHAPTER FORTY-SEVEN

Nick Petrucci found Henry Armstrong in the studio behind his house, a simple shingled old cottage in Wainscott where he was nearly as tall as the old front door.

At the back of the property was Armstrong's studio: a red barn concealed behind a line of mature arborvitae trees nibbled at the bottom by deer.

Petrucci erroneously summed up Armstrong just by his surroundings: trust-fund gay man whose rich friends bought his paintings.

But Petrucci had to admit Armstrong had done a great job of preserving the old building since it looked just like it must have when cows and horses called it home.

When Armstrong let him in Nick realized that the front of the building was nothing more than a façade of the past. It opened onto an enormous space with the first third given over to a full kitchen and a conversation area that was at once orderly and chaotic yet inviting. The rest was his massive studio with the entire back wall double-glassed sliding doors that opened onto a loading area with an unobstructed view of beach grass and trees in the distance.

Rich sons of bitches.

Nick showed Henry his badge and said he needed to ask a few questions.

Henry, of course, remembered Nick from the night before when he took Mary to meet that other detective.

"Right now?" Henry asked, running a paint-speckled hand through his hair leaving a thin streak of blue.

"That's why I'm here." Nick offered a grim smile. "Unless, of course, you think I should come back at your convenience." His brows went up and the corners of his mouth down.

"No, no of course not," Henry said stepping aside to let the officer in. "Please come in. I'm just finishing a piece, that's all." That's all, you bloody imbecile.

Nick's face remained blank as he took in the barn that felt larger than his own property, house and grounds included.

"Please, have a seat." Henry gestured to the sitting area with a large, worn sofa on which Gert snoozed, and two armchairs around a coffee table. "Can I get you anything? Espresso? Tea? A smoothie?" Henry asked.

"No thanks," Nick mumbled as he looked more closely at the cluttered coffee table realizing it was painted in vibrant colors to look like the face of a dog.

"That was Beau, my old lab who died," Henry offered.

As if sensing competition, Gert raised her head off the sofa pillow and sighed, which made Henry chuckle until he saw Nick was not a dog man.

"Why don't you sit down, Henry," Nick suggested, taking ownership of the situation. Henry might have been taller than him and it was his house, but Nick needed to take control and he did.

He waited until Henry was seated, then cast the artist a cold look, pulled out his notebook, opened it to a blank page, slowly withdrew his pen and sighed. "Tell me, Henry, how long have you known Corliss Blines?"

As it turned out Henry Armstrong had known Corliss Blines very well. Very well indeed.

CHAPTER FORTY-EIGHT

Statistically speaking, Sheryl Strickland's death was no big deal; it was an event that occurs approximately ten times daily in the United States.

Had fate not intervened Sheryl Strickland might have simply died of old age and been buried, ultimately forgotten as the past so often is.

But no.

It is strange, and perhaps sad to think that dying could be the most colorful event of an individual's life, but the possibility that this was the case with Sheryl was enough to cause an exciting stir among her family members and friends and most certainly the locals. In the end she would be remembered for having been murdered; not for being a mother, wife, daughter, or grandmother, and not for being one of the dullest people that had ever walked the planet, but for having been drowned deliberately.

Because homicidal drowning is almost impossible to prove by an autopsy, unless there are obvious signs of injury or struggle, in all likelihood Sheryl's death would have passed completely unnoticed by authorities as another tragic accident had it not been for her cellphone.

Cell *phones.*

Detective Gabe Lasworth held evidence in hand, both hands. In one hand was a much-used, battered, pink-sheathed iPhone and in the other a spanking new small, grey, nondescript Nokia. Both had evidence leading to a familiar common denominator. "Call her in," he told his assistant Donald as he shook his head.

CHAPTER FORTY-NINE

As Richard Sarcoff walked Mary and Camille to the door he handed Camille a tiny wire outline of a tree, something he had tinkered with during a call to his banker, something to be tossed out with the garbage. "For you, my dear. A true believer." He then turned to Mary and said, "I believe I have given you all I have to offer. Good day, ladies."

Forty feet down the driveway in the car Camille set the wire onto the dashboard and laughed. "Oh my God, I thought I was in the middle of a Tennessee Williams play! Can you believe that guy?"

"I believe he didn't have the wherewithal to kill her." Mary said as she pulled out of the driveway. "*Speaks to both the sociological as well as the emotional*? I nearly died when you said that."

"When you go to as many openings as I do, it starts to come naturally. The bizarre thing about artists is that as long as you're talking about them, they assume it's positive. Actors are just the opposite."

"Yeah? What about writers?"

"They listen better, I'll give them that, but ego in any artist is a fragile thing. Now what?"

"Sarcoff could be her biographer but not her killer," Mary said.

"Agreed. But he could afford to hire anyone to do anything."

"Which leads us to motive. I thought what he said about Marcus Schulman was telling. Corliss not only cost him a lot of money, but she humiliated him."

"Did you know that before?"

"Some of it." Mary said. "I had heard that they were thinking about partnering in a restaurant. Then Marcus told me that she made him look bad with some heavy hitters."

Camille laughed. "Well, if what Dickey said is only half true I'd say that's an understatement."

Mary smiled. "You know, you have to wonder why she did that." Mary shook her head. "I mean it's just plain malicious."

"You know why she did it," Cam said.

Apparently Corliss had said she was on board in a partnership with Marcus and two other deep-pocketed investors he had brought to the table, but when they were all gathered at a final meeting she pulled out, taking the other investors with her. Richard Sarcoff said she had walked into the room and dramatically presented proof that Marcus was a drug addict who would blow the profit up his nose, and she had decided he was too high a risk for her to partner with. Then she partnered with them in an overseas project.

"There are always two sides to a story, Cam, you know that. And he was a risk. Even if her timing was deliberate to do the most damage, no one had the right to take her life. Especially like that."

Cam agreed. "I tell you one thing though; whoever killed her has got some nasty rage in them. You hire someone to kill a person it's a job, right?"

"Yeah, impersonal. So whoever killed her really hated her." Mary sighed. "Okay, Marcus is number one."

Camille shook her head. "Imagine living a life that at the end there could be a tally of people who hated you enough to want you dead?" She shook her head and looked out the car window at the passing hedges—natural screens defending the inequality of wealth.

"You knew her, Mare." Cam said, old friends talking shorthand.

"Yeah," she sighed. "She wasn't very nice. I mean it was more than not being a warm and fuzzy type. Honestly, I'm baffled about her and Di. But clearly they connected. I've known Di a long time and never have I seen her so smitten with anyone before."

"Is it because she's dead?" Cam asked with a brief look of apology crossing her face.

Mary thought about it and shrugged but before she could answer her phone rang.

Gabe Lasworth's gentle voice filled the quiet interior. "Wondering if you could stop by to see me, Mary." It was not posed as a question but more as a given and she agreed without a second thought. "The Huntting Inn?" she asked. She was ten minutes away and that was fine for him.

"I'll wait for you," Cam said knowing their next stop was Tristan's studio.

"Ok. It shouldn't be too long," Mary said confidently. But she was wrong.

CHAPTER FIFTY

Based solely on gut reaction Nick was convinced that Henry was somehow involved with Corliss's murder. However, unlike Detective's Lasworth's instincts, which had been cultivated over years of experience, Nick's investigative intuition was in its infancy and unreliable at best.

To Nick Petrucci's untrained eye Henry appeared relaxed, too relaxed. He interpreted Henry's calm posture as deliberate arrogance: legs crossed, one arm resting on the back of the sofa, the other petting his old dog. Within the limitations of Nick's myopic vision he could only perceive Henry's poise as a challenge.

An hour into the questioning Nick now knew that Corliss had been Henry's lover (for a brief spell when they initially met), his agent (until she played with the numbers of two sales) and then, naturally, his nemesis. But now Henry expected Nick to believe that he and Corliss were friends.

"Holding on to hurt or anger does no one any good," Henry explained when Nick asked how they could forge a friendship after she had siphoned ten thousand dollars from the sale of his work.

"That's a lot of money," Nick said with tight, crooked smile.

"I make a lot of money," Henry said. "But that's not the point," he added. "Corliss's short sightedness in screwing me out of ten thousand dollars only hurt herself. True, she never imagined I would find out, but I did and she lost the lucrative honor of representing me."

Nick just didn't like him. What he interpreted as arrogance was confidence and if he took half a step back and peered just inside himself, he would have seen that the two men were very similar and that what he didn't like was the reflection of himself.

"Honor?" Nick asked.

"Yes, honor. Would you prefer I say 'position'? Look, if an artist is lucky they can sell their work. If they are very, very lucky they can actually make a living at it. It's difficult, actually quite impossible to be creative *and* productive *and* represent oneself all at the same time. Fortunately, there are people out there who love art and have an eye for what might sell and have the amazing gift *to* sell. Corliss had a very good eye and the gift. And she had contacts and energy and was hungry in the beginning, so she worked like a demon. But as happens too frequently with too many people she got greedy."

"Sounds like a motive to me," Nick said, sounding more like Barney Fife from Mayberry than himself; so much so even he heard it and cleared his throat as if to erase it.

"Indeed," Henry agreed. "But as I said, she hadn't represented me for years. What reason could I possibly have for wanting Corliss dead? Absolutely none. As a matter of fact it was Corliss who brokered my sale to Diane Ajam for the piece now in her den."

"So you *have* had recent contact with Corliss."

"I never denied that."

"Never offered it, either," Nick thought. "Go on."

"It's quite simple, really. Diane was looking for a piece to fill a space, thought she would like a local artist and asked Corliss for a list."

"And Corliss suggested you? That seems unlikely since she didn't represent you."

"No, she did not. You would think with her list of extremely talented artists she would have been able to provide ample possibilities for her friend, but apparently not. Diane found the piece she wanted on my website and Corliss called me directly to see if she could broker a discount for her friend."

"Did she?

"Of course. As I said, the past was the past. A sale is a sale and it was a good sale."

"Did you share the profit with your current representative?"

"How is that relevant?" Henry asked.

"Okay. Who is your current agent?"

Henry told him.

"How long have you known Mary Moody?" Nick asked without missing a beat.

"Two weeks?" Henry was starting to think this policeman was wasting his time and he had much to do.

"You met through Diane, is that correct?"

Henry nodded.

"That was a lucrative introduction, wasn't it?"

Henry stared at Nick in response. The man was fishing and trying to get him angry, though why he didn't know.

"She's one of the big movers and shakers out here, isn't she? I mean to simply know her would be a step into a very refined circle. Wouldn't it? *And,* as I understand it, she kind of fancies you. And I mean why not? You're talented, wealthy, and you have a nice spread here. And let's face it; being with a woman like that would open lots of doors for a man like you, wouldn't it?"

"Detective, perhaps you need to do your homework. I assure you I do not need Ms. Moody to open doors for me." Henry's voice was even, but Nick did notice him pinching the piping of the sofa cushion until his nails turned red.

Nick chuckled softly. "I mean I know it's crazy but if you think about it this could actually be an updated version of your relationship with Corliss. Friends. Lovers. *Associates* ..." Nick drew out the last word and sighed.

"Yes, well now we've seemed to come full circle and if you don't mind, I really must get back to work." Henry stood.

Nick smiled and took his time standing. He was shorter than Henry but felt as solid as stone as he studied the artist's eyes until the taller man looked away. Nick was on to something and he knew it. He could almost taste the success of his theory that would elevate his stature not only within his department, but perhaps more importantly in Gabe Lasworth's eyes.

CHAPTER FIFTY-ONE

When you love what you do hours can fly by like minutes and before you know it the light has changed or you're suddenly hungry.

Tristan Cooper was a very lucky man for in this one single life he had been blessed with such focus several times over: first as a teenager with surfing, which brought him to this area, next with wood crafting, which led to his current and powerful body of work, and finally with what he knew to be his likely unrivaled skill as a lover.

But today he was watching the clock as he put the finishing touches on the fourth piece in his latest series. At the base of each piece was a womblike cube. The first piece, a prototype, really, was no more than eight inches in diameter with delicate limbs protruding limply from the base. A delicate gold band ringing a slender, wilted, almost skeletal finger seemed to be pointing upward and any passerby, even one with no interest in art, would feel powerful, nearly overwhelming emotions emanating from that simple, graceful gesture.

The current, fourth and final piece in the series was perhaps its most powerful, incorporating for the first time the clarity of a face straining against the cube. Unlike the sharp details of a hand, an arm, a shoulder, and the base of a foot where the detailed physical acuity of muscles, veins, nails, scars, and even hair was frighteningly real, the tormented face was muted as if a thin sheath could soften the acts of life or death. It was impossible to distinguish between fear and rage. Was the face running from or to something? It was Tristan's goal that the very subjectiveness of the piece—the need of the viewer's reaction—created a different complexity of viewer participation: the artist created something neither black nor white, only the viewer would make such a determination and in that define the piece. Coming. Going. Frightened. Enraged.

He was excited to show his work to Mary and her pretty black friend, but they were late. Big surprise, he thought as he lit a cigarette and leaned against the door frame looking out onto a beautiful day.

Which happened to be his birthday.

His fiftieth.

Fifty, which really meant he was starting his fifty-first year of life.

When he awoke that morning to the screech of hungry birds he was thinking about age and wisdom and how he had mellowed so much in the last three years.

A soft latticework of light filtering past the trees outside his windows swayed against the wall and the floor and instead of jumping up as was his way; he simply piled his pillows high behind him, lit a cigarette and studied the graceful shadow of nature.

He smoked and considered Oscar Wilde's platitude, "*With age comes wisdom.*"

"Crock of shit," he muttered. With age simply came the tempering of expectations. Was that wisdom? Well, maybe. He chuckled.

Everyone knows disappointment. That's life. He was old enough to be jaded and jaded enough to have lost the ability to fully trust.

This was a subject Tristan knew very well. One of his most powerful works, indeed a seminal point in his career as an artist, was a piece titled *Ow* made with rusted metal, nails, rosary beads, and fabricated skin.

Again he looked at his watch. She was forty-five minutes late and hadn't called. The prospect of a new buyer, perhaps a new rep in Mary, who was embedded with the real wealth, was so enticing he had allowed himself to actually hope that this might be a turning point. Corliss and her dumbbell Ruggiero had cheated him, he knew that, but other avenues had failed to materialize. Her death could likely be his final undoing as a selling artist and the thought was compelling enough for concern. Okay, maybe low-grade panic. Well certainly anxious enough to start considering financial alternatives.

Living in the Hamptons on the two-acre property his mother had helped him purchase in the '80s for a fraction of its current value was now in some ways a detriment: a deceptive billboard in a way. People assumed that the location, the property, indeed his historic freewheeling lifestyle, meant that he was flush. That assumption made idiots think he didn't need to sell his work or even take a job like that poor schmuck who hung himself. In reality he was property rich but dead poor. Up to his ears in debt for his art supplies and liquor tab at Atlantic Wines where Paul let him ride for long stretches of time, he had been racking his brain for ways to get an influx of dough.

Mary seemed to be the light at the end of the tunnel.

But she stood him up.

He took a final drag of the cigarette and returned to the comfort of work.

Something will work out. It had to.

CHAPTER FIFTY-TWO

As Leah led Lillian, Jack, and Missy through the magnificent property where the wedding would take place in a matter of days, she was struck by the lethargy of the threesome. Clearly the tour was biting into the father's day, the pouting bride-to-be said nothing and the mother, well the mother tried in vain to rally some excitement from her family. Leah felt sorry for Lillian, couldn't have cared less about the girl, and played to Jack who was about to sign a very large check of which she would receive a useful commission.

It helped that the space was absolutely stunning, from the select furnishings and lighting to the artwork and mirrors.

Because time was of the essence and the bride was apathetic, together Leah and Lillian decided on the best spot for the outdoor ceremony and how they would turn the grand room into a dining hall. Mary had already explained that during cocktails after the ceremony the waiters would bring the chairs from the ceremony to the dining tables. Leah and Lillian were getting so excited it actually infected Jack, but alas not Missy.

"I assume the owner will provide ample toilet paper," Lillian said as they gathered around one of the kitchen islands to complete the paperwork.

"Oh of course," Leah said making a mental note to go to Costco.

When the papers were signed Leah walked the family to their car and waved them away saying she needed to close up the house. Inside she called Mary and gave her a complete update including where the ceremony would be held and parking logistics.

"Leah, you have no idea how grateful I am to you. Things have bottlenecked here and I just can't get away."

"Believe me, I understand. I'll help you in any way I can." Like Mary, Leah had the innate ability to put others at ease no matter how panicked she might be about a situation. Life had shown her repeatedly that for the most part things always had a way of working out.

That's when Mary asked to hire her for the next three days as her liaison to the space. Since Leah knew the house and the logistics she would be able to keep things flowing on site.. The sum Mary offered was extraordinary; it was enough to cover the broker's expenses for a month and a half. Add the commission on top and this was more than worth three days of headaches.

"I'm not normally this removed," Mary started, but Leah cut her off.

"Listen, I get it. The girl is a pain in the neck and I can't imagine the stress of changing everything last minute. I've thrown two weddings of my own; well, not mine but my daughters'. I'm here for you. Why don't you email me the names and numbers of all the purveyors and I will be happy to be your on-site person."

"I asked Lillian to call the tent company as soon as they signed the papers but can you lead that?"

"A tent?" Leah asked knowing her client would likely burst a blood vessel at the potential wear and tear on her property.

"And a dance floor," Mary said, knowing the problem.

"Oh, that's not good," Leah mumbled more to herself than Mary. "No one mentioned that."

"I'm sorry. I don't know how that got overlooked. Look, tell her we'll tack on another ten."

They both knew she meant thousand. Mary had no choice thanks to the little bitch bride.

She gave Leah the information and was assured that Leah would call them and also let Lillian know she was on top of it.

"I owe you," Mary sighed, feeling the weight lessen if only a bit.

Within minutes after their call Mary had emailed an impressive, comprehensive document which calmed Leah's concern over what she had gotten herself into. Her first call was to the renowned caterer, a rock star in the industry. Making a contact like him alone excited her. It would, she knew, impress her clients.

Next, she contacted the tent company who said they would be there in an hour. She had more than enough time to grab a cup of coffee and a yogurt after which she would call the house owner about the tent and Lillian about the increase. As she locked the house she realized she was smiling. This was different.

This was going to be fun. Or so she thought.

CHAPTER FIFTY-THREE

Mary sat across from Detective Lasworth, clearly stunned. "I had no idea," she said, and it was obviously true.

"I'm sorry. I thought you knew."

"How could I know?" she asked.

"Well, you exchanged calls with Sheryl Strickland twice yesterday." He shrugged a shoulder. "As a matter of fact, yours was the last call registered on her cell phone at 11:38 last night. Can you explain?"

Mary frowned and cast her eyes about as if looking for an answer. "I called her because one of my clients needed her services."

"An emergency?"

"Yes." She nodded once.

"For a maid." It was a statement.

Mary nodded.

"At eleven thirty at night."

"That's right." Mary knew how screwy it sounded, knew she had to explain, but also knew she had to protect her client. She took a deep breath, leaned closer to Gabe and spoke softly. "I know it sounds ridiculous but there was a housekeeping emergency last night and Sheryl is my client's maid, so naturally I called her."

"Okay. Let's start at the beginning."

"Detective Lasworth, if it is possible, I would really like to keep my client out of this."

"Mary, Sheryl Strickland was likely murdered last night -"

"You said she drowned." Mary interrupted. When he said nothing the gravity of the situation hit her so hard she felt sick.

"Oh my God." She swallowed several times and calmed herself before telling Gabe everything about the night before.

When she was finished Lasworth nodded as he considered her story. "That doesn't explain her earlier call with you."

"That was the only time I called her."

The corners of his mouth drew into a deep frown. "My records show that she had called you earlier in the day. The call lasted under ninety seconds. How do you explain that?"

"Are you sure it was me she called?"

He read off her cell phone number. "Is that you?"

"Yes. But I never spoke to her. I swear that's the truth."

Gabe wanted to believe her, but he had proof in hand.

"What time was the call?" she asked. He told her and she went over the day and all the calls she had received. "Oh my God," she finally said.

"What?"

"That's around the time I got a call about the reward. I thought it was a man." She described the call and how the person sounded like Darth Vader and said to meet them at Cittanuova at ten o'clock. "I remember that it was from a private caller."

The redheaded assistant with a tic called Gabe away and Mary was left alone with her thoughts. If Sheryl was calling about the reward she likely knew who killed Paulo. And if she was killed it stood to reason that the killer knew Sheryl was about to blow the whistle because who on earth would kill Sheryl for any other reason? Yes she was irritating but she was innocuous. And she was a really good maid, who spoke English, a difficult combo to find in the Hamptons. Replacing her was going to throw a dozen different rich kudzu girls into a tailspin. Mary could just hear the cacophony of their plaintive whines, "Oh my God, what am I going to do without her? I mean I'm sorry she's dead, but *really*? It's summer! I need help!"

Mary knew she was in imminent danger, which meant Cam was too. Think. Think. Think. Sheryl was likely killed because she knew an identity, but if she was dead wouldn't it make sense that the killer would think they were free, that no one could trace them? But clearly that wasn't the case. Or maybe it wasn't the killer leaving her these insane warnings. Maybe it was just a local looney who thought this was fun. It wasn't beyond reason. But why did the killer kill Paulo? For the same reason? Did Paulo have something on the killer? And if so, what? And why was Corliss killed? Think. Think.

"Mary?" Gabe said her name for the third time, finally rousing her from her contemplation.

Startled she recovered quickly. "Well, I was lost in space wasn't I?" she said too loudly.

"Seems so." His serious face revealed nothing but his eyes still shone kind and concerned. "I want to go over a few things." He sat across from her, his little feet planted firmly between them. "You up for it?"

"Yes, of course," she said completely forgetting about her appointment with Tristan to see his work.

During the next forty-five minutes Mary learned a lot more than she had to offer and when they were done she was exhausted.

Finally Gabe took a deep breath, leaned back in his chair and said, "Now, let's talk about you and this morning's event. You've stirred up something. Because of that stupid reward you have made yourself a target."

She tried to cut him off but he held up a hand. "And it's not just today is it?"

Mary shook her head as she looked down. "I know they're just sending a message but ..."

"*Just* sending a message. Is something wrong with you? Consider the messages: four flat tires and the note. Those are strong messages which reminds me of an old Italian proverb: 'Beware of one who has nothing to lose.' You have no idea what can of worms you might have opened here. And sadly neither do I." He sounded tired. "I had a feeling something like this would happen."

"Well then can't you use me?" she asked in earnest.

"Oh! You mean like bait? Dangle you in front of someone who has a history of killing, if not two, then at least one person? There's an idea! How could I have possibly missed that?" His mockery was loud and clear.

"The last thing I meant to do was intrude in your investigation." Mary apologized.

"Bullshit. It was the only thing you meant to do. You thought for some inane reason that you could do my job better than me."

"That's not true," she interrupted.

"Yes. It is." He stood and though he was not a tall man he seemed to tower above her. "You thought the local police are boobs and if you gave them a little assist you might be able to move things along. But at what cost? I am not happy with you right now. I would not assume to interfere with your work so what makes you think it's okay to intrude in mine?"

There was nothing Mary could say to better the situation and she knew it.

"I am going to assign an officer to you. Until they are available, I want to know where you are and who you're with every moment of the day, do you understand?"

When she said "Yes," her voice cracked.

Gabe considered for a fleeting instant to let this sophisticated yet seemingly real person know that he was only concerned for her well-being and not as angry with her as he seemed, but because of that he said nothing. Maybe a little fear would keep her out of trouble.

He pulled a notepad from his breast pocket and set it in front of her. He then offered her a pen. "I want you to write down every number of every person you will have contact with today and tomorrow. And addresses if you plan to be at a client's or a friend's."

Without hesitation she did as he requested.

When she was done, she handed him the pad and his pen. "You have to know that I have all the respect in the world for you, Detective. I will admit that I have never had much confidence in the local police, but you're not a fool and I am sure you can understand why I have felt that. But I do have the highest regard for you." Standing, she loomed over the detective and yet he was still in command.

"Mary, I don't need you to like me. I need to keep you safe. Put my number in your speed dial right now," he said poking his chin at her.

"Okay," he said when she had done so. "Now expect a call from someone on my staff within the next hour. Do everything they say and don't give them a hard time. You understand?"

"I do."

"Good. Now get outta here, I have work to do." He softened the order with a gentle smile.

CHAPTER FIFTY-FOUR

Agda sat at the counter of John Papas coffee shop knowing that Ruggiero would never look for her here. She needed to be alone and she was hungry. Anxiety always had that effect on her. She pretended to read the newspaper while she sipped a lusterless cup of coffee and waited for her breakfast of eggs, bacon, pancakes, sausage and a toasted bagel.

She could no more concentrate on the news than fly to the moon. Fucking Ruggiero. That sniveling, stupid son of a bitch, *jävel feg*. She always knew he was a chicken but to throw her knowingly under the police bus, so to speak, was even lower than she thought he could stoop.

"Disgruntled," the policeman had quoted Ruggiero as saying when questioned about Agda's relationship with Corliss.

She who had always prided herself on her Swedish calm was taken aback. She had thought Ruggiero was her friend. For the last two years they had been practically inseparable. How could he do this?

"Miss Eck?" She remembered how the policeman had jarred her from her thoughts in the cramped trailer.

"Oh yes. No. Corliss has been selling my work for two years now," she had said and then with quick calculation explained how with the last two sales Corliss had said the canvases had sold for one amount when Ruggiero had shown her proof that they had sold for more.

Her plate of food arrived and she dug into the pancakes first, not bothering with the pre-packaged syrup.

The fat little policeman had scared her. And he had scared her because Ruggiero gave him the opportunity by pulling her in where she didn't belong. She ripped a bagel half in half, slathered it with butter and drove it into an egg yolk without benefit of salt or pepper. She tasted nothing.

And he hadn't even warned her, even after she had been there for him last night trying to soothe his fucking fragile dirty soul. *Jävel.* Fucking bastard.

Now they probably thought she was somehow complicit in Corliss's death and it was all Ruggiero's fault. She stopped chewing. Maybe, just maybe he was deliberately pointing a finger at her to take suspicion off himself. Was it possible? Could Ruggiero have killed Corliss? He certainly hated her enough. But he was a *feg.* She shoved a rasher of bacon into her mouth and chewed on other cowards from history: Judas, Bin Laden, Newt Gingrich at his wife's death bed talking divorce, Saddam Hussein. The list could go on and on and on, and most of them were men. Of course! Ruggiero. You sniveling little bastard, did you kill Corliss?

She popped a whole sausage link into her mouth and without finishing the rest of her breakfast threw a twenty on the counter and left. She had to confront him right this minute.

She cut through the parking lot and stormed over to the gallery where she found him sipping his stupid trenta caffè Americano that she slapped out of his hand.

"Wha—," he sputtered as he flinched away from her. Between his massive hangover and immediate panic that the coffee might have splashed onto a canvas he grabbed the leather wastebasket to retch but there was nothing: he was like an old cat working a hairball.

Out of the corner of his eye he saw Agda swinging her arm back to cuff him again. She missed but he let out a scream and staggered backward tripping on his feet and landing on his backside.

"You!" she yelled. "I thought you were my friend!"

"I *am* your friend!" he screeched trying to scooch away from her raised boot. Terrified she would hit his face he rolled into a fetal position, covering his head with his arms.

Agda stood on one foot, arms aloft, her other knee bent for the kick and then just froze. What was she doing? No. No.

She knew what she was doing. He deserved it. But the steam had been spent. She let out a long breath, turned away from Ruggiero and dragged her fingers through her hair. She would not be lowered to his level.

Having braced for the kick with closed eyes, when Ruggiero felt nothing, he stole a glance up and crawled far enough away before struggling to his feet.

"What are you, crazy?" he panted pressing his hands against his chest.

Facing away from him Agda shook her head. "I thought you were my friend," she said softly as she started for the door.

"What are you talking about? I *am* your friend. Agda, you're my best friend. What did I do? Tell me," he pleaded.

"It doesn't matter," she said turning to face him. "If you don't know ..." She couldn't even finish her sentence. She took one last disgusted look at him and left.

What neither of them knew was that in the heat of their altercation a window-shopper had gotten an eyeful.

When Agda barreled blindly out of the gallery Cam looked to be calmly strolling up the street trying to temper her pace to meet Mary, who was at the Palm with the police.

CHAPTER FIFTY-FIVE

"Mary Moody was here." Richard cradled the phone between his ear and chin as he played with a slim piece of wire.

"When?" Marcus asked.

"Just a little while ago."

"Yeah, well she came to see me yesterday … or maybe the day before. Shit, I don't know. I don't care."

"She wants me to help her."

"Help her what?" Marcus asked knowing perfectly well what she wanted. The concierge was making the rounds, having hit him the other day and now she was trawling.

"Investigate who killed Corliss." He was practically breathless.

"Get the fuck out of here." Marcus feigned surprise as he bent over his desk for a breakfast line of coke.

"I know, but trust me, it's true all right. We talked for *hours* and she took copious notes and we're going to have dinner together." The strange thing was that, though he was elaborating on the truth, in Richard's mind, it was absolutely accurate which is why it trickled so easily off his tongue.

Marcus lit a cigarette and scratched his dirty hair. Richard was like a love-hate thing. As annoying and starchy as he was, he was also smart and rich. Marcus worked the friendship for one reason: the old faggot had no family and when he died Marcus expected to be rewarded handsomely. In the meantime he did his due diligence and for the most part Richard could be very entertaining.

"Yeah, well, I hope you have dinner here," Marcus finally said.

"Ach, if I know you you'll put ex-lax in her dessert," Richard twittered.

"Ground glass," Marcus replied. "So what'd you talk about?"

Richard gave him a longwinded rundown of their conversation, told him all about Camille, whom he simply *adored*, and finally let it drop that, "She asked about you."

"Why?"

"Oh Marcus, simply *everyone* knows that you two hated one another ..."

"So did you," Marcus interrupted.

"Well yes, of course, and I was very upfront about that. But aside from the fact that I despised the bitch, I have no real motive for killing her."

"And she thinks I do?" Marcus asked.

"I don't know what she thinks." There was no need to mention that he had detailed the enmity between Corliss and Marcus.

"Yeah, well like I said she was here the other day looking for Corliss. I think the two of them had something going on."

"Oh no," Richard countered confidently. "Her lover is the most magnificent black woman I have ever seen, prettier than Lena Horne or Diana Ross. I mean absolutely exquisite."

"All right, well I gotta get back to work." Marcus sighed. "Just one thing, Ricardo." He paused. "How bad did you make things for me?"

Richard was finishing a wire figurine that resembled Camille and said, "Oh Marcus, would I do a thing like that?"

"Yes."

"Not too. She needed juice. I poured a little. You're fine."

CHAPTER FIFTY-SIX

After Mary left, Gabe Lasworth ordered a member from his team to keep an eye on her.

The officer tapped for the job received his orders and all pertinent data while returning in an unmarked car from Yaphank.

It was perfect since he was planning to stop in the town of Shirley, which was right on the way.

The prescription was waiting for him at the doctor's office but the drugstore was crowded: he was sixth on a slow line.

Once he handed in the prescription he was told to come back in half an hour. Naturally this made him more anxious but fuck it, he'd get to East Hampton when he got there.

To fill the wait time he went across the street and had two quick tequilas while he concocted stories to explain his tardiness.

The clerk behind the counter was new but after only three days, with accolades from the pharmacist at the end of every day, she was cocky and flirted with the customer as she slid him the bag of pills and his change.

If she had been paying attention she would have seen that the name on the bag was Anderson, with an O, not Andersen with an E.

If the police officer had been in less of a hurry for his fix he might have looked at the bag or the label on the bottle, but no.

Without looking he popped two pills and pulled away from the curb confident that the oxycodone would soon have him mellowed.

But digoxin is a funny drug.

By Eastport his vision started to blur and then a mild dizziness set in. Going off course he pulled onto a side street in Remsenburg and tried to catch his breath. This was different. Not bad, just different. He pushed the car seat back and shut his eyes.

Five minutes, that's all he needed.

He shut his eyes and drifted into the high.

CHAPTER FIFTY-SEVEN

Cam was pacing the parking lot when Mary finally emerged from the police trailer looking at her cell phone. She didn't look happy.

"You're not going to believe this," Cam said, unable to stop herself.

"Shit. I forgot about Tristan," Mary said pressing a button on her cell and bringing it to her ear as they headed to the car.

Cam listened silently as Mary apologized and promised that they could be at his studio in fifteen minutes.

Once in the car Mary took a deep breath and held onto the steering wheel as if it could center her.

"I saw a big white woman beat up a man at Corliss's gallery," Cam blurted.

It took Mary a second to take in what had just been said. She slowly turned to Camille, who was flushed with excitement and asked her to repeat that.

Cam did.

Not knowing any of the players by sight Camille described the two and Mary knew precisely whom she meant: Corliss's assistant Ruggiero and the artist Agda Eck, whom she had met at several art shows.

"Okay," she said putting the car into reverse. "Tell me everything."

As the women drove to Tristan's Cam told Mary everything she had seen at the gallery.

In the meantime Tristan was getting ready for her. He wondered who *they* were, hoping it wasn't Henry. Every time he envisioned showing Mary his studio it ended with them fucking on his good-luck couch where he had pleased many women in the past, including a seventy-three-year-old collector who had a surprisingly supple body, large breasts and had purchased two pieces for her children.

He stood in front of a mirror and winked; he really was a handsome man. *"Fuck, if I were a woman I'd want me,"* he thought. *"Certainly more than Henry."* But Henry and Mary had something already. So what? A roll in the sack meant nothing, just a bodily urge satisfied.

"Whoa, buddy," he warned his reflection. "This is business. Not pleasure. The objective is to sell. Just remember that. Don't let your dick get in the way. Okay?" He nodded. "Okay."

He took a slab of clay and pretended to work; wanting her to find him so engrossed he wouldn't even hear her enter.

But it was impossible. Her car rolled over the gravel and he came out to greet her. Them. Holy cow. Well, it sure as hell wasn't Henry.

"I am so sorry we're late," Mary said.

"No big deal," he lied. "You're here. That's what matters."

Mary introduced her friend and the three of them stood in a clutch before entering the studio.

"This is a beautiful property," Mary said, admiring the mature trees surrounding the run-down studio, and twenty feet away a copse of massive rhododendrons one could actually walk into—a perfect haven for a child's imagination.

"I've lived here a long time," Tristan said as he led them into his studio. "Welcome," he pronounced as he stepped aside for the ladies.

Mary thought he seemed different from the two previous times she had met him, more subdued, and she wondered if this was the real Tristan Cooper.

Canvases lined and leaned against the walls, one atop another; there had to be close to a hundred. The studio was divided into what looked like three distinct work areas, one for painting, one for sculpting with shelves of sculptures in varying degrees of completion, barrels of clay, an enormous table and a kiln at the far end and finally an enclosed tent-like structure. The place smelled like turpentine and clay and smoke and beer. It was like an explosion of creativity, as if the occupant had no sense of order, and yet the work was staggering.

Slack-jawed, the two women slowly walked the circumference of the room flipping through the mostly abstract paintings. All of the canvases were bold, mostly stark white, muted greys and blue-black but all had a streak of red somewhere on the canvas ranging from bold to a *Where's Waldo* search for the mark. Tristan kept his mouth shut and studied them. Their familiarity with one another, the way one would touch the other to point out a piece and the other's seamless response. He could easily picture the three of them on the couch.

"So," he finally said when they were only halfway through the work, "what do you think?"

"It all has quite an impact," Mary said. "And you seem equally comfortable with clay, oils, and metal. The piece at the gallery was metal, wasn't it?" she asked.

"Bronze." He nodded.

"What's in there?" Camille asked pointing to the tent.

"I do the silicone work in there. You have to keep it contained because it's so toxic. Part of a process." He waved off further explanation. That was where his current work was in development.

"Tristan, what will happen to the artists Corliss had been representing?" Mary asked.

He took a deep breath and shrugged. "We have to look for other agents or reps. For example, you mentioned the other day that you had a client who might be interested. If you were to make the connection and a sale occurred, you would receive thirty percent of the profit." He knew legally fifty percent would still be owed to Corliss but she didn't need to know that and he could probably fudge it.

"That actually sounds like fun," Camille said, rolling through a list of friends and associates in her own head who could be likely clients.

"Not to me," Tristan laughed. "Can I offer you ladies a beverage?"

Mary shook her head, obviously preoccupied. "No, thanks. Busy day ahead. But I might have a potential buyer for the piece I saw in the gallery. Do you have others like it?"

He glanced at the tent. "I'm workin' on the last in that series right now. It's larger and, I think, more powerful." He strode over to the shelves and pulled down two pieces, his first and third piece from the sequence which he placed on the table and stepped back for them to inspect. He pointed to the smallest piece. "This was more or less the prototype for my final in the series. But I actually like the unimposing size of it, something you could place on a mantle or a shelf, rather than needing floor space for a pedestal." Then he nodded to the third, somewhat larger sculpture, already bronzed: it was the first one in which he had included the shadow of a face.

Mary barely heard what he was saying, her mind still on what she had learned from Detective Lasworth concerning Henry. Why hadn't Henry told her the truth? True he hadn't lied per se but isn't withholding information as good as lying?

Cam continued the conversation with Tristan, obviously interested in either the man or his work or both.

By the time Mary reemerged from her thoughts Cam and Tristan were shaking hands.

"Great, I'm thrilled," she heard Cam say.

"It couldn't have found a better home," Tristan said, a wide smile creasing the entirety of his face.

Cam sat on a stool at the table, pulled out her checkbook and took the pen Tristan offered. When she handed him the check he offered to put the larger work in the car.

He had sold the piece for a fraction of its worth but he considered it an investment. Camille was not only a woman he knew he would bed one day but she was enthusiastic, and enthusiasm was the first step for any rep. She tells a friend, a friend tells a friend and before you know it a whole new network of potential buyers are knocking on your door. But right now the unexpected check in his shirt pocket was an omen that things were about to change for him, and it couldn't have come too soon.

Before they drove off Mary promised to talk to her friends.

Tristan kissed Cam's hand and waved as they backed out of the driveway and up the road.

When they were out of sight he pulled the payment out of his pocket, kissed it and returned to work.

CHAPTER FIFTY-EIGHT

In the aftermath of Corliss's murder Diane had stopped eating much of anything. In mid-bite tears would swell up and spill out, extinguishing an already lackluster appetite. So she drank and she smoked. And she waited, waited for someone to tell her who was responsible for tormenting her lover and obliterating their future. A peaceful death was hard enough but knowing that Corliss had been murdered and had been frightened before she died was unbearable.

She was old enough to know that time ultimately does heal most wounds, but this was something altogether different. In this there was no comfort, not now and not in the foreseeable future.

But instinct was another thing altogether and her strongest drive had always been her creativity, her emotional buoy.

She was not a writer. Writing required a different set of creative tools than she possessed. The writer could be alone for hours on end and hide in broad daylight whereas Diane needed to know she was in control of a room and with energy alone boom "I'M HERE!"

Solitude for a woman like Diane is akin to death.

And yet she had spent the night before, well into the morning, working on a screenplay in her study. Unable to stop thinking about Corliss's last moments of life, she put her imaginings on a page, one leading to another, to another. She believed with all her heart that when Corliss died she had been thinking about Diane, and the story became her catharsis.

When she finally awoke in the afternoon she was, for the first time in days, hungry.

In the past she and close friends had joked about the grief diet, but in truth there was something so empty inside her now that she wanted to explode.

Checking the cabinets and fridge for something to eat she found nothing. She reached for a cigarette but after the long night the pack was empty.

Instead of just jumping in the car looking like one of Macbeth's witches, she showered and threw on a shirt and sweats which were suddenly loose.

She turned east on Montauk Highway with no destination in mind.

The straight, flat road led to one place only: Montauk. "People from Queens go to Montauk," Corliss had once said, basing her calculation on miles: "New Jersey residents will go as far as Westhampton or Southampton (if they have dough), Manhattanites to Bridge or East Hampton and people from Queens will go to Montauk."

Diane smiled at the simple mathematics, which proved oddly accurate.

She drove focusing not on the road but on conjuring memories of the good times with Corliss. Not the end. Not what would never be, but the good times and the good that had come from their time together.

Good had come from it.

She pulled into a parking space in front of a deli where without thinking she ordered a liverwurst, onion, lettuce, mayo, mustard, and peanut butter on white bread, a sandwich she hadn't had since her grandmother died. Nanny's concoction was only one of their many connections. Nanny; she hadn't thought about her in months. Every six months Diane lit a yahrzeit candle for Nanny, a candle of remembrance, as if she could ever forget. Nanny would have liked Corliss because in many ways they were cut from the same cloth. Both were independent, stubborn, fun-loving women who didn't give their love easily, but gave it fully.

Sitting on a stretch of damp, empty, vast Montauk beach Diane took out the sandwich, placed it beside her on her bag and lit a cigarette. The town of Montauk may be the only one in the area that felt like a tacky beachside hamlet, but the beaches are deeper than any of the others along the Hamptons shoreline, which makes it magical. It was a perfect day; wisps of fast-moving clouds, the ocean the color of celadon with a steady flow of whitecaps.

To take comfort from all this felt like a betrayal to Corliss, and yet it *was* comforting. It was the very thing she loved about life: the simple, natural beauty of the world which they had been gifted.

So engrossed was she in studying the horizon she hadn't noticed the visitor sitting silently and politely beside her.

Normally such a thing would have scared the daylights out of her, but when Diane realized she was not alone, she simply said, "Well hello. When did you get here?"

The emaciated black lab sat straight and proud despite the sadness in his eyes and his evident ill health. He blinked yet kept his gaze straight toward the ocean.

"Listen," Diane said as she unwrapped the sandwich, "Most people find this gross, but let's face it; you could use something in you, right?"

She extracted a slice of liverwurst and placed it in the palm of her hand. She had to encourage him to eat but after he took a cautionary sniff he gently wolfed down the meat in one inhalation. Knowing most people wouldn't touch this sandwich and in all likelihood this poor dog would get sick from it, she picked off the onions and laid out the rest of the sandwich on its wrapping in front of him and waited.

"What happened to you, little guy?" she asked as he lay down and inched toward the sandwich, choosing to lick at the peanut butter first. While she had always liked dogs she had never been one to fuss over them. As a matter of fact it was only in that moment as she watched him slowly down Nanny's sandwich that she even remembered Beanie. "Wow. What's that about?" she asked the dog. And then she told him everything that had happened in the last week including her having completely ignored Beanie. "How could I do that? I mean, am I that wrapped up in myself?"

The dog sighed.

"Yeah, you're right. I guess I am." She took the empty sandwich paper, fashioned it into a bowl and filled it with bottled water, holding it steady in her hands as he drank.

When he had had his fill he stretched onto his side and Diane touched him for the first time. The poor thing was skin and bones but he didn't seem to object to her touch.

"Hey!" a man called out as he approached them. "You must be a magician," he said to Diane as he gestured to the dog.

"Why?" she asked, shielding her eyes from the sun with her hand.

"I've been trying to help that guy forever. Everyone has. But he's so skittish you can never get close enough. Look at him. You must have a special touch." He kept his distance, not wanting to spook the dog, and told her how he had appeared a few months ago and they figured someone had abandoned him because the community had done due diligence in trying to find the owner. "Several people, myself included, wanted to adopt him, but he would never let anyone get close enough. Even animal rescue couldn't help. Looks like you have yourself a dog. Congratulations," he said before continuing on his way.

About to object, Diane simply watched helplessly as he walked away apparently more confident than she that the dog had found a home.

"You know," she said to the dozing dog, "I travel a lot." In his sleep his feet started twitching which she took to mean that he did too. "This is crazy. I can't have a dog. I'm selfish and myopic, and I'm depressed. See, I'm still focusing on me and not you. I mean if either of us should be depressed right now it's probably you, but no, I'm thinking about myself." She continued to pet him as she spoke and he seemed so calm under her touch. "You know what you need? You need love. Love like that man would give you. I bet he's retired and would walk you every day two and three times a day. I could never do that."

The dog lifted his head and stared at her as if to say, "Calm down, just calm down." As irrational as it was, Diane took this as an invitation to lie beside him, which she did. She tentatively spooned the little guy and in turn he pushed his painfully thin back against her belly and sighed contentedly.

Resting her cheek against her arm as a pillow, she cried softly, but it wasn't for loss this time. This time it was for the love welling up inside her for this lost creature who had been found, not knowing whether she meant the dog or herself.

CHAPTER FIFTY-NINE

By the time they got back to the house it was not yet two, which was insane considering how much they had already accomplished.

Cam set the new sculpture in the center of Mary's massive square coffee table and smiled. "He's good. Ain't no question about that," she said, arms akimbo.

Mary let the dogs out back and continued into her office not even bothering to look at Cam's new pride and joy. She stood staring blindly at her white boards.

"You want to tell me what's on your mind?" Cam asked leaning against the door frame.

"Aside from the fact that I want you to go home?"

"Yes, because that's not going to happen so don't start again. I am not about to leave you until I know you are really safe and that's it. No more discussion. Look, you said we're under police protection now, right? And you trust that detective, right?" Cam wasn't dumb enough not to be concerned or to trust anyone, even the police, blindly. But two targets were a lot more challenging than one especially since they had both taken self-defense classes in the city.

"He and Corliss were lovers," she said softy trying to temper the anger she had been fighting since she learned this little tidbit from Gabe Lasworth.

"Who? The *detective*?" Cam was stunned.

"Henry."

"When?"

Mary turned and Cam saw the full force of her friend's upset. "It doesn't matter. He never said anything. Omission,

Cam. Think about it." Her voice was hard.

Cam didn't have to think about it; she knew how it looked for Henry and more importantly how this could affect Mary, who was already struggling with trust.

"Honey, I think you need to clear your head. I haven't seen you relax once since I got here."

"I have work to do."

"Right. And you know as well as I do that your head is not into it right now which only means you'll ultimately wind up doubling your efforts."

Mary couldn't argue.

Cam continued. "The most pressing client you have is that idiot bride and there really isn't anything you can do about that right now. You said you trust the broker, so here's what I think: I'm going to take the dogs for a walk and I want you to go out, Mare. Get a massage, go to the beach; just get out of here. No work. No me. No nothing. Okay?" She came up behind Mary and wrapped her arms around her. "It will be fine. Right now you only have suppositions and you know how dangerous those are."

Mary put her hand on Cam's forearm and squeezed.

"Okay, I'm out of here," Cam said. We'll be back whenever. Just be sure and lock the door, okay? I have a key."

"No!" Mary yelled coming to her senses. "For all we know that asshole is out there right now."

"Okay. But thanks to your dealer we have two cars again. I'll take them to the dog park where there are loads of people and I'll be safe. The police will be following you so you're safe. Is that okay?" she asked gently.

Mary nodded and stood in place another five minutes after they had gone without moving, trying to ward off thoughts of Henry and her ex, Marshal, and figure out what would make her feel better. The office phone ringing startled her and she left the house before hearing another whiny client in need of something.

She found herself pulling into the parking lot of the funeral parlor where Paulo would still be laid out, the final day of his wake.

Inside she read the board and realized that it was between hours. She entered the room expecting a final private farewell but found Lina and Paulina seemingly deep in conversation.

It was Paulina who saw her first and she cast her deep brown eyes uncertainly at the stranger. Lina stood when she saw her and, taking Paulina's hand, went to greet Mary.

Lina introduced Mary as, "Poppy's friend, Miss Mary." The child was a clone of both parents, with her father's face and her mother's slender build. Unlike other children her age who might hide behind the safety of their mother's leg, Paulina offered her hand in a firm little shake.

Lina bent down and whispered in her daughter's ear. The child nodded and hurried out of the room. Lina smiled as she watched her daughter run to the bathroom.

"She likes the hand drying machine," she said as she gestured to a row of seats.

"How are you holding up?" Mary asked.

Lina gave a little shrug.

"I don't know how you recover from something like this," Mary said softly. "But you will."

Lina nodded. "Every night I dream about him. Good dreams. We're laughing and, and when I wake up I roll over expecting him to be there." She brought her opened hands to her face and pushed her hair back through her fingers. Dark circles underscored her tired eyes.

They talked like old friends, discussing the wake and the people there, the turnout that had surprised Lina. They talked about Paulina's reaction to her father's death. "It's very odd. She sits in bed at night and talks to him like he's still here," Lina said. "I tell you it would be scary or funny if it didn't break my heart. I listened at the door last night and it was like she was having a normal conversation with him. She was telling him about everything that was going on here and then she would pause and respond as if she was answering a question. I went in to sit with her and she told me not to worry, that Poppy was okay. And yet she wakes in the middle of the night screaming." Lina shook her head.

Mary took Lina's hand and they sat in silence for a long

moment. And then without prelude Lina told Mary how she and Paulo had met. "I was raised out here with my aunt. My mother died when I was five and the family thought it was best if I lived with my aunt. It was a wonderful childhood. She was as good to me as my own mother would have been and she encouraged me to reach for the stars. The summer after high school I worked part time and went to community college. That's when Paulo came out to visit his family—a family my aunt knew since childhood. At first I barely noticed him. He was a goofy-looking boy who seemed to spend a lot of time on his own, even though he was here to visit family and friends. But one day he hands me a little wooden statue of the sun and the moon that he had carved. He said, 'This is for you. I hope you like it.' It was so beautiful. Delicate, whimsical, and powerful at the same time. Just like him. By the end of the summer we were married."

"What are you going to do?" Mary finally asked.

Lina's eyes were uncomprehending.

"Ready or not, you have to keep moving forward. Do you have a job?" Mary asked.

Lina shook her head. "Paulo was doing so well we decided that I would stay home." She pressed her lips tightly together and brought her hands to her belly. "No one knows but … I'm pregnant."

"That's wonderful," Mary said sincerely, despite the fact that Paulo would never see his new child or the complications that would arise for Lina, now having to raise two children without him. "No one knows?" Mary asked.

Lina shook her head. "We were waiting for the Fourth of July party to tell everyone. We always have a big barbeque with about fifty people." She rubbed her still-flat belly. "And now, I'm just, I don't know. It's too much."

"Do you know what it is?" Mary asked, her hand resting on Lina's knee.

"Not yet. We thought about not knowing, but now I want to know. I want it to be a boy." Lina inhaled sharply and whispered, "I don't know what I am going to do. Two babies, no job. It's not good."

"Well, it's not as bad as you might think. I have another check for you from Diane. With the other check it should be enough to get you through a year."

Lina stared at her. "Why? She gave me too much before."

"Diane is a good woman. The fact is she cares." There was no sign of Paulina. "I'm thinking, though, that you will need to work. Not only for the income but for your sanity. Do you agree?"

Lina nodded. "Absolutely, but who would hire a pregnant woman?"

"Me." As soon as she said it Mary knew it was the right thing. "I need an assistant and I think you would be the perfect candidate for the job."

Lina's eyes widened, making her face look like innocence personified.

"I mean, I don't even know what the job entails, but my friends and clients have been bugging me to get an assistant and honestly you're the only one I think I would want to work with. Are you interested?"

"Are you crazy?" Lina asked.

"Maybe. But you know, now that I think of it, I'm getting excited. We can sort out all of the details later, but this might be a perfect solution for both of us. I mean, you have to deal with lots of difficult, entitled people who can be rude. Most of my clients are actually very nice, but forewarned is forearmed. Some will treat you like a speck of dust. And it's an anxiety producing job." As Mary said this she realized how true that was but thought that Lina would be steady and unimpressed by celebrity. "Will you think about it?"

"I don't have to think. I am honored."

"You're going to be okay, Lina. You have a great support group, you are a strong woman, and I promise to be here for you in any way I can."

Paulina ran into the room and threw herself on her mother. Lina kissed the child's head and asked in Spanish if she was hungry, which she was. Mary waited as mother and daughter said good-bye to Paulo before leaving.

Mary took a moment to assure her friend that she would

look after his family as if they were her own.

Finally, with Paulina secure in her car seat, Lina walked Mary to her car and asked if she had had any response from the reward.

"Yeah, but it didn't pan out," was all she said. Sheryl was the caller and Sheryl was dead. The thought coursed through her body like dry ice.

CHAPTER SIXTY

Shortly after Cam and Mary had left there was a knock on Tristan's door. Thinking it might be Camille Logan—whose name was on the check in his breast pocket waiting to be deposited—coming back to thank him properly for the great deal he had given her, he opened the door with a sultry smile.

This quickly faded when he saw a small, roundish man in a suit standing before him.

"Tristan Cooper?" the man asked.

"Yeah," he said but it sounded more like "Maybe." Just past the little man was a Ford sedan with a carrot-topped man in the driver's seat.

"I'm Detective Lasworth," Gabe said showing his identification. "May I come in?"

Tristan looked confused but stepped aside to let the officer in.

Gabe walked several feet into the space and looked around. "I understand you knew Corliss Blines."

"Knew?" Tristan asked. "No, I *know* her. She's my agent." He squinted at Gabe.

"Why don't we have a seat," Gabe suggested, motioning to the worktable where there were two stools. He strolled slowly around the studio, glanced in the tented area and finally back to Tristan.

When both men were seated Gabe studied Tristan and finally said, "I'm sorry to tell you this, Mr. Cooper, but Miss Blines is dead."

"Oh my God. How? When? While she was on vacation?" His distress was undeniable.

"I was hoping you could tell me a little about your relationship," Gabe said offering no response to Tristan's questions.

"Um, well ... sure. What do you want to know?" He chewed his lower lip.

It was a story Gabe had heard before. Young artist meets young rep, a quick affair; she becomes their agent and ultimately cheats on them with something more valuable than their feelings—their work, their income.

"We recently went through a phase where she said she was having a hard time selling me, but she would try overseas. And she did, she's sold a couple of things. But her assistant Ruggiero told me—or rather *suggested*—recently that she was getting a lot more for my work than she was reporting. She said it was going to a Russian collector who insisted on anonymity, but who knows."

"That must have made you angry." Gabe said sympathetically.

"Yeah, sure. And apparently I'm not the only one she cheated—*if* that was even true. Ruggiero has insinuated himself between her and a lot of her artists. He certainly has with me. Either way someone had me by the short hairs. When you're selling nothin' anything is good."

"You were recently at her gallery?"

"Yeah. I stopped in for an overdue check."

"But you knew she was on vacation."

"I did. But Ruggiero handles all that. For the last six months or so he's been the one to hand off a check. What are you getting at?" He leveled a look at Gabe as he wrapped his lips around the filter of a Winston.

"Did you know you were in her will?" Gabe asked rolling a discarded piece of grey clay between his thumb and index finger.

Tristan stopped before he could light his cigarette and stared at Gabe.

Clearly he hadn't known.

It took a moment before Tristan said, "What did you say?" There was a hint of a smile, but he kept in it check.

"I think I said you're a wealthy man," Gabe responded.

Tristan huffed his disbelief and then the smile hit. "Get outta here. You're shittin' me, right?"

"Nope. It looks like she left you half her East Hampton business. That's a considerable inheritance."

Tristan's smile faded as he considered this. He then frowned and finally lit his cigarette. "Why would she do that?" he asked.

"I was hoping you could tell me," Gabe said.

"Fuck if I know." Tristan crossed his arms over his chest and tucked his hands under his armpits. The cigarette dangled from his lips. "I'm an artist not a salesperson. What was she thinkin'?" He pulled the nearly fresh cigarette out and ground it into a jar lid.

"I would have thought you'd be pleased," Gabe said.

This seemed to confuse Tristan. He sputtered before getting out, "Well fuck, man she's dead. I mean shit I might need money, who doesn't? But I'd rather be sparring with Corliss than burying her."

He and Gabe talked for several more minutes before Gabe stood and said he believed Corliss's lawyer would be in touch.

When the door closed between them the two men had very similar thoughts. Gabe thought it odd that Tristan didn't ask who owned the other half of the business and Tristan wondered who the other inheritor was.

CHAPTER SIXTY-ONE

Mary paused before she knocked on the door to Henry's house, a simple shingled old cottage in Wainscott where she was nearly as tall as the old door. Only yesterday she would have thought it was as charming as the owner. But now, not so much. Now it was almost too perfect, like a Hollywood set.

Funny how perception can change on a dime.

Though she looked up his address she had not called to say she was coming. She knew he was here because his car was out front, but for all she knew he was sleeping, or hated unannounced visitors, or—worse still—had company. *"This was a stupid idea,"* she thought as she stood frozen in her indecision.

As if an omen, the sunlight was dimmed by an ominous cloud.

She had three choices: leave, knock, or call.

"Okay." She sighed and knocked.

Nothing. She knocked again and still nothing. She turned to leave and argued with herself that she had come this far because she was this angry, so she might as well confront him and be done with it.

She headed to the back of the property where she found his studio.

She paused. Then mustering all the courage she had she strode up to the open entrance and heard voices inside which stopped her in her tracks.

Go or stay? Confront or run? The lady or the tiger?

It was in this indecision that a surprised voice called out her name startling her from her final decision to flee.

Before she could move in any direction goofy Gert was

smiling up at her doing a little *Oh-Boy-I'm-Excited-To-See-You* dance. Mary's response was Pavlovian: a returned smile, an issuance of love, and a scratch behind the ears.

Henry had come to the entrance wearing a broad smile and said, "By God, this is a nice surprise! Come in, come in," he repeated when she hesitated.

She slowly entered the enormous open space and was surprised to see Tristan sitting on a kitchen stool sipping from a mug.

"Look who's here," Henry said too loudly. Mary didn't know if he was talking to her or Tristan.

Tristan smiled and teased Mary. "Are you followin' me?"

She pressed her lips into a tight smile and raised a brow. She turned to Henry and apologized, "I'm sorry. I shouldn't have come without calling …"

"Don't be ridiculous. I'm thrilled you're here. Besides, Tristan was just leaving."

"I was? I was." Tristan said, rising from his seat. "I get to see you twice in one day, Mary?" he said as he approached her. "Indeed, the Gods have smiled on me on my birthday."

"Happy birthday, Tristan."

He stood before her. "Thank you. Well, I'm off, unless, of course you would like me to stay and chaperone?"

"I feel like I'm the one who's interrupting," she said.

"Don't be silly," he said glancing at Henry. "We're just two old artist friends comparing paintbrushes." He gently placed his right hand on her left cheek and kissed the other. "And make no mistake;" he continued as he made his way to the door, "my brush is bigger. See you later."

"Get out of here you crass bastard," Henry said good naturedly.

Tristan was gone, leaving behind only a short, resonant laugh.

"Well now," Henry said waving her in, "I can't tell you how glad I am that you're here. Please, come in."

Unlike Tristan's studio which had been all work, Henry's space was more inviting with the initial section dedicated to comfort and the other a surprisingly pristine workspace.

"Do you live here?"

Henry laughed. "You'd think so from the mess, but no. I live in the house. This area is homage to my laziness. I knew there would be those winter days when the last thing I would want to do is trudge into the house for a cracker or a visitor."

In the studio she saw that the floor-to-ceiling windows were actually sliding doors. In the middle of the room were two ten-foot-long tables pushed together, covered with the tools of his trade. Large, colorful canvases covered every inch of wall space. Though his was abstract like Tristan's, their work was night and day. Each canvas cried out with emotion, defying you not to feel, and feel mostly joy. The vibrancy of the colors actually had her entranced. She slowly studied each one until she stopped in front of a canvas that was resting on an easel.

After what felt like an eternity, Henry finally said, "Well, say something."

Yesterday she might have said, "I could love a man with this talent and soul." But instead she simply smiled and offered, "You're very talented, Henry." In truth she couldn't take her eyes off the piece. Varying shades of blue and green seemed to be taking shape to be more than an abstraction. Mary saw the bay and the horizon beyond, and yet it could have just as easily been representational of a woman's pubis. "*Who are you?*" she wondered.

"Is this a work in progress?" she finally asked.

"It is. Do you like it?" he asked.

"Yes."

"Good." He came up behind her and set his hands on her shoulders. There was no need to tell her that this was for her. No need to reveal that she was the inspiration for this piece, which was unlike his other work. Not yet, anyway. "I'm rather fond of it myself." He squeezed her shoulders gently and said, "So, Miss Mary Moody. What brings you to my humble abode?"

She slipped out of his touch and turned to face him. "I had a little time. I was thinking of you."

"That's good. Would you like some tea? Coffee? An espresso? I have actually mastered the little machine."

"No. Thanks." She drifted back into the living area.

"Are you all right?" he asked, following her.

Gert was sprawled out on half the sofa.

Mary took a seat on an armchair and smiled as Gert snuggled against Henry once he had settled on the sofa and rested his feet on the coffee table.

"So," he said drawing out the word. "You want to tell me what's on your mind?"

"Why didn't you tell me you knew Corliss?" She asked bluntly for there was no way to approach it gracefully.

"I assumed you knew that Corliss had been the middleman in my sale to Diane."

"That's not what I mean and you know it," Mary said holding his gaze. "You were with me throughout the chaos Henry, and you never said anything. How could you think that was right? I thought you were ... different." She shook her head and looked at her hands in her lap unable to face him.

"Mary, I don't understand. Are you angry at me?"

"Yes."

"But why?"

"Because you haven't been fully honest with me."

"About what?" He seemed truly baffled.

"About Corliss."

"Mary, we've known each other less than two weeks," he rationalized. "In that time we've seen each other maybe five times and most of it—with the exception of that first wonderful dinner at Dockside—has been spent with other people. When should I have told you that I knew Corliss a long time ago?"

"That you were intimate?" It came out all wrong.

After a long pause Henry said, "Well, quite honestly if you thought I was different, imagine how I feel right now." He looked down at Gert and rubbed her head. "I didn't think jealousy—" he started but was immediately cut off.

"This is not about jealousy," Mary assured him, uncertain that there wasn't an element of that in the mix.

"Well then what is it?" His tone was stone cold and his gaze equally hard.

It was hard for Mary not to look away, but she didn't as she tiptoed over feelings searching for words.

Hurt is such an easy thing to misinterpret.

"Henry, you were lovers," she finally said. "Given everything that's transpired since we met, don't you think it looks suspect that you kept that little tidbit secret?"

His jaw twitched. "Suspect?" he asked. "Tidbit?" Both words were equally offensive.

She said nothing.

He shook his head and shut his eyes before speaking. This was a fine pickle. After all these years he finally meets a woman a cut above the norm, a woman he could actually see himself with and she accuses him of murder, because that was obviously where she was leading. There were two very clear paths before him: to explain his position or ask her to leave. Either way led to a dead-end for them as far as he was concerned because lack of trust is a broken bridge he had no energy to try and traverse again.

"You know, over the last two weeks I have watched you theorize, speculate and conjecture, all very logically and admirably I might add. And what little we know of one another, I was really starting to trust again, which I know doesn't come easy for either of us." He slowly pulled his legs off the table and flattened his feet on the floor. "But now I feel as if I must either defend myself against what I know is coming—baseless charges of murder and mayhem—or protect myself emotionally." He stood. "I choose the latter. I'd like you to leave now."

If he had slammed her in the head with a two by four it wouldn't have had as powerful an impact.

She wanted him to prove to her that … what? That he was innocent? Innocent of what? Murdering one, two, three people? Sleeping with Corliss? Surely, she wasn't going to accuse him of murder; or was she? Was it remotely possible that Henry was capable of murder? She didn't know. In fact, she didn't know who he was. Not a clue.

With a final lock of eyes, both of them searching for something but not knowing what, she left.

CHAPTER SIXTY-TWO

"Where the hell is he?" Gabe growled at his assistant, Donald, whose head twitched to the left.

"We can't find him," he answered.

The sun had set and Detective Andersen hadn't been heard from since initial contact; given the situation Gabe had good cause to be concerned.

As a stopgap measure he had asked the local police to step in to follow Mary Moody. Like a game of telephone where communication dwindles to gibberish, his objective to protect her was ultimately seen as a directive to keep an eye on a potential suspect. With Nick Petrucci in the mix Gabe was confident Mary would be safe, which eased his burden, but now he had to devote team members to finding Andersen.

Damn it.

What had started out as a simple suicide had swiftly turned into a knotty mess, but Gabe knew that if you follow one thread and loosen it from the bind, strand by strand, you will ultimately find clarity in the undoing. It just takes time and patience.

But time, Gabe thought, was the one thing they might not have.

CHAPTER SIXTY-THREE

It would have been so easy to kill Moody but playing with her was proving to be too much fun. Like a cheetah after a gazelle.

Sheryl's fear made the kill surprisingly fun. So far they had all been fun.

But Moody was always with her nigger friend. And now the fucking reward was getting real news coverage which made it worse. Enough with the games. Something had to be done. People like that had to be removed, those self-righteous sons-of-bitches with their holier-than-thou pretenses. They were the real scourge of the planet imposing themselves in everyone else's lives like they had a right to have a say. If Moody was stopped everything would stop. Who did those two think they were, fucking super heroes? Like Batman and Robin? Nick Fury and Dum Dum Dugan or the Green Arrow and Green Lantern? Fucking brilliant Asterix and Obelisk? No fucking way. No fucking way. No fucking way were they going to continue to be allowed to live their sanctimonious lives putting others at jeopardy.

"You're going to die bitch. Both of you."

CHAPTER SIXTY-FOUR

"Aren't you going to eat anything?" Cam asked as Mary sat motionless with fork in hand for a good minute.

"I'm not hungry." Mary put her fork down and sat back.

Cam mimicked Mary. In truth she wasn't hungry either.

"Maybe you should go downstairs and work out," Cam suggested. She had only seen Mary this low once before and it hadn't been good. "Take your feelings and batter them out on that ugly elliptical machine."

Mary tried to smile but quickly dismissed the pretense.

"You know what bothers me most?" she asked and continued without waiting for a response. "He was so logical. I mean he's right, I've only known the man a week—"

"Two," Cam corrected her.

"Whatever. It did sound like I was jealous."

"Are you?"

"No! At least I don't think so. No, how could I be?"

"Stranger—."

"It was rhetorical," Mary cut her off knowing all of the possible answers. "I'm just wondering if I was more damaged by Marshal than I realized. Maybe I'll never be able to trust again."

"You trust me," Camille noted.

"No, I mean new people. Do you realize I haven't made a new friend since I left the city? Not one. There are acquaintances, but no real friends."

"Cultivating friendships takes time."

"And trust," Mary added onto Cam's point, to which her friend could not argue.

Not knowing how to respond Cam said nothing.

Suddenly Beanie jumped up and started barking wildly as she raced into the living room and focused her attention to the street, scaring the hell out of both women. They followed her and by the time they were halfway to Beanie, there was a knock at the door.

They froze with one solitary thought: maybe it was the killer. They shared a glance and Mary finally said, "Well it can't be a bad guy. They wouldn't knock." She used logic.

Cam didn't say that many a victim has opened their door only to regret it in the end.

Holding hands they inched toward the foyer where Mary called out, "Yes?"

"It's Henry," his voice slurred behind the closed door.

"And Tristan," a clearer voice added.

The women let go of one another and Mary opened the door.

"I should very much like to talk with you," Henry said, bleary-eyed and swaying almost imperceptibly. Tristan linked his arm through his friend's and smiled.

"Boy's had a bit too much to drink and there was no stopping him, so I am his designated driver." As he said this he pushed his chest out like a peacock revealing through his own goofy smile that Henry had not been alone in his imbibing.

"I'll make some coffee," Cam said, peeling off from the cluster.

"Come in," Mary said, fully opening the door so both men could enter at once. Tristan steered Henry to the kitchen, despite Henry's protest that he could walk perfectly well on his own.

Safely deposited at the kitchen table and the untouched dinner, Tristan said, "Food! Oh my God I'm starving."

Mary pushed her plate toward him and said, "It's all yours."

Henry looked up at Mary and said, "We have to talk."

"Let's have some coffee first, okay?" Mary sat across from him and felt herself relax for the first time since she had been asked to leave his house that afternoon. This was crazy, she barely knew the man and yet … and yet.

"Can I have a beer?" Tristan asked, already halfway through Mary's dinner.

"No." Cam was emphatic. "You're the designated driver, remember?"

"But it's my birthday." He played the role of a pouting seven-year-old perfectly. In fact he had been celebrating all day since this was markedly the day when his world had turned around. From the sale to Camille to discovering his bequest from Corliss, he knew that from now on he would never have to worry about solvency. Yes, poor Corliss, but in the end he saw the inheritance as an admission of guilt: she knew that she had hurt his livelihood and wanted to make it right.

"Happy birthday, enjoy your coffee," Cam said, pouring two strong cups.

Mary studied Henry and realized he wasn't as bombed as she had initially thought. He politely refused her offer of dinner, drank his coffee, and listened as Cam and Tristan admired how perfect his sculpture looked on Mary's coffee table and the new direction he planned to take his work.

"May we talk privately?" Henry finally asked Mary, ignoring the flirtation evolving between Tristan and Cam.

Otis followed as she led him to her office where she shut the door.

Here Henry took in her office as she had his studio. Much to his surprise her desk was piled high with towering stacks of papers and books. It seemed to belie her appearance of organization personified, and yet, the rest of the space was both calming and inviting. As he entered he faced a dark-blue wall where five large white boards hung, all neatly written upon in obvious color coding: notes on work and what looked to be her makeshift investigation. To his right was her very messy desk with windows behind it facing the yard. To his left, facing the street, she had custom-built open shelving in front of a wall of sea-green bricked glass. It was sparsely furnished with comfortable seating for two clients and a sofa and coffee table near the windowed wall. Otis's large bolster bed was situated next to the desk; though it was clear he preferred the soft leather couch. Who wouldn't?

"I am sorry I asked you to leave today." He got right to the point and sounded preacher sober.

"Thank you," Mary said holding back from blurting out her own necessary apology. She sat at one end of the sofa and waited for him to alight somewhere, wondering if he would choose the safe distance of a chair or the other end of the sofa. He chose safety. She didn't blame him.

"I like your office," he mumbled. "It's so you." This garnered a smile from her.

"I felt the same way about your studio."

He nodded, eyes downcast, not seeing much of anything because he was so focused on how to reach past their divide.

He started to say something but stopped himself. You upset me? She knew that. I'm sorry I caused ... Malarkey. He hadn't caused anything.

"Henry," Mary took the reins. "I really like you. I haven't been open to letting anyone new in my life in a long time. And suddenly there you were and without a moment's hesitation I just fell right in step with you. It felt as if I'd know you a long, long time and so the question of trust never really came up. And with all the chaos that's been going on I found myself leaning on you in some measure, which I suppose subconsciously at least, meant that I did trust you. "

"Too quickly," he said, knowing the answer.

She didn't respond but her face said it all.

"You ought to know I feel the same way. And while we're both old enough to know better, from the moment I met you I was smitten. Schoolboy's crush one-oh-one. But that's not what I want now. I want whoever I move forward with romantically to be first and foremost a friend. I don't know if we could have that but I think I'd like to try."

"Me too," she said. They stared at one another a moment before she stood up, held out her hand and said, "Hi. I'm Mary Clyde Moody. Nice to meet you."

"Clyde?" he asked.

"Family name. And you?"

"Henry Armstrong. No middle name I'm afraid." He shook her hand and gestured to the sofa. "May I?" He asked and took a seat at the far end, keeping his distance. "Now then," he said when she had settled in and faced him, "Many years ago Corliss and I tried to fornicate on three different occasions, and it was painfully unsuccessful each and every time."

"But Detective Lasworth said they found a photo of you in Corliss's house."

"Yes, they showed it to me. Have you seen it?" he asked. When Mary shook her head he said, "It's quite silly, really. It's in an antique frame cluttered with silver cherubs so strikingly ugly that there couldn't possibly be two like it. The photo was taken when I was twenty-six, after a racquetball tournament. It is of me and three friends beaming at the photographer who, by the way, happens to be the woman who tried to hone in on our dinner at Dockside, do you remember?" he asked.

"Yes, kudzu."

"Exactly," he said as if this explained everything.

"I don't get it," she said. "You make it sound like this exonerates you when in fact it's damning evidence."

"Perhaps it's not *me* she wanted to be reminded of daily," he suggested.

"Who is?"

His jaw tightened. What difference did it make now? His initial objective to protect Becky was now moot. "Becky Sims, who is now Sister Frances living in Edinburgh. They were in love but it was a different time then. I stood in as Corliss's beard and she seemed perfectly fine with that but Becky couldn't do it. She was over-the-top in love with Corliss but couldn't get past her self-hatred for it. So she joined a convent."

Mary held her breath. It made perfect sense.

"But Diane said this was the first relationship either of them had had with another woman."

"I'm afraid Corliss lied to her." He rubbed his forehead feeling the effect of his two scotches. "But I'm not lying. The police may not believe me, but I am hoping you do."

"I do," she said and quickly edited with, "I want to."

Henry nodded. "I understand. I think. Look, we both know we want to move forward, right?"

"Right."

"We both have trouble trusting, right?"

"Right."

"I propose in moving forward we never ever knowingly lie to one another no matter how much that might hurt. If I hurt you, no matter how, you tell me and visa-versa. All right?" he asked rising from the sofa.

"All right."

"Now I am going to have that jackass drive me to my car so I can walk Miss Gert, who sends her love by the way."

Before he could reach for the doorknob Mary put her hand on his cheek and drew close. She brought her mouth to his and he responded as if he had found home. When they both pulled apart for air, she said, "My God, Henry. Just imagine."

He felt weak in his knees and pulled her closer.

Mary laughed as she felt his growing desire and pulled out of his embrace.

"You are cruel," he said.

"Some things are worth waiting for, don't you think?"

He issued a low growl before Mary reminded him that Paulo's funeral was the next day. He didn't know if he could be there, but he promised to see her somehow. Somehow.

CHAPTER SIXTY-FIVE

Unless you live close to the ocean where the constant drone of waves lapping or crashing against the shoreline create white noise, the Hamptons in most neighborhoods is intensely quiet in the witching hours.

So when a brick was hurled through Mary's living room picture window at three a.m. it shattered her sense of security along with the stillness.

The noise of the crash and Beanie's frightened barking, then Otis and finally car tires screeching away—was it two sets?—thrust Mary heedlessly toward the sound.

Cam was right behind her holding a struggling Beanie and screamed for Mary to "Stop!"

Barefoot, Mary did stop and prevented Otis from going further.

"What the hell was that?"

"Wait here," she told Cam and firmly ordered Otis to "Stay." But her voice was shaking. Her whole body was shaking as she eased into the room and saw a large hole in the broken window backlit by moon glow as powerful as a klieg light.

"Put shoes on," she told Camille as she gently took Beanie and led Otis to the back door where they would be safe in the yard.

In the seconds that it took for Cam to return, shod and with Mary's slippers in hand, it was clear that the damage had been caused by an ordinary red patio brick.

"Oh my God," Cam whispered as they hurried out of the living room into the kitchen out of sight.

"So much for police protection," Mary said and with a trembling hand dialed 911.

When the call ended Mary turned to Cam and spurted, "And you don't think you should go home?"

"Okay, I'm officially spooked," Camille said and looked it.

Mary took a deep breath knowing it was about to happen. "Stop it," she said, fighting the first burble of a laugh.

"*You* stop it. Don't you laugh, Mary. That little maid is dead and the way things look we're next." Cam shook Mary knowing her friend's propensity to laugh at all the wrong times. "No, no, no, not now. This is bad timing."

Mary had the terrible habit of laughing whenever she was nervous. It was a problem she and her sister had inherited from their mother's side of the family. Once when an aunt had slipped on wet pavement in the middle of a busy street and her husband took one arm and her son the other and both went off in different directions to avoid oncoming traffic, Mary and her sister nearly peed they were laughing so hard—an unfortunate moment their aunt always remembered with acrimony.

"Stop it," Cam warned. "What's wrong with you, girl? This is not funny."

"I'm not laughing," Mary said barely able to get the words out. "This is fear," she chortled doubled over holding on to Cam to try and stay upright. "This is like crying only different." The words came out like a hiss as her face reddened and she literally guffawed.

"Stop it fool, you're scaring me. Oh sweet Jesus this is all so wrong."

This only made Mary laugh harder until the phone rang and scared her to silence.

It rang again. "What if it's him?" Mary asked.

"Who?" Camille asked.

"I don't know. The crazy person. "

"Pick it up for God's sake," Cam ordered pointing to the landline which kept ringing.

Mary walked to the phone and picked up the receiver "Hullo?" She sounded like a dullard.

"Mary, its Nick Petrucci. Are you okay?"

"Yeah. Yes." But before she could say anything else the sound of three gunshots shattered the tenuous calm as more glass shattered. Mary had stepped into open view to answer the phone. Both women fell to the floor screaming.

The dogs barked in the backyard.

Nick yelled her name into the phone.

Cam crawled to Mary and together they scrambled to the deepest part of the kitchen where they were either safer or trapped. Someone was out there with a gun.

Nick continued yelling Mary's name until she was able to bring the phone to her ear and say, "Help."

"I'm on my way. The police will be there any second."

"We have to get out of here," Mary whispered.

Just as they started crawling to the back door they heard the sirens.

The killer, already starting toward the house, heard the sirens too and slowly disappeared into the shadows cursing bad luck.

In a matter of moments the house was surrounded with police. Three curious neighbors watched from the street and answered questions but offered no information.

Both women, still trembling, felt safer when Nick walked through the door. Cam was clutching Beanie and Mary looked dazed. He told her to start some coffee knowing that having something to focus on would be the best thing for her. He oversaw the investigation, studied the three bullet holes in the kitchen wall, discussed trajectory with a lanky man in khakis and a tee-shirt and finally joined them in the kitchen table.

Nick had received a call from the officer posted outside Mary's house when the first event occurred. It all happened so quickly that the officer had to make a choice between following the perp or checking on Mary. Yes, maybe he had fallen asleep but at least he caught the culprits: Sheryl Strickland's two sons, who had heard a rumor that Mary was somehow responsible for their mother's death. "They're young and drunk and stupid," Nick said at the end.

"Poor kids," Mary said as she filled their mugs with coffee.

"They damaged your home," Nick reminded her.

"Glass can always be replaced," Mary said.

Nick didn't think it was worth mentioning that the older Strickland kid, who was plenty a man at twenty-eight, had vowed to get even with Mary.

"Are they the shooters?" Cam asked.

The phone rang again. What the hell? It was four in the morning.

Nick held up his hand and had Mary answer so he could hear.

"Mary? It's Lillian. I'm sorry to call so late but have you heard from Missy?" The brat bride's mother sounded stressed.

Clearly not the shooter. Nick nodded.

Mary quickly moved to her office. "No. Why? What's going on?"

"I can't find her."

"Since when?" Mary asked with dread. Not another one.

Mary missed Lillian's response. "Lil? What was that?" she asked loudly, as if it were the fault of the phone and not her own thoughts.

"Since today, or yesterday. After we met Leah. We all came home, I called the tent company and I haven't seen her since. No one has."

Well, this wasn't good. "The wedding's tomorrow," Mary said.

"I know. I'm terrified," Lillian whispered.

Mary was livid. This little shit thought she could do anything and get away with it and she was right. Mary finally took a deep breath and asked, "Lillian, when I left the other day, did you two talk? Did she tell you what's going on?"

"We did. But she was tight-lipped. I got the sense that she's in love with someone else, but she denied it absolutely. Nevertheless I told her I love her and that nothing could be so bad. I assured her that we could easily cancel the wedding, no big deal: it was just Mulford then. Even still. I mean really, what could be so horrible? Different race? Gender? I don't care."

Mary thought species, but kept it to herself. The idea of Missy with a horse or a bull mastiff was just too ugly.

"I mean nowadays everything goes, right?"

"I suppose. What about Patrick?" Mary asked about the groom.

"He's holding up amazingly well. He knew she was conflicted but he's such a nice guy, he was just giving her a wide berth. He's been upstairs all night looking through her computer."

"Have you called the police?"

"Jack's calling them now. Oh God, Mary. You were my last hope. Do you think something's happened to her?"

"Lil, she's probably with this person she's in love with," Mary said not adding, *God forbid the little brat would consider that her folks would worry.*

But then Mary was guilty of the same self-absorption because all she could think of after the call was that the one common thread in all recent police activity in the Hamptons was Mary Clyde Moody.

"Lillian, I hate to do this right now but I need to know if you think she might return for the wedding or if we should cancel it."

There was a long pause and Mary felt Lillian's struggle. If it were up to Mary she would just cancel it and if Missy showed up she could suck an egg. But it wasn't her decision to make.

"Most of the guests are already here," Lillian moaned. "The rehearsal dinner is tonight."

So Mary jumped in and suggested they cancel the wedding yet still have the dinner for the out of town family members and friends that night where Mary would explain everything to the gathered.

"Tell everyone we'll cover their expenses," Lillian said and was then distracted by Jack calling out to her. "I'll talk to you later." She hung up.

By the time Mary returned to the kitchen most of the police activity was over and Nick and Cam were talking quietly at the table.

When a tired silence fell Nick suggested that the women go back to bed to try and get some sleep. "I'll be here should anything else happen, which I doubt it will since the sun's almost up."

"I couldn't do that," Mary said, fighting her eyelids to stay open.

"I'll keep him company." Cam promised.

And she did, for about twenty minutes before she drifted off on the second sofa facing the window that was free of shards. Beanie draped herself over Cam and Nick, despite his better judgement, took a picture of the sleeping beauties.

Mary fell dead asleep before her head barely hit the pillow.

CHAPTER SIXTY-SIX

Despite being full the house was quiet. Lina had been awake since before dawn dreading the day ahead. Today they buried Paulo.

She had tiptoed into Paulina's room before sunrise and watched her daughter sleep. The pull to slip in beside her was strong but she didn't want to wake her child.

Instead she simply listened to the rhythmic breathing of a life force she and Paulo had created from love. She remembered the night they conceived Paulina; they both knew it. "We will be together forever mi amor," he had promised that night, kissing her belly. With Paulina and the new baby, they always would be.

But it didn't lessen the pain.

"Life is not fair," her mother-in-law had repeated over and over again since Paulo's death. "It is not fair I should bury my baby," she cried throughout the day until it sounded like an invocation. The sentiment was true enough but Lina was already tired of the old woman's performance, for that's what it felt like. The loss was real, yes, but the loss seemed to be about her and how it would affect her, not the fact that Paulo would never smile again or breathe in the scent of his newborn child.

Lina was bone-tired, a term she had heard but never understood until now.

Ever since Paulo went missing the house had been filled with family and friends, all meaning well but as it is with good-intentioned people, there is an overwhelming need from them to know they are making a difference. Their needs become a cloaked burden the recipient must shoulder in silence.

Lina sat on the front swing with a cup of coffee and watched the birds gather at the feeder Paulina and her father had made together. Cardinals waited for the blue jays to leave, who in turn made way for the woodpecker, who was content to share the space with the others, but only the titmice and chickadees dared. A single mourning dove fed contentedly on the ground. Such a perfect day for such a horrible task.

Eduardo's car pulled up to the front curb and he emerged looking, as he usually did, angry. It was not yet six in the morning and she was not in the mood for talk.

He stopped and looked up at her without climbing the three steps. "You're up early," he said softly.

"I don't sleep much."

He nodded.

"Why are you here now?" she asked gently.

He shrugged. "I can't think of where else to be." Again he shrugged.

She nodded. In the silence that followed she willed him to be gone, but she knew the others would now start stirring and it would all begin anew. "Coffee?" she asked.

"I loved him," he said softly.

"I know."

"I am so sorry."

Again Lina said, "I know," but in truth she didn't know what exactly he was sorry about. Was he sorry he no longer had his best friend? Was he sorry that she was alone? Was he sorry that this is an ugly world in which we live, where innocents are slaughtered daily? Or was it just the whole damned platter of misfortune?

She kept her eyes on a male cardinal sitting on a shrub who let out three long whistles and then a series of quick chirps. The female landed on the feeder, clearly plump and ready to lay her clutch. Cardinals were Paulo's favorite because they mated for life, no matter how short or long those lives might be. Lina couldn't help but smile at the recollection of Paulo's imitation of a cardinal's whistle when he just wanted her to know, in their own secret code, that he loved her.

The female cardinal chirruped back and Lina held her breath.

The front screen door opened and Paulina scrambled up beside her mother, sleepy-eyed and frowning. She snuggled against Lina, who wrapped her arms around her daughter, still warm from sleep.

"I hate today," the child pouted, feeling better though in her mother's arms.

"Me too, baby." She kissed the top of Paulina's head. "Me too."

CHAPTER SIXTY-SEVEN

Rugs would cover shoddy but expeditious workmanship, and he could live with that.

Now before the sun had fully risen he sat upon the last remaining chair in the silence of what had once been a suffocating, chaotic place and inhaled the calm.

He thought, as he had almost obsessively for the last several days, of the woman he had discovered at Landing Lane. And as he did his thoughts invariably drifted to his mother. In his mind's eye when he remembered the lifeless body in the marsh it was no longer a stranger's form but rather his mother's, and in some bizarre but deeply satisfying way, it empowered him.

If he had been another man, a man of action and not lethargy born from fear, his own hands might have held the old woman's head under water until the empty, mean life she had lived seeped out of her body with his guidance. It had not and he could only imagine.

But the fantasy was good.

As if stealing someone else's act of rage or bravery, he was able to reap the reward without any risk.

The killer had saved the conservationist's life. No longer at his mother's beck and call, he only now realized that he had options, and he considered them all with great deliberation. His father had left them comfortable, and the conservationist's own investing acumen had generated very cushy padding as long as he lived within his means which, apart from his recent spending frenzy, was easy enough.

But what to do? The four walls of home had been essentially

without egress for his entire life and now there was a door that opened and closed at his will.

He could work. Granted this meant interacting with people on a daily basis, a concept that was absolutely revolting but suddenly an option. Option. As the word rolled around and around in his mind it was almost intoxicating.

"*Slow down*," he silently warned himself.

What kind of work could he do that would assure him the least amount of contact with people?

Again the killing came into play. He could dig graves. That would be nice. It would afford him physical labor in the fresh air with little or no contact with others. Or he could drive a hearse and be completely anonymous. He liked the idea of chauffeuring dead people to their final resting place.

It would, of course, be intellectually beneath him, but who was to know or care?

Gardening was another possibility. All of the landscapers he knew, and there were many out here involved with the conservation movement, were always complaining about the lack of manpower with a brain cell or command of English. He filed that one in the forefront of his mind. He now had two viable options.

As he was formulating another possibility, something in a library perhaps, the house phone rang, a sound so foreign it startled him clear to his core. His hand was still shaking when he finally lifted the receiver from the wall cradle and tentatively asked, "Hello?" To a perceptive listener it might have sounded as if he had never used, let alone seen a phone before

The caller, however, was not perceptive. It was Carla Winnow, the police officer whose number he kept extracting from and returning to his pocket ever since they had met.

"I'm checking up on you. Are you okay?"

His dry mouth fought to get the simple word "yes" out, but once successful he added, "Thank you."

"Well, no one should have to go through what you did. I was concerned. I hope I haven't called too early."

The pause that followed, of which there would be many in the road ahead for the conservationist and the cop, was based on his awe that she was so comfortable and articulate, and her concern that she sounded like an idiot.

"I have been meaning to call you," he said as he stood ramrod straight by the kitchen counter tethered to the spot by the long-out-of-date beige phone cord. "I wanted to thank you for your kindness," he stammered.

And thus began the awkwardly adolescent courting of two elder virgins.

CHAPTER SIXTY-EIGHT

It was early but Ruggiero sat in his car outside Agda's house mustering the courage to knock on her door. He had just finished his second trenta caffè Americano—thanks to Corliss he could now afford the indulgence—and was silently repeating that the objective outweighed the means of getting there and he had to stay focused.

He loved Agda as much as he had ever loved anyone except, perhaps, Mr. Gold, his fourth-grade teacher and first lover. Agda was his best and only friend. He would do whatever it took to mend their broken fence. He couldn't be without her. That would leave him completely alone.

But he couldn't seem desperate; she loathed desperation. Who didn't?

Out of the corner of his eye he saw movement on her deck; she was filling the birdfeeder. That meant she had not yet had her first coffee as it would be brewing.

He continued to plan. If the bonds of their friendship didn't push her to forgiveness—for whatever infraction she imagined—he would offer her a solo show and sixty percent of the sale rather than the customary fifty. Seventy-five? No, sixty. Then again with their recent transgression—selling her beautiful piece *Odium* under Corliss's name without her knowledge—Agda had received eighty percent and he a mere twenty. It hadn't struck him until this very moment that the stress of worrying that Corliss would find out had been wasted energy.

Finally resolved to make things right he strode swiftly to her front door.

Agda was waiting. She had seen his car sitting there for the last half hour which had allowed her time to prepare, but for what? Reconciliation? Well she certainly wouldn't make it easy for him that was for sure. Truth was, however, that she loved Ruggiero despite his black humor, bitterness, and inability to censor himself. Hell, she loved him because of those very things. Unlike almost everyone else on the planet she never had to guess where he stood. And while he was irritating to most people she found those specifically objectionable traits refreshing. And endearing. Yes, endearing, what a loathsome word.

She opened the door before he could knock.

"What?" She asked.

With mouth agape and eyes bulging he pushed past her and cried, "I have to use your bathroom!"

Damn that second trenta caffè Americano.

CHAPTER SIXTY-NINE

As Mary slept she dreamed. Throughout her life, even as a child, she would problem-solve in slumber.

In the two fitful hours she had before being awakened by the glassman's call, there was something she was trying desperately to remember. She knew she was dreaming but every time she moved from one image or person to another in the string of disjointed impressions, her mind went blank and she felt panicked. She frantically tried to hold on to something, but what happened a moment before was lost in the next and by the time the ringing phone startled her awake all she had was a headache and a nagging sense that she had just left answers behind. Answers she thought that had something to do with a body part.

She knew something; she just didn't know what. And time had proven over again that this would gnaw at Mary until she worked through it.

CHAPTER SEVENTY

Marcus Shulman stood before his bathroom mirror and admired his reflection running a hand over his thick stubble. Unlike most men he knew, shaving was a ritual he had always loved; from the first time when he was fifteen and his father showed him how much cream to apply, which direction to pull the razor against different parts of his face, which angle to hold the blade. Now it was a Zen-like part of his day when he emptied his mind of everything and simply savored the act of shaving.

But today he was back in time standing at the sink next to his father.

Dad had pulled out his Gillette razor, twisted the bottom of the handle, and it opened like a flower. His father took a two-sided blade from the pack, grabbed it by the ends, and slipped the center hole over the peg in the middle of the razor. He then twisted the bottom of the handle the other way until it closed tightly around the blade.

"Take the razor and slowly pull it down your cheek scraping the shaving cream off. Do not put too much pressure on the blade or you might cut yourself. And always pull the razor downward, as that is how the hairs grow, so it's safer and you will get a better shave."

As Marcus now went through the process he could see his father standing at his side, an experience that had probably lasted five minutes, but had taken on mythical proportions for him. His father had always insisted he didn't remember the moment, but Marcus was convinced he did. He had to believe that since it was the last time they ever shared such intimacy.

Everything from that point forward seemed to change between them thanks to his mother's indiscretion and his father's resulting rage.

"Shit," he muttered as he nicked himself thanks to a shaking hand. But even the resulting blood couldn't stave off his good mood. He wiped his face and sang, "Ding dong the bitch is dead."

He had hated her and now she was gone. Poof. Though it had been a struggle to get there the restaurant was doing amazingly well and he made sure the assholes who had backed out with Corliss in the lead knew it. The only thing better than vindication was retribution and he had both, a delicious cause for celebration.

If Marcus knew and loved one thing, it was himself. He was well aware that he was a bright man but one bogged down by grudges and hatred. Not an hour could pass without him saying at some point, "I hate that." And whether he was referring to a soup or a person, a book or a political point it was always an accurate assessment from his heart. He knew he had a drug problem, but he didn't care; the high outweighed the low. He understood why some people loathed him while others loved him and usually for the same reason: his brash honesty. He loved and loathed himself in equal parts.

But what he didn't know, in part because of his preoccupation with himself and in part because others were doing their job remarkably well, was that for three days he had been under the watchful eye of Suffolk and East Hampton police and about to be hoisted by his own petard for drug distribution in his successful new venture.

CHAPTER SEVENTY-ONE

It took a moment for Tristan to realize where he was when he awoke smelling of scotch and feeling cotton-mouthed.

He reached for the pack of cigarettes, in which there were none, so he fished out a respectable butt from the plate Henry had supplied as an ashtray the night before and lit up.

He thought of Corliss and her surprising, indeed profound generosity in leaving him half her business. He let out a soft laugh in appreciation for her humor as well; having to share anything with that weenie Ruggiero was sure to be a shit show.

But he had something now.

Pinching the cigarette between his thumb and index finger he took a long draw and gave a silent thanks to Corliss. Being a Have-not in the land of Haves had had its toll on him. But now, now he was a bona fide Have.

He squashed out the cigarette, stood and stretched smelling his own rankness. He wouldn't bother Henry who was probably still sleeping in the house. Nope, he'd go get a pack of smokes, some coffee, shower, and perhaps call on that lovely, lovely Camille. Who knew? With his luck changing maybe, just maybe he would even settle down.

He was planning a future he never could have imagined, not in a million years. There was a bounce to his step as he headed to his car feeling hopeful for the first time in what had to be a decade. You never know what's around the next corner. You just never know.

CHAPTER SEVENTY-TWO

For the first time in her life Missy felt free; absolutely and utterly free. Life as she had known it was over and she was headed toward a higher calling.

Settled into her first-class seat with a glass of champagne in hand she silently checked herself for feelings, much like an athlete might pat down after a nasty tumble, only her search was invisible to any passing eye. Too sheltered to fully understand that fear will inevitably accompany drastic change, she assumed she was fine.

And as far as she was concerned she was right; she was fine. She had planned extremely well, even to the point of throwing everyone into a tizzy over the stupid wedding. Rush here. Rush there. Rage about this and that to the point where they would be so distracted that by the time of her departure it would likely be welcomed.

This thought stopped her like a bullet. She took a deep breath and kept her head down as others around her found their seats. Lillian, she knew, would not welcome her stealthy exit. Mom. She hadn't called her that in close to six months, believing that by removing the word from her lexicon she could extract herself emotionally.

Okay so maybe she was wrong about that, but it didn't alter the certainty that life had led her to this moment for a reason. And didn't her father always say, "Sacrifice is a part of life." When she was a child he would say it in a bone-weary way and just as quickly swoop her up in his arms and like a pirate promise her, "Yours will be few if I have any say in it!" Then he would hoist her up on his shoulder and pretend to be a buccaneer and she his giggling parrot as he limped around the living room shouting, "Yar! Yar!"

Missy smiled at the recollection.

The thought that she was hurting them, and she knew she was, was awful but it was a small price to pay in the long run. She was sacrificing the life of privilege and in that she was forcing the sacrifice of her upon them, but wasn't that how life worked? When one's actions affect another, wasn't that part of the flow of life, how it was supposed to be? The challenges presented to one person were often a result of another's act: love, politics, war, religion, loss.

She raised her head, took a sip of champagne and studied her fellow passengers. She considered that this flight might never make their destination. A lazy or farsighted mechanic might have overlooked a missing screw, the pilot could have a heart attack or be suicidal, or a bomb might shatter the airborne craft: one person's act affecting others. The logical assumption and only comfort is it was thus meant to be.

A mother held her sleeping baby as she made her way down the aisle, her right shoulder weighed down by a monogrammed canvas satchel overflowing with her child's needs. Missy followed them with her eyes and was struck by the peace of the slumbering little girl whose face was framed with tight red curls.

She guessed there were about three hundred passengers aboard this flight. If they all died what would be deemed a "senseless" death, she wondered if any of the scores of those impacted in the aftermath of a loved one's passing would conclude that this was how their wife or daughter or husband was meant to pass into the next higher realm. Would anyone feel comforted?

Perhaps only when a reparation check came in the mail.

He was fucking his wife's best friend. She was suffering from cancer. The baby had an inoperable brain tumor. Their daughter had abandoned them.

She finished the champagne, sat back and shut her eyes.

CHAPTER SEVENTY-THREE

When Leah arrived early at the Briar Patch house to let the caterers in for set up, she unpacked the trunk of her car and schlepped in the over-abundance of toilet paper she had purchased the day before.

She marveled at the transformation of the backyard, at how quickly they were able to put in the tent and dance floor. No question, it was a perfect setting for a wedding. Leah never ceased to be amazed at the power of money; it both fascinated and disgusted her. Money could work miracles. Imagine if the one percent really put it to the proper use and not personal folly.

As she waited Leah sipped her coffee and considered how skewed things were in the Hamptons. Everyone in the universe seemed to think it was wall-to-wall gazillionaires and celebrity tour busses. She laughed out loud as she now remembered having once, when she and an old friend had gotten high after years of abstinence, considered various ways of making money out here including offering private tours of where the rich and richer lived. And yet she knew that her own concept of financial security was skewed by living here. Everyone's was, even the illegal workers packing four families into a house meant for a family of four. Her housekeeper drove a BMW but went to the local food pantry to feed her family and her kids wore designer clothes, albeit from T.J. Maxx and outlets, but the kids—like all the kids out here—had a sense of landed entitlement fused with the frustration of not having as much as the next kid. It was crazy-inducing.

And it was pervasive throughout the East End, even within herself. Oh sure, she had savings, but enough to retire on? No way. But what was enough? Her modest house, which had cost under two hundred in the eighties, was her only real security as it was now worth well above that, but how much would ever be enough? How many nights had she stayed awake worrying about the future and the litany of what-ifs?

Oh well, she sighed, that's life. And this, she thought as she sat in the fifteen-hundred-square-foot kitchen that would soon be a hive of activity, was another life. And a life she truly considered excessive. No one needed this. No one.

Her cell phone and the doorbell rang at the same time. Mary was calling and the caterer had arrived. Leah asked Mary to hold as she opened the door for the caterer who was as handsome as his pictures, told him she'd be right with him and motioned him in.

"Sorry about that," she said to Mary. "The tent and dance floor look great," she started.

"I have bad news," Mary said and then proceeded to tell Leah that the wedding had been cancelled.

As Leah listened she knew it was a mixed blessing for her and wondered if it was the same for Mary. Leah would still get the commission but not have to deal with any complaints of wear and tear on the house. "Do they know where she is?" Leah asked as she held out a hand to the caterer to wait. He nodded and took a seat at the kitchen island.

"No, but I have to go to the rehearsal dinner tonight and break the news to everyone."

"Oh, I don't envy you," Leah said sympathetically and immediately asked if she had yet spoken with the caterer who was here with her.

Mary hadn't, so Leah passed on her phone and listened until the doorbell rang again when Joe the tent man arrived to check all final fittings. As Leah led him into the kitchen she explained that the wedding had been cancelled, which didn't seem to faze him in the least.

The caterer passed the phone back to Leah, and Mary asked if she was still willing to work with her because she had to go to a funeral.

"Sure. I'll do anything I can for you."

Mary went through a long list, even asking her to talk to the idiot planner whose job was to oversee the guests. She should assure the florist she would be paid but find out first if she had finished any portion of the job. If she had, Mary suggested that Leah get the flowers and distribute them among her friends.

"Seriously?" Leah asked.

"Seriously."

When the call ended Leah and the caterer—who had already contacted his office and cancelled the job—and Joe the tent man commiserated briefly about the craziness of the bride and all agreed they'd kill her if she was their kid.

And just as soon as it started, it was over. Leah made plans to be there the next day for Joe's team to take down everything. And that was it.

She left a message for the owner of the property, locked the house, and stuffed a year's supply of toilet paper back in the trunk of her car.

Oh well. Easy come, easy go.

CHAPTER SEVENTY-FOUR

The eleven o'clock funeral was well attended, though without the crowds from the wake.

Mary saw the *East Hampton Star* reporter, Patty, in the parking lot and after introducing her to Camille they started toward the church together.

"So how are you?" Patty asked, adding, "I heard about the Strickland woman and your problems. They connected?"

"Are you asking as a reporter?" Mary's eyes darted around the area, feeling ever vigilant.

Patty shrugged. She covered politics and was trustworthy. "Unless you found Jay Schneiderman wearing a pink tutu, my lips are sealed."

Envisioning Jay, a local politico, in such a get-up made them both laugh. It was hard not to like Patty and while Mary had considered the two of them having a drink together, it never happened.

"In that case, I'm tired," Mary said illustrating it with a half-smile.

"Yah, imagine how we'll all look on Tumbleweed Tuesday," Patty laughed referring to the day after Labor Day when the locals had traditionally been able to palpably breathe in the serenity that was lost in the summer. "But even that's changed," she added. "Some idiot must have told them that September and October are the best months out here."

"Damn them," Mary offered, though her attention had been pulled to Diane, who was trudging up from the parking lot.

She excused herself and she and Cam walked back to meet

Diane, who greeted them with, "Don't you think it's odd that an anagram of funeral is real fun?"

"I never thought of it," Mary said.

"Me neither," Cam agreed and then asked Diane, "How are you?"

"Dandy. And you?"

Though Diane's hair looked better than before—actually clean—she wore loose sweatpants, a large Oxford shirt with a streak of dirt down the front panel, and a pair of sneakers.

"You're wearing your pajamas," Mary noted casually.

Diane looked down and shrugged. "Only you would know that. And technically they're not pajamas, though I admit they are a tad casual for a funeral, but really who cares? They're perfect for real fun. Besides, the idea is to be here. I finally talked to Core's sister about the funeral."

"Does she know about you two?" Cam asked.

"Now she does." She dug her hand into her purse and pulled out a cigarette and lighter. It was a picture Mary still couldn't wrap her head around. Diane lit the cigarette and exhaled as if it had been years and not fifteen minutes since her last one. "She actually sounds like a nice woman. I surprised myself."

"How so?"

"I was so prepared to ... I don't know ... dislike her on Corliss's behalf but I didn't. I kind of felt sorry for her. She'll never have a chance to make things right with her sister and she knows what a loss that is. She assumed that they'd make up one day. Now they won't."

"Where is she?"

"Pound Ridge. Husband's a cardiologist. Three adult children, a couple of grandkids." Diane seemed to lose steam.

"When is the funeral?"

Diane shrugged. "They still haven't released the body, or whatever they have."

It was impossible to forget or mention that Corliss's head had still not been retrieved.

"Her sister wanted to bury her with their parents in Ohio for fuck's sake, but she can actually listen to reason. When I explained that Corliss had wanted to be cremated and have her ashes spread at the bay she said that sounded nice."

If Corliss's body hadn't been found at the bay it might have been nice but the thought made Mary uneasy.

Diane continued. "I also spoke to Core's publicity person who I think is going to spearhead the whole memorial thing. I mean, I can't get too involved but at least everyone knew we were friends and let's face it, publicists like to make people like me happy."

Several people walked past them nodding a silent, somber greeting.

"So, are you or the police any closer to finding out who killed her?" Diane asked, taking a deep drag off her cigarette.

"I don't want to discuss that here."

"Of course not, I'm only your client."

"No Diane, you're my friend. You are also a pain in the ass who thinks the whole world revolves around you, which—news flash—it doesn't. Whereas others are actually concerned about *my* safety—*our* safety," she said, nodding at Cam, "you are so self-involved that the only thing you can focus on is how things affect you." Then, without another word, Mary turned her back on her friend and stormed into the church.

Diane stood in stunned silence looking helplessly at Camille. Mary was right, of course, she wasn't so deluded not to know that. She dropped the cigarette and saw that the front of her shirt was stained from the dog's paw. Her sneakers poked out under sweats too baggy to wear in public and yet here she was, frozen now in indecision.

She was here. She should go in. She looked like a fucking bag lady. She didn't know the guy. What difference would it make to anyone if she was here or not? But she was here. Thirty steps tops to go in, sit at the back and be done with it. But what for? She gave them a check. That was more than enough to make up for her not being here. No one would care. No one would know. What the hell was wrong with her?

"I'm an asshole," she told Cam.

"No you're not. You're hurting."

Diane nodded and brought her hand to her forehead, raking her hair back with smoke-infused fingers.

No. It was time to go home. Time to start from scratch. To reinvent who she would be from this moment on.

"Thanks," she said, and turned back to the parking lot where the dog waited for her in the car.

CHAPTER SEVENTY-FIVE

Much to his delight and fear they were meeting for an early lunch at Pussy's Pond, a serene spot in the heart of the Springs. Not knowing what Carla would want, the conservationist had stopped at several local delis so she could have her pick; ham and cheese sandwiches from Springs General Store, one with brie and honey mustard, one with American and mayo; her choice of a tuna or chicken salad on whole wheat from Old Stone Market; and finally, a mozzarella and tomato or a roasted veggie panini from Luigi's.

Despite his rounds of delis, he was still twenty minutes early and entertained himself by watching a three-year-old and his mother feed the diverse variety of ducks, along with a few geese. The little boy would hold his arm high in the air, fling a piece of bread, stomp a few times and run away. The routine never varied. That is, not until the ducks grew braver than the boy and approached as if to say, "Come on, come on, we're hungry here." This scared the child, who dropped what he had and was swiftly scooped up by his mother, who comforted her son and easily shooed away the birds.

Alone again the conservationist glanced at his watch and wondered if he ought to run over to Kristi at the the General Store and grab some sodas. He had only purchased water. Maybe Carla preferred Coke or Pepsi, or maybe even ginger ale.

"Am I late?" He heard her voice behind him and was stunned by her sudden arrival. He hadn't even heard the cruiser drive up, but once he jumped to his feet and spun around, there it was and the uniformed officer was almost upon him.

She was beautiful as she swaggered toward him, her wide

hips bearing the load of her official regalia, gun and all. The peak of her cap was set at a jaunty angle shielding her eyes from the sun, but her smile was not in shadow; no, it was beaming happily over her several chins. The conservationist stood in speechless awe.

He tried to smile back at her but he could only clear his throat. "I was early," he stammered.

"That's good," she said, joining him. "You got us front row seats." She gestured to the bench and saw the four different, bulging paper bags.

He saw her look at the bags took in her confusion and quickly said, "I didn't know what you would want."

Her smile revealed a wide space between her two front teeth and relieved him of his fear. No one had ever taken such effort with her, at least no man. And unlike with most men she didn't feel awkward with the conservationist. He reminded her of her grandfather, a tall lanky stick of a man with old-world manners who was more at ease in his garden than with people—well, everyone except her.

When they were seated he handed her a napkin and recited the menu, which seemed to delight her. She chose the ham and cheese with mayo. He went for the veggie panini, though he didn't think he would be able to take a bite.

He had never in his forty-six years eaten alone with a woman other than his mother or a few relations. This this was completely out of his safety zone. This was a date. At least he thought it was. Not that it was official; as a matter of fact, the plans had been so casually made that he had called her back to make sure.

"I'm starving," Carla said as she attacked her sandwich with gusto, leaving an errant glob of mayo on her upper lip as she chewed, and studied the birds.

"You know, this pond is actually the freshwater springs that our fair hamlet is named after," the conservationist said as he held his untouched sandwich.

She nodded and wiped her mouth, missing the mayo. "Beautiful, isn't it?"

"Yes," he said, and without thinking reached across with

his napkin and removed the mayonnaise.

"Christ, that's embarrassing," she said as she rubbed her lips free of any other offending lunch remnants.

"No," he assured her.

They ate in silence, he taking a tiny bite and she finishing the first half of her sandwich as he said, "I've never done this before." She might as well know.

"What?" she asked, wiping her hands and reaching for a bottle of water.

"You know, had lunch with … with a woman. Alone." He shook his head in silent reprimand. He should just keep his mouth shut, let the meal end and be done with it.

"Me neither. I mean with a man." There had been Barney, but that was back in grade school, before he became cool in high school and ignored her.

They both ventured a look at one another. She couldn't believe that this wonderfully thoughtful man was still single and he—well, he was amazed that she wasn't married with a gaggle of children. She was so compassionate and round, as if she could embrace the entire universe in her arms.

He nodded.

She nodded.

He took a big bite of his sandwich and she watched as he chewed.

She just watched.

CHAPTER SEVENTY-SIX

Tristan entered the Gallery where he found Ruggiero on the phone and Agda Eck wandering the space taking in the various works.

"Tristan," she said with no inflection.

"Agda." He nodded. "Nice piece," he added, motioning toward her newly hung canvas.

"Thanks. I like it too." Here she granted him a smile.

Ruggiero bent into the mouthpiece of the phone and took his call in the back away from their chatter.

"I might be able to get us a buyer for that," Tristan said with a taunting sense of ownership over her work.

He saw the flash in her eyes before she feigned an ah-ha moment and said, "That's right, you own part of the place now."

"That's right. Half." He was examining the other pieces, other artists who would soon be bringing him income. With Corliss's gracious gift he had been placed into the ten-percent puddle of Americans able to retire without worry. The daily gnawing fear of *how can I survive* had been miraculously and seamlessly replaced with newfound confidence that extinguished his first instinct to attack. This epiphany came to him as he studied Jerry Schwabe's piece and he smiled at his kinder, gentler self who was actually affected by Jerry's graceful work.

"Tristan." Ruggiero's greeting sounded like an accusation.

"Ruggiero," Tristan said with a smile. "How's my partner today?"

"Busy. Have you spoken with Corliss's attorney?" He picked up a short stack of papers from the desk casting off the words as if they were nothing more than a second thought.

"Not yet. Thought I'd call him today. I mean she's not even buried yet." The pointed chide did not go unnoticed.

"Yes, well be that as it may there are legal issues we need to deal with and life does go on."

"We will," Tristan said slowly.

"So why are you here?" Ruggiero asked.

Tristan raised his brows and sauntered from piece to piece, hands in pockets, in no hurry to be rushed by Miss Prissy Pants. He made a deliberate tour of the room ending near the front door before facing Ruggiero and said, "We're partners now Ruggiero, whether we like it or not and I think it would be prudent if we got to a place of mutual respect. Now you and I both know that's not gonna be easy, but if we're gonna survive as business partners it's something we gotta do. Corliss threw us together for a reason, though I'll be damned if I know why. Bottom line is we gotta make it work. Think about it." Without another word he let himself out of the gallery and sauntered away.

Ruggiero and Agda watched until Tristan was long past the windows.

"He's going to find out," Ruggiero said.

"It doesn't matter," his friend assured him. "She's dead and I doubt anyone is going to be looking for traces of arsenic."

Ruggiero rubbed his eyes. The plan had been so simple. A little arsenic every now and then to compromise but not hurt Corliss, just enough so she would be distracted by headaches, confusion and stomach distress which would make her rely more and more on him. That had been working as planned for the last three months. The first real test of selling a piece out from under her while she was on holiday had been moot since she would never know.

"I just hate the thought of having to give him any piece of my profit," Agda sighed.

"Yeah, well, maybe it won't come to that." Ruggiero picked up his keys and said, "Come on, I need a drink." With that they closed up shop and headed to Starbucks.

CHAPTER SEVENTY-SEVEN

Lillian felt and looked like hell. She paced the living room listening as Jack conferred with an FBI agent.

Though Missy had deleted her emails, dear Patrick the groom had been able to retrieve them, and the revelation had been astonishing, so much so that Jack had called the FBI immediately.

It had now been twenty-four hours since they were aware of Missy's departure.

In that time they had learned things about their daughter they never would have imagined. While Lillian couldn't understand how her daughter had come to this insanity, she finally understood Missy's incomprehensible behavior of late. But how? Why? She wrapped her arms around herself and squeezed as if the touch were proof that this was not a horrible dream.

"Okay," Jack said to Lillian. "They were able to track her to a flight to Paris."

"Paris?"

He nodded grimly. "It was a one-way ticket."

"She has friends in Paris," Lillian interrupted hopefully. "Marie and Ava and—"

Jack shook his head, "Stop, Lillian. Just listen." He glanced at the FBI agent who was at the far end of the room on his phone. "We already know that she has a new passport they supplied her with, but the agent is concerned that they are using her unwittingly as a ..." He paused his mouth trembling around the word. "...as a suicide bomber."

He caught his wife as her knees buckled and gently lowered her onto a chair where he kneeled before her as she sobbed uncontrollably in his arms.

CHAPTER SEVENTY-EIGHT

After the funeral Mary and Cam went back to the house exhausted and depressed. The front window had been replaced and apart from three small holes in a wall the place looked perfectly normal; no one would have known that less than twelve hours earlier it had been a hub of chaos. Cam flopped down on the sofa in Mary's office and listened to the messages from wacky clients, amazed at her friend's patience and the fact that she could focus.

One woman wanted hotel reservations for two couples for the weekend. "I mean they could stay with me, but honestly, I hate having company. I'd rather pay for them to stay somewhere else. You decide where. I think you have my credit card number, right? Whatever, call me and let me know where they'll be staying."

Two calls were from a client throwing a summer carnival themed party and *had* to have an elephant, no *two*; one call was from Gabby DuBois's manager complaining about her clients, Bob and Bob, at whose wedding she was to perform; one from the billionaire baby Annabelle; and the last call was from the Montauk concierge gossiping about the difficult clothing designer. "She called at six this morning screaming that there was a duck in her bathroom and I had to come and get it out," the Montauk concierge laughed.

First, she called the 1770 House and arranged for her client's guests to stay in their Carriage House, a beautifully appointed building at the back end of their East Hampton Main Street property, just blocks from Lee Street where the client lived.

After a quick glance at her emails and Cam snoring softly

on the couch, she got up and erased the brat bride's white board.

"What are you doing?" Cam asked sleepily pretending to be fully awake.

"Someone killed Corliss and I promised Diane I'd figure out who it was. Well, I've been avoiding it long enough." At the top of the board she created three columns, and started each row with the name of the deceased: Corliss, Paulo, and Sheryl.

"Now, we know Sheryl was killed by the same person who killed Paulo because she was Darth Vader, right?"

"Right."

Mary drew an arrow between the two names.

"But we don't know who killed Corliss. Right?"

"That'd be right." Cam stretched.

"Now what did these three people have in common?" Here Mary scribbled every detail that linked the three coming to the conclusion that while Corliss had a firm connection with the other two, it was an unknown as to Paulo's and Sheryl's connections.

"But there has to be," Cam said, still prone on the couch.

"Why?" Mary added names to each column: individuals who knew each victim, often repeating the names.

"Because she was Darth Vader. She obviously knew who killed Paulo." Cam hoisted herself into a sitting position.

"Or did she?" Mary asked.

"Why else would she have called?" Cam asked.

"Maybe, just maybe she was calling about Corliss and not Paulo."

As they looked at the lists of names Cam sighed.

CORLISS	PAULO	SHERYL
Paulo	Corliss	Corliss
Sheryl	Diane	Diane
Diane	Henry	Ruggiero?
Richard Sarcoff	Tristan	
Henry	Ruggiero	
Marcus Schulman		
Tristan		
Ruggiero		

"I mean look at this, Sheryl didn't even know Paulo," Mary said, tapping the board with the marker.

"But we don't know that. Hell, they could have been lovers for all we know," Cam countered.

"The only name that crosses all three columns is Diane." Mary took a deep breath.

"Well that solves it. Let's make a citizen's arrest." Cam slapped her thigh.

"I think it's a man."

"Wait, it could be Ruggiero. He's in all three columns too."

"Oh yeah, you're right. How did I miss that? Well, whoever did it has strength and knows how to use a knife."

"The police know that, Mary, but they haven't done anything more than question everyone on that list, which means they have no solid evidence against anyone."

"All right, someone hated Corliss enough to not just kill her, but chop her up; that's rage."

"That's Richard," Camille said. "Of everyone on that list I think he hated her more than anyone."

"More than Marcus? She really screwed him over with the investors. And let's not forget, my tires were punctured at his place."

Cam shrugged. "Richard certainly has enough money to hire someone to kill her, but why Paulo and Sheryl? Unless we've been chasing our tails thinking that they are somehow connected when they're not." Cam crossed her long legs into a yoga position.

"Marcus and Richard are friends. Maybe they combined resources."

"But neither of them had anything to gain other than the gratification that someone they didn't like was dead. Who had something to gain?"

"Ruggiero," they said at the same time.

Then Mary smiled.

"What?" Cam asked.

"There's no way." Mary chuckled.

"Why?"

"Have you met that guy? I mean he may have motive and he may even be evil, but there's no way he could have committed any of these murders. He's a lightweight."

"Girl, adrenalin is a crazy drug. Go online. There are dozens of stories of women who have lifted cars off people. I am telling you, *cars*! This Ruggiero knew everyone on that list. He had to know Sheryl; you said she was Corliss's maid, right? I wouldn't laugh at him if I were you."

"Huh."

Beanie came into the office, jumped onto Cam's lap and let it be known that she was ready for a walk.

And as it turned out, so were they.

CHAPTER SEVENTY-NINE

Unaccustomed as he was to excessive imbibing, Henry's day had gotten off to a slow start. By the time he reached the studio and the stench of Tristan's stale cigarettes it was nearing noon.

He was glad to see that Gert was getting more comfortable in her new home and instead of following on his heels chose to explore the property and carefully mark the perimeter of her home.

It took twenty minutes before he had straightened the place and removed all signs of Tristan's disgusting habit, but he nonetheless smiled when he considered how changed Trist was now that he had a little security. Over the months he had watched as his friend had gradually lost his spark but yesterday, his birthday, had been a turnaround day starting with the sale of a piece to Cam.

Fifty years. Half a century. Why, fifty years ago the world was a totally different place: politically, technologically, medically, and socially. Hell, Henry hadn't even been born.

He smiled. Espresso in hand he was finally ready to work.

He thought of Mary and the night before as he took brush to canvas. He couldn't remember the last time he had been so smitten. Perhaps a boyhood crush once upon a time, but not this way. No other woman had ever ignited him like this before.

He painted guided by feelings, surprising himself with some of the twists and turns the work was taking. He heard Gert's nails tapping on the hardwood floor and called out, "Welcome back my love. Have some water."

He continued working until he heard a plaintive little cry

escape Gert, who was sitting at the threshold of the room with something hanging from her mouth.

"Oh crikey," he mumbled as he set down his brush thinking it was a creature she had bested or more likely an already dead creature she simply found.

"What you got there, princess? Let's have a look."

Unlike any other dog that would have held steadfast to their trophy, Gert dipped her head and dropped it on the floor.

Nothing more than a filthy piece of black, ragged cloth. "Well thank you, that's disgusting." He held the rag between the tips of his thumb and middle finger and held it up for examination. Nothing. A torn piece of what was once nice fabric now stained and filthy.

He commended Gert for having brought him this and not a chipmunk, tossed it in the garbage under the sink and rewarded her with a nice big piece of chicken jerky which she strangely refused. Instead she looked from the cabinet door hiding the garbage to him and back again all the while issuing little cries.

"Absolutely not," he said firmly leading her to the sofa. "Here you go; a treat, your favorite toy and the best seat in the house." Reluctantly she did as he bade letting the tasty treat sit untouched on her paws for the longest time. Her old soulful eyes looked so worried that Henry took time to sit with her and reassure her.

Unlike some unevolved people, Henry was of the mind that in their own way dogs try to communicate with people. One just has to be mindful and listen. Something was upsetting Gert; he didn't know what, but to just walk away from her felt wrong. So he sat with her for another twenty minutes until she seemed to calm down and fall asleep.

Her eyes were closed tight as she fell into a fitful sleep not dreaming of chasing squirrels, as Henry thought, but the scent that lingered.

CHAPTER EIGHTY

"So where is he?" Camille asked after they had walked half a block.

"Who?"

"Your shadow, the policeman. I don't see him." They walked arm in arm.

"That's the whole idea. You're not supposed to see him. I have to say I do feel safer knowing he's out there. You?"

At the stony bay beach where the water was so calm it looked like a mirror, the dogs took their time sniffing, marking, and snacking on a fresh bouillabaisse.

"God, it's beautiful here, isn't it?" Camille asked as she watched violet and lavender clouds shape-shift.

"That it is."

Mary shook her head as she watched the dogs. "They're good together, aren't they? You know Diane hasn't asked once about Beanie. Not once. I figure Otis needs a companion so I believe little Beanie's found a new home. What do you think?"

Camille said nothing.

"What?" Mary asked.

"Nothing."

"No, no, that's not nothing. What?"

"It's stupid," Camille demurred.

And then it hit Mary. The whole time Camille had been staying with her she and Beanie had connected so strongly that the little dog even slept with her and not Otis.

"Oh my God, you want her, don't you?" Mary asked.

"It's a stupid idea. I work. I live in the city. My life is constantly on the go. This is a much better home for her, I know it." She knew it, but it didn't make it easier. Camille had fallen head over heels in love with the goofy little dog and had been daydreaming about taking her back to the city and bringing her to photo shoots.

As if on cue Beanie came rushing up to them and threw herself at Camille's legs.

It was clear that Beanie had found a new home and it wasn't with Mary or Otis.

On their way back Camille linked her arm through Mary's and said, "And now if we live through this you might even have yourself a boyfriend."

"Oh I don't know."

The two women froze as a pickup truck passed them, slowing for the dogs.

"Baby you deserve it," Camille said, breathing again. "It's been way too long since you had yourself a good man."

"Honey, I don't know that I've *ever* had a good man!"

Camille's phone rang and she sighed when she saw the caller ID. "Work," she said as she took the call and slowed her step.

"A gig in Amsterdam," she told Mary when she was back in stride.

"You sound bored."

Camille paused. "I don't know. Maybe a little. I'm getting too old for this shit. I've been thinking about it since I got here. I think I need a challenge, you know what I mean? You're challenged every day with those crazy people. But I don't know what I would do."

"God, Cam, you could do anything," Mary said.

They continued in silence until Mary stopped abruptly, swung Cam around and blurted, "Be my partner!"

"Yeah, right."

"No, seriously. I mean you would be a sensation out here. Between us? My God, we could make a killing."

"Don't use that word," Camille said.

"No, really. This is something you could do with your eyes closed and you could still take the modeling jobs that interested you. Honestly, this is a great idea. And you could keep Beanie because I would always be there to help you out when you had to leave town. Oh my God, I'm serious. This is perfect. And with Lina agreeing to work for us, you and I could focus on creating more business and the clients. We could even get a real office!"

"Don't be silly," Camille cautioned, but she was starting to feel the excitement herself. Now they were speed-walking the last block with the dogs huffing behind them.

"And the best part is we'd be together again. I mean don't you miss me?"

Mary's enthusiasm was contagious. As much as Camille wanted to pooh-pooh the idea, the truth was it seemed like a viable option. With her career and her financial acumen, money wasn't an issue. She could afford to take several years off without drawing any kind of salary, but she knew what Mary made and it was considerable. With her contacts she knew they could grow the client list and spread out from the Hamptons to the city and maybe beyond.

It was tempting.

"I need a drink," she said when they reached the house.

"Champagne!" Mary said.

"God no. Coffee. Look, we don't know that I'm going to do this."

They both glanced out the front window and were relieved when they saw an unmarked car park just up the road.

"You may not, but I do. Camille, for God's sake, you know the Clintons! You have their private phone numbers!"

"Slow down, girl. In a minute you'll have us selling in-ground pools on the moon."

But Mary couldn't slow down and before she knew it she had lost herself in the possibilities that lay ahead and had completely forgotten about everything else swirling around them.

It almost felt like a brain vacation.

Until the doorbell rang.

CHAPTER EIGHTY-ONE

When she left the funeral, Diane made a beeline home where she spent forty minutes shampooing, soaping, and shaving, all in all washing away her mood. She emerged feeling like a different person. The pain was still there, along with her desire for a smoke, but so was Beau, the dog from the beach who now had unheard of carte blanche in Diane's house.

After their meeting on the beach, Diane took Beau straight to the vet, simply waltzing in without an appointment, but Dr. T., a gentle soul, had fit her in and given Beau a clean bill of health along the necessary shots and a suggested a diet to get the likely five-year-old up to a healthy weight.

"Hi." Diane stood naked in the bedroom as Beau, freshly washed by the maid the day before, lay on her bed having eschewed the soft carpeting, where she had told him to stay. "All right, Beau, this is me, like it or not." She went through the process of getting dressed all the while talking to her new companion. "But at least I'm clean, just like you."

He cocked his head.

She told him about Mary and what had happened at the church and how mad she was at the world, and herself for just about everything imaginable from her weight to the smoking to her insecurity and being what she now deemed a creative fraud.

When she was dressed and finished with her self-excoriating diatribe, Beau jumped off the bed, went directly to her and gently jumped on her, his back legs firmly on the floor and his front paws pressed against her chest. He was hugging her.

As she gently hugged him back she cried but this was different from the flood of tears she had shed in the last week or two. They were neither tears of rejection or loss. This was love. A deep unshakable love she had only known once before and this time she wasn't going to lose it.

CHAPTER EIGHTY-TWO

"I hate that son of a bitch," Ruggiero complained as they took a seat in the gazebo at Herrick Park in the center of town where they felt certain they wouldn't see Tristan. "I wish he was dead."

"All things considered I'd say that's not a prudent thing to voice in public," Agda said.

"You know what I mean."

"I do and it wouldn't solve anything." Agda unscrewed her bottled water.

"There is no way the two of us will be able to work together. Did you see how he strutted around the gallery? Like a wild turkey in heat."

"Peacock," she corrected him.

"He's not that handsome," Ruggiero assured her.

Agda wasn't so sure but kept quiet.

A line of children crossed Newtown Lane from the middle school coming to use the park for recess. "Oh shit," Ruggiero sighed. "Kids. Let's go."

"Stop." Agda put a hand on his arm. "They're fun to watch."

Ruggiero yanked his arm away and faced off. "Agda, you don't seem to understand, everything is changed! That maggot is going to find out what we've done and … and …"

"And what? Calm down. She's dead, Ruggiero. She can't do anything. You own the place now. Yes, yes, I know—" She held up a hand to shush him before he could object. "You own it with Tristan, but the truth is after all the paperwork is done one of you might buy out the other or choose to be a silent partner or I don't know—die! But listen to yourself. You're crying like a big baby because someone you didn't like left you an amazing lifeline? What's wrong with you?" She released his arm and waved him away. "Go on, go and cry by yourself, but me? I'm going home to make the next great piece *you* will sell." She stood up, stretched and as she walked away she said, "The past's the past, Ruggiero. Let it go."

She was right, of course.

So he stole from Corliss. So what? She deserved it. And it was unlikely that Tristan would ever understand the paperwork even if he did look at it, which Ruggiero doubted he would.

He had to relax. He was buzzing, his whole body was jittery. But Ruggiero, like so many others, didn't really know himself. While he could run a business his common sense was skewed: he would never consider that four coffees with no food would have an effect on his nervous system.

Silly man.

CHAPTER EIGHTY-THREE

It should have been so easy. In Missy's carry-on was everything she needed to complete the metamorphosis except for the passport, which she had glued between two identical postcards and tucked between the pages of the book she finished on the flight: *The Birth of Venus* by Sarah Dunant, a story of another woman in another time who had her own secrets which she wore as a second skin.

She would slip into a ladies' room at the Charles de Gaulle airport and change into her lighter weight custom-made niqab. Despite having been tailored with Japanese crepe it was still a heavy, hot garment but one she had come to love. Slipping into the niqab was like donning anonymity: sheathed in black from head to toe with only her eyes showing she might as well have been wearing Harry Potter's invisibility cloak. Contrary to her initial fears that people would stare, it turned out that most people would look and then just as quickly look away, either embarrassed or frightened.

Over a period of months she had trained herself and finally grown accustomed to the dress, testing it many times in the city: walking the streets, using public transportation, walking slowly through all kinds of stores and of course the most challenging effort of dining. Recently she had arranged a lunch date with several girlfriends, called when they were at the restaurant to cancel and sat at a nearby table to watch them and see if they recognized her.

They did not. And while Janie, the most emboldened of the three, stared at her while she ate, no one seemed the wiser.

That's when she knew she was ready.

The flight had been uneventful; the food while good was hardly worth the price of the ticket, but it was her farewell to ostentatious living.

She could never have anticipated what awaited her at the airport.

As she filed off the jet bridge with her fellow passengers it was with heightened anticipation and newfound confidence. She wasn't an idiot; she hadn't come to this moment lightly. Her interest in Muslim history had started during an art class at Vassar. Online connections are like neurotransmitters only better, taking you seamlessly to places you never knew existed … to people you might otherwise have never known.

The thought of meeting him after all these many months, of actually hearing his voice unencumbered by the distance of miles clouded every other thought she had or concern for those she left behind. He had become her addiction.

At the gate she was met by two somber men in dark suits who politely asked if they might speak with her. When she saw their badges her heart sank, but her entitled upbringing was a part of her DNA and her response was chilling, confident and haughty.

She would not simply comply. No. She continued toward her destination, the ladies' room where she would change and slip past them unnoticed.

But the young woman was no match for the seasoned agents and in the end she was escorted to a quiet room down a long sterile corridor where unanswered questions were asked.

Ultimately a female agent joined them. It was she who subjected Missy to a humiliating body search which proved the young woman was clean. The agent was kind, almost maternal as she began a dialogue with Missy who opened up, slowly allowing glimpses of herself and her ambitions.

"Missy, sometimes people are not who we want to think they are," the agent said softly as she set coffee in front of the clearly shaken girl. "The man you have decided to align yourself with is using you."

"You don't know that."

"Unfortunately, I do." Here the older woman sighed and

picked up a remote control which she aimed at a small TV on a rolling cart. "This is Amir," she said when a photo of a young man with fiery eyes and a dark beard appeared. "His real name is Brian James. He was born and raised in Indiana until he found the calling five years ago."

"So?"

"I just want to show you some of the things he has done along with evidence of his intentions with you. Are you okay?"

"Why shouldn't I be?"

The next five minutes revealed such barbaric acts of violence that Missy thought she might be sick.

The agent paused the video. "Should I continue?" she asked.

"That could be anyone," Missy said softly.

"Not really." When the video started again the man who had just beheaded a child pulled off his mask and winked at the camera revealing his bright white teeth in a joyful smile.

Missy covered her face.

"Look, you're a good person," the agent started softly as she paused the video again. "He's not. Maybe he started out like one, but acts like this, taking pride and obvious delight from something so heinous is evidence of evil." She let the word sit between them like an entity in the room.

"It is no secret that women in his society are abused; raped, beaten, handed from one soldier to another. They have no will of their own save for how they privately maintain their own dignity. It is likely you were to be a hostage held for ransom until your father paid—and they are well aware of his finances; it is one of the reasons you were wooed. You would have been wed, had no say in any aspect of your life, and never been returned. Of course at first he would have treated you well enough, but once the ransom was paid you have to understand your usefulness would have been over."

Missy folded her hands in her lap and turned to stone. He was different, she knew that. They didn't know him the way she did. But she didn't know him the way they did. And that was enough to scratch the smallest chink inside her which would ultimately create an emotional tectonic shift that would take years to repair.

CHAPTER EIGHTY-FOUR

When Cam opened the door she was surprised to see Tristan standing there with a boyish grin and cleanly shaved.

"I hope this isn't a bad time," he said offering her a small bouquet of flowers. "For you," he said.

Her smile was radiant. God she was beautiful.

"No, we just got back," she said, stepping aside to let him in. "Thank you. They're lovely. Come on in."

Tristan followed her into the kitchen, taking in the house in the daylight and his piece on the coffee table. He was good. Yeah, he had sold it at half the price, but with any luck—and his was changing—he could envision a future with the same sculpture in *their* home.

"*Whoa, boy, slow down,*" he silently warned himself.

As Mary walked through the living room, hearing Tristan's voice in the kitchen she stopped to take a look at his artwork on her coffee table. Seeing as though he was here and she had barely looked at it, it would only be polite to tell him how much she liked it.

"Well hello," Mary said as she entered the room.

"Mary! What a nice surprise."

"Really? I live here," she reminded him.

"Well yes, of course. I was just hoping ..." he paused. "Well if truth be known, I was hoping to get Camille all to myself." He had discovered long ago that women liked disarming honesty once they recovered from the shock.

He glanced shyly at Cam who was at the sink putting the flowers in a vase. She didn't turn around so he couldn't see her smile. Maybe she should take up Mary on her offer to partner;

maybe this was an omen to stay. She could have a job and a sexy, talented man who was neither a businessman nor a politician. It could be interesting.

"Oh well," Mary said. "You're stuck with a chaperone. Want some coffee?"

For the next twenty minutes they sat outside drinking in the sun along with the coffee. When there was a pause Tristan turned to Cam and said, "I came here thinking I could give you a tour of the area. You know, see places you might otherwise miss. Or maybe just see my Hamptons."

Cam demurred. "That sounds like fun but I'm getting a massage in …" She checked her watch. "Oh my gosh, ten minutes! Can I have a raincheck?"

He held up his hand and said, "Any time."

Mary stared at his palm and noticed a small, perfectly round scar.

As a lawyer she was experienced at showing nothing, so keeping her face passive was not a problem. She smiled when she said, "Oh my, that's an unusual scar. A sculpting accident?"

Tristan looked at his hand. "No, childhood. I fell on a nail."

"Yikes, that must have hurt," Mary said as she got up from the table.

He shrugged. "The good thing about pain is that one forgets."

"That's true. Well it was nice seeing you, Tristan. I have to get back to work. I need to find two elephants."

He smiled and turned to Cam. "Elephants?" Mary heard him ask as she slipped away.

In her office she hit speed dial and called Gabe Lasworth. God damn it, it was him. The face in the sculpture: yes it was merely suggested but it had to be fashioned after Corliss. There was no mistaking it. And the scar; that's what she had seen in her dream. She must have noticed the small round mark before but it hadn't registered. "Pick up, pick up, pick up," she repeated as the phone rang, ultimately going into voice mail. Damn it. "Gabe, it's Mary. I know who killed Paulo."

CHAPTER EIGHTY-FIVE

After lunch with Police Officer Winnow the conservationist didn't know what to do with himself but before he knew it he was at the cemetery standing before his mother's grave. He had passed the cemetery earlier when he saw gravediggers preparing a plot for burial and had pulled over to watch. It was a beautiful day for a funeral.

To work in the sun in such tranquility; it must be comforting.

But what about the days when it rained or snowed or was so hot the earth was like stone? Something to consider. At least with landscaping he wouldn't have to work on days like that. Well, in the heat, yes, but he liked the heat. He liked the way sweat rolled down the length of his body and clung to his clothes; how the slightest breeze had the power to cause a pleasurable shiver.

Standing there alone by the grave he had visited every week since her death he remembered that grey, gloomy day when Mother was given to the earth. It had been a very lonely parting.

He tucked his hands into his pockets and rolled back onto his heels.

"Well Mother, you'd probably hate it but I'm happy for the first time in my life," he said softly to the headstone. "I met a girl. Well, not a girl, a woman. That's right. You said I'd never meet anyone didn't you? You said over and over again that you were the only girl for me you crazy ..." He took a deep breath of the fresh June air, shook his head and sat on the ground to be closer to her, so she could hear every word he had to say.

"You were wrong. I want you to know that. I also want you to know that as much as I loved you—and I did—I'm glad you're dead. I only realized that recently. And you want to know why? Because you only loved yourself. You needed me, yes, but love? I don't think so. You kept me boxed in to that shitty—yes, shitty—life with you so you wouldn't be alone. You taught me to distrust everyone and you were very successful. I hate you for that. I've been thinking about the dead woman I found, and if the poor son of a bitch who killed her hated her half as much as I hate you it was justifiable homicide. That's right. I hope whoever did it gets away with it. You think that's crazy?" He ran his palm gently along the blades of grass.

"Not crazy at all, in fact it's a kind of vindication." The conservationist sealed his lips, closed his eyes and raised his face to the sun. "I won't be coming back," he said, eyes still shut. "I have nothing more to say to you. I'm done."

But much to his surprise instead of getting up and walking away as he wanted to, he started crying for the first time since her passing. He issued no sound but tears streamed down his cheeks and it felt strangely good.

CHAPTER EIGHTY-SIX

Cam went to her room to get ready for her massage. By the time she came out, the masseuse was there and Mary decided to wait to tell Cam what she suspected. No, what she knew.

But she had to tell someone: Lina.

As she drove to the house she emotionally slapped her forehead that she hadn't put two and two together before.

Lina, however, wasn't home. She had gone back to the cemetery.

Without giving it a second thought Mary got back in her car and started for the cemetery, not noticing that at the halfway point between Lina's home and Paulo's resting place they passed one another going in opposite directions.

Mary's mind was not on her driving, but Tristan Cooper. He knew Corliss and he had met Paulo. She remembered their meeting and Henry's nearly unbridled enthusiasm to Paulo's work while Tristan had been more reserved. But Paulo had been enthralled to meet Tristan; he had known his work and was obviously a fan. If Tristan had gone back there, as she suspected he did, Paulo would have been honored and welcomed the artist.

Tristan was one of Corliss's artists. Since she had a reputation for cheating it was likely she had cheated him as well. There was no proof of anything, but she felt certain that all Gabe needed was one shred of evidence.

She stood at the foot of Paulo's fresh grave and spoke to the flowers and mound of earth.

"You will be able to rest in peace, my friend. Of that I'm

confident. I don't know why he did it but I promise you he won't get away with it."

"Well look who's here."

The voice startled her and Mary jumped.

"Good God, you scared me. What are you doing here?" Mary asked trying to control her fear and glancing around the cemetery for the police.

"Didn't you know great minds think alike? I came here to say good-bye to Paulo, apparently just like you." Tristan studied her trying to get a handle on what she knew, if anything. One could never be too sure. His hands were in his pockets and he lifted his chin toward the grave. "He had a lot of promise. Too bad he couldn't handle it."

"What makes you say that?" Mary asked almost casually. There was no room for a misstep. Having been trained in a courtroom she had learned to never show doubt. Despite her alarm Mary was able to call upon two central parts of herself, intellect and anger, which she had trained to work as one when needed. Now was one of those times.

"He killed himself," Tristan said as if stating the obvious. "I know *you* don't think so, but I think you're wasting your time."

"Oh?" Again, Mary looked for the police car and saw a nondescript car parked no more than sixty feet away. Though it was hard to see in the sunlight, there seemed to be a shadow of a man in the front seat, which gave her courage.

Indeed there was a plainclothes officer in the car, but she couldn't know he was preoccupied with his girlfriend on the phone who was threatening to tell his wife about their affair, and barely paying attention.

"Yeah. He was a bull of a little man. There's no way anyone could have killed him. Honestly I've thought you've been on a wild goose chase from the start." It sounded like a friendly observation, no threat, no edge. "But I do know you were fond of him and I am sorry for your loss," he added.

Mary felt a flash of deep rage at his condescending tone. She took a step away from him and, feeling confident that the police were there, asked, "Why did you do it?"

"Do what?" His smile was tight, his eyes cold.

Her phone rang but she ignored it.

"Paulo was a good man, Tristan."

He studied her face and knew now was the time. If he didn't stop her before she could contact the police, everything he had recently gained would be lost. He took a deep breath.

"He was. Wasn't he? Loving family. Promising career. Impressive talent. Just like all the other little burritos coming into our country who take what is rightfully ours. I am a talented man. I am an American, born and bred in this fine country with a God-given talent and what ought to be a natural citizen's birthright to make a living and not be afraid of getting old and having some foreigner take work away from me. Corliss owed me that job."

"What job?"

"The fuckin' armoire for your friend. She'd been selling my work, then showing me false receipts for half of what she was getting and pocketing the extra profit for herself. That's what she did when she got tired of having to sell an artist instead of their work flying off the walls. Recently she hadn't been selling shit. She knew I was hurting financially, and she knew my skill as a woodcrafter. And as insulting as it might have been for me to do *that* kind of work, I would have taken it gratefully because I have been runnin' on empty for way too long. Because of her. And when I saw what that little bastard was doing, I dunno, it made me crazy. He was good, real good, but not as good as me and I had known her for fuckin ever; she owed it to me. It hit me that my future was over. That was it and I was mad."

"So you killed him?" Admission was imperative.

"Sure I did," he answered easily. What difference did it make now? To any outsider it would have looked like two people were having a conversation, not a confession wherein one was trying to think how to most expeditiously dispose of the other.

"Corliss, too." Now there was a sparkle in his eye. His creativity of incorporating pieces of Corliss into his work had been nothing short of genius and Tristan was proud of this; it actually felt good to be able to brag about his ingenuity. And so, knowing she would never have a chance to share his brilliance, he told Mary how he had meticulously planned and executed Corliss's end.

"I loathed her. You know as well as I do that she was not a nice person, Mary. In her own way she was just as bad as those Wall Street bankers and brokers who butt-fuck the population with serrated objects and say, 'Like it?'" He shook his head barely noticing her look of disgust. It didn't matter what she thought anyway. She had to go too.

"Well, I didn't like it. So I did something about it. The planning took forever. With each sculpture in the series your pretty nigger friend bought I planned how I would do it and use her or bits of her anyway. I molded her hands and then burned them and her feet in the kiln. But her face, that's where I was fucking brilliant."

"She's in your sculpture." Mary was horrified.

He chuckled. "Yeah. You have to admit that's genius. It would have stopped there but when I saw that she had hired that little spic to do a job that should have been mine, I knew he had to go too. Trusting little son of a bitch welcomed me in like I was the second coming."

"What about Sheryl? Did you have anything to do with her death?" She asked hoarsely.

"Ah, Sheryl. Yea, well, we knew each other from the deli, which means not at all, but she made a stupid mistake. She was a busybody and had a big mouth. She saw me leaving Corliss's house and told me so. Now I couldn't have that, could I? Just like I can't have you wandering around after this, and I'm sorry for that, Mary. You're a nice girl and Henry will be heart broken, but I promise you this: I will be a great comfort to both Henry and Cam when you are gone. Fucking is always a great release, don't you think?"

"The police are watching us, Tristan." She nodded to the car.

In the second he took his eyes off her and saw the car Mary screamed and started to run, but she didn't get far. Tristan clamped on to her wrist and yanked her back. "Mary, Mary, Mary," he whispered in her ear, pressing her back against him as he placed her in a choke hold. "This is what's going to happen. I am going to break your neck and walk you back to my truck as if nothing happened; just one grieving friend helping another. Then I am going to take you back to my studio and lay you on my couch."

Here he glanced at the police car but there was no movement.

Mary tried to call out but the vise-like hold on her throat was too tight. She tried to claw at his arms but he had her in a hold that made it impossible to do more than flail like a rag doll. Where was the policeman? She picked up her foot and slammed it down on his but he was wearing construction boots. She threw her heel back and caught him hard on his tibia but not hard enough to stop him.

Oh my God, where are the police? He applied more pressure, which is when she heard a ringing in her ears and her head felt as if it was about to burst.

And then, out of nowhere was a flash of movement to his left that Tristan didn't see until a second too late and hit him like a ton of bricks, catapulting Mary out of his hold and sending all three of them sprawling.

Unable to move Mary gasped for air as the conservationist kicked at Tristan with all his might. Had he been wearing more than Birkenstock sandals it might have had an impact, but as it was Tristan grabbed his ankle and gave it one good twist issuing a snap from a bone and a shriek of pain from the conservationist.

Fuck, it was all going wrong. Mary was crawling away desperately trying to get to her feet, but Tristan grabbed her by the hair and yanked her back. He didn't know what to do but there was no way this stupid bitch was getting away.

"Get up God damn it!" He hated her. This was all her fault, the son of a bitch. He pulled her hair to lift her off the ground but she tripped and screamed which pissed him off so he kicked her in the back of her thigh and used his free hand to hoist her up by the waist of her pants.

"Hey!" a man's voice called out. "It's over man. Let her go." It was Nick Petrucci.

Tristan spun around and now saw that there were six cars where there had only been his and Mary's. He pressed Mary against his chest to use her as a shield against the three cops who had guns trained on him.

Despite her own searing pain Mary could feel him shaking.

The conservationist passed out.

More officers aimed guns at the ready. Another car arrived; Gabe Lasworth got out and slowly started walking toward them. "Listen to me, son, this isn't necessary." His voice was firm and gentle at the same time.

Tristan tightened his hold on Mary and took a step back. "Back off!"

Gabe seemed no real threat—he was short and old—but the little man kept inching his way closer to them.

"I'm telling you: Back! Off!" Tristan's voice cracked.

Gabe stopped. He was twenty feet away.

He looked impassive yet kindly. "It won't do any good to hurt her," he said, sounding off-handed.

"Fuck you. It's people like her that cause all the problems and you know it." He tightened his grasp on her hair, pulling out strands from the scalp.

"Maybe but hurting her won't do you any good, Tristan. Listen, you're a smart man. Look around you. There's nowhere to go."

This was true enough. Tristan knew that even if he were to get the two of them into his car there was only one road, two fucking lanes that led in and out of the Hamptons.

"But there is," Tristan whispered to himself. Mary could hear his breathing become shallow as he considered his options in silence. There was only one way, really. He didn't want to live the rest of his life in a fucking cell. And while killing Mary at this point would be a perfectly justifiable thing to do this was about him now. There was only one viable objective, but how to assure it?

He leaned close to Mary's ear and said, "You tell Cam I'm sorry it didn't work out. She and I woulda been good together." With that he shoved Mary to the ground and started toward Gabe, reaching his hand into his pocket and drawing it out quickly with a small sculpting tool in hand.

No one could have known what was in his hand. It could have been a gun or a lighter, but Nick Petrucci was taking no chances since Tristan was within feet of Gabe. He squeezed the trigger and before the echo of the report stopped, Tristan was down.

CHAPTER EIGHTY-SEVEN

Mary cradled her head as she sat in a heap near the tall, pale man who had come to her rescue.

She flinched when Gabe squatted beside her and wrapped his arms around her. "It's over, Mary. You're safe."

She was suddenly cold and trembling. Gabe knew shock had set in and motioned for help. He would talk to her later. When an officer wrapped her in a blanket and was ministering to her, Gabe walked to where Tristan lay, assessed the situation and led Nick away from the activity.

"He didn't have a gun," Gabe said.

"I didn't know that."

"Where'd you learn to shoot like that?"

"I started hunting when I was nine."

Gabe nodded.

Two ambulances pulled up and gurneys were wheeled to the conservationist, who had come to and was crying in pain, and Tristan.

Carla Winnow ran from the line of officers to the conservationist's side where she knelt beside him and cradled his head. "Oh Clarence," she cooed. "You were so brave. So wonderful. You're a hero. I promise I'm going to take good care of you." She cried as she kissed his forehead and he mumbled, "It hurts."

"Take a look at her," Gabe called out to an EMT who nodded and went to Mary.

The scene was now swarming with police, technicians, a reporter who had a friend on the force, cemetery workers, and a growing number of onlookers.

"I want them to take her to the hospital for a once-over," Gabe told his assistant Donald, with the tic, who had joined them. Donald went to tell the paramedics.

"Mary will need her friend, Nick. I want you to go get her and take her to the hospital. Make sure they get home safe."

Nick nodded. "Okay." He started off.

When he was six feet away Gabe said, "By the way." He waited until Nick was facing him. "Good job."

Nick nodded and left.

Gabe watched as Mary was escorted to an ambulance, oddly compliant.

He then walked back to Tristan where the medics were just about ready to get him on the gurney.

He smiled down at Tristan. "I'm guessing that hurts," Gabe said nodding to Tristan's now bandaged knee.

Tristan glared up at the detective.

"Didn't get what you wanted, did you son?" Still Gabe smiled. "I'm guessing that's going to hurt the rest of your life, which I hope is very long and otherwise healthy."

"Fuck you."

Gabe chuckled. "Get this garbage out of here."

Hoisted onto the gurney, Tristan was cuffed to the railing.

It would take hours before the scene was cleared, but it would be cleared and Gabe would be reunited with his wife that night. He texted her to let her know.

Twenty minutes later she responded: PICK UP MILK.

CHAPTER EIGHTY-EIGHT

By the time Mary, Cam, Nick and Henry got home from the hospital, Diane was there, having let herself in to the unlocked house.

She hadn't wanted to leave Beau alone, so she brought him with her but knew well enough that dogs had to be introduced carefully, which much to her surprise she did, all by herself.

And they all seemed to get on, which astonished her. She started in the garden where Beau made a round first sniffing and then marking and Otis followed him calmly reclaiming his own territory.

When Mary and the others got back Diane had laid out a spread from a local Japanese restaurant thinking they would all be hungry. Of course they'd be hungry.

Mary and Henry arrived first and Cam, who had stopped to retrieve Mary's car from the cemetery, a short while later followed by Nick.

Diane wrapped Mary in her arms and in an odd reversal of roles insisted on taking care of her friend, directing Mary to the sofa and getting her a drink.

"Who's this?" Henry asked about Beau who was sitting on the threshold between the kitchen and the living room while Otis whined practically in Mary's lap.

Henry offered his hand and was rewarded with a quick lick.

Diane explained their story and proudly detailed how she introduced the three dogs.

Beau's presence initially made Mary nervous, but he was a gentle soul who followed Diane everywhere. When she brought Mary a drink, he sat quietly by her feet with his head bowed waiting for a pat. Otis's calm acceptance clinched Beau's initiation to the group.

When everyone was gathered Mary recounted almost everything from when she first noticed Tristan's scar and called Gabe to the angel who flew out of nowhere to try and help her. She told them of his confession, leaving out the details about Corliss. "And then Nick, this brave man, shot him."

"Why didn't you kill him?" Diane asked.

"There was no need to. He'll have to live with what he's done. He'll spend the rest of his life in jail. I think that's worse."

"Amen," Camille whispered.

"Right, and we get to pay for his room and board," Diane complained.

"Di, did you know Corliss left Tristan half the business?" Mary asked.

"Not a clue."

"Why would she have done that?" Cam asked.

Diane shrugged. "I don't know. But last night I remembered a conversation we once had about the play *No Exit* by Sartre and who we would cast it with from our own lives. She was stuck in hell with Tristan and Ruggiero. We couldn't get much beyond that because we were laughing so hard." She paused. "Honestly I think she did it as a placeholder, really, and a joke because she expected to live a very long time. With me."

Diane was done. She cleared away dinner and decided it was time to go so they could talk freely. She didn't want to hear anything that bastard had said about Corliss. Not yet anyway. Gathering her purse and leash she said, "Well you did it, Mary. You fucking did it. Thank you." She stood before Mary and said, "I love you. I gave you a hard time, but I love you and appreciate what you've done."

"I didn't *do* anything," Mary said, shorthand for *I will not take pay for this.*

"Whatever." Diane's shorthand was *We'll see.*

As they embraced Cam cried out, "Hey, you haven't had a cigarette!"

"I know and I'm dying for one! Gotta go. Come on Beau."

"Can you believe she has a dog?" Cam asked when Diane was gone.

"She still didn't ask about Beanie," Mary said. "So that's cool, you both got dogs this week."

"We don't know that," Cam said snuggling Beanie who was asleep on her lap. "So what did happen to Corliss?" she asked.

"He burned her hands and feet in his kiln and mixed the ashes into the clay he was working with. Then he used her head to form the piece he was working on."

"The one in the tent?" Cam asked.

Mary nodded.

"No wonder he wouldn't show it to us." Cam shivered and glanced at the sculpture on the coffee table. "Oh my God, do you think ...?"

"No. He did that a long time ago," Henry said.

Mary shook her head. "I hate to tell you but this was a prototype as he planned how he would kill and dispose of her."

Nick excused himself to answer a call from Gabe, with whom he had kept in touch throughout the afternoon and evening.

Henry was stunned. Cam threw a napkin over the artwork.

"Mary," Nick said entering the room. "Can you meet with Gabe in the morning?"

"Absolutely. I can do it now if you want."

"Slow down tiger. You need to rest. But I have to get back to work," Nick said looking at Cam.

Henry got up and walked to the officer he had had such a dislike for. He held out his hand and said, "Thank you for everything. You're a surprisingly good man."

Nick smiled, feeling the same about Henry but only offered, "Just doing my job."

Cam walked Nick to the door.

"It's funny how things happen, isn't it?" Henry said almost to himself. "Honestly I had no idea how cracked Tristan was. And I've known him for years. I mean he was always a little off, but that seemed to be part of his artistic charm."

"I wonder what will happen with the art gallery," Camille said walking back to her seat.

Mary shrugged. "Dunno. Don't care." She sighed. "I'm pooped."

"You should be." Henry held her hand. "I'll leave you."

"Yeah, Gert's been alone too long."

"She's with my neighbor."

Cam got up to take the dogs out back.

Mary stared at Henry. She didn't want to be alone but …

"You okay?" He asked but didn't wait for an answer. "I understand if you don't feel safe. I am more than happy to take the sofa, just so you know you and Cam are not alone."

"Honesty, right?" she said.

"Yes."

"I would like you to spend the night, but…."

"I understand. Sleeping buddies." He smiled.

"That's right."

"You have an extra toothbrush?"

"Yes."

"Well then I'd say this is the start of a fine romance."

EPILOGUE

"Okay, no wait!" Mary yelled at Camille and Henry, who were holding the six-by-four-foot canvas against the wall. "I'm not sure," she mused.

"Really?" Camille said. "Well then get your behind over here and *you* hold it up. This thing is heavy."

Henry told Camille to let it go and stand next to Mary while he held it aloft. "Mary, remember this is the first thing your clients will see when they walk in."

"I like it," Mary said.

"Yeah, but do you like it there?" Camille asked. "I'm not so sure. Maybe a little higher."

"Or lower."

"Just try higher," Camille directed Henry.

"Or in the office. Maybe this shouldn't even be out here," Mary suggested.

"Oh no," Lina piped up from the far side of the room as she hoisted herself up from her seat. "I think it *has* to be in here. It makes a statement. It's powerful. It lets whoever comes in know that they have arrived at where they are meant to be." She rested her hands on her very full belly temporarily housing not one but two little boys in the making.

Mary and Camille glanced at one another.

"Do whatever she says," Mary said, poking a thumb in Lina's direction. She was finally in her new office, a small cottage she had modernized. Renovations had not taken as long as anticipated, owing to the fact that the contractor was beholden to Mary several times over. Now the once-adorable cottage was a spacious two-floor studio on a quiet street in Sagaponack.

She had crazy Charlie design the space including an upstairs apartment for guests. Though the grounds were intimate, the landscape architect, Jack deLashmet, had designed a natural setting with a wonderful entrance: a green gate nestled in high hedges to ensure clients' privacy.

"Fine," Henry said, gently placing the canvas he had titled *The Day After* on the floor.

"Diane's coming back tomorrow," Mary told Camille who followed her into the office with its sliding doors opening out onto a large brick patio. "There's someone she wants us to meet." Mary waggled her eyebrows.

"A love interest?"

"Dunno."

"Man or woman?"

"Dunno."

"Biped or quattro?"

Mary shrugged.

"I'm headed to Moscow tomorrow night, remember?" Beanie followed after her and jumped up on the white sofa, ignoring the throw meant for her little paws.

"You know, I renovated this place with you in mind. The upstairs is yours. You could easily live here until you find your own place—."

Camille cut her off. "Stop it. I told you I'm not ready."

"Yes you are."

"No I'm not."

"Yuh huh," Mary said taking her seat behind the desk.

"Nuh uh," Camille flopped down next to Beanie. "But I had a long talk with Beanie who has agreed to behave like an angel while I'm gone, isn't that right?" Taking the dog's paws in her hands and making it look as if Beanie was gesticulating Camille said, "Oh yes, Miss Mary, I promise to be a very good girl," then added an evil laugh.

Mary's cell phone rang, she glanced at the caller and held up a finger to Camille and said, "Gimme a second."

"Mary, its Hannah." Hannah Miller had become one of Mary's first friends in the Hamptons when they met while walking their dogs.

"Hey Banana, how are you?"

There was a pause. "Mare, Cash is dead."

Mary felt herself freeze over. Good God, not another. Cash was the owner of The Little Inn, the most neglected inn in the Hamptons. Hannah called it the Last Hope Inn because it was the last place people could find on a summer weekend. "How? When?"

"Heart attack. Yesterday."

"Oh honey, I'm so sorry."

"Thanks. I just wanted you to know about the funeral." She gave Mary the information.

"I'll be there." After the call Mary picked up with Cam where she had left off. "How long are you gone?"

"A week."

Henry poked his head in the door and said, "Come on girls, I'm busy. It's not always about you. Ninety-twelve percent of the time but not always."

The phone rang as they entered the outer office where Henry had hung the painting precisely where he wanted it to go.

"Green Door Concierge, how can I help you?"

"I love it," Mary said.

"It's perfect," Camille agreed.

"Could I ask you to hold, please?" Lina looked up at Mary and said, "This is nasty. There's a screaming Kardashian on the phone."

"Which one?" Mary asked.

Lina shrugged. "She says her dog was kidnapped."

Mary stared at Lina in disbelief.

"What?" Lina asked. "It's true. What should I tell her?"

"I'm leaving," Henry said rousing Gert off the mini dog sofa designed to mimic the client couch.

"Thank you," Mary said with a hug. "I love it."

"You know, so do I. It looks good there. Will I see you soon?" he asked at the door, allowing Gert to go through first.

"Yeah. As soon as the Full Moon Party is over. You sure you don't want to go?" One of her clients, a Thailand entrepreneur's son, was hosting an enormous Full Moon Party as a lark for four hundred guests. "There will be fire rope skipping," she added as an incentive.

"Yes, appealing as that may be, I think I'll pass. Bye love," he said to Camille as he kissed her cheek. He waved at Lina and was gone.

"You're an idiot," Camille said when the door closed behind him. "You're not getting any younger and that man is as near to perfect as you're gonna find."

"Oh stop it. We're fine, thank you very much."

"Mary," Lina said, holding the receiver in the air.

"Oh God, tell her I'll call her back," Mary said, wandering back into the office. "Can you imagine working for a Kardashian?" Mary asked.

"Can you imagine being Bruce Jenner?" Camille replied.

They both laughed.

"Lost pet," Mary scoffed. "How ridiculous is that?"

"Well you do love dogs and let's face it, you see yourself as Nancy Drew."

"That's not true," Mary fibbed.

"You best start telling the truth girl." As Cam squatted to kiss Beanie good-bye the front door opened.

Both Mary and Cam stared at the newcomer, a thin young woman who looked ready to back out the door but thought better of it. She looked directly at Mary, took a deep breath and said, "Mary? I don't know if you remember me, but I'm Missy."

"Of course I remember you," Mary recovered quickly. "How are you doing?"

The Missy they knew was changed; she had lost the plumpness and grown her hair out to reveal a very pretty shade of chestnut. The edge was gone and what remained looked to be a very subdued young woman.

"I'm doing much better, thank you. It's been an interesting odyssey to say the least."

An uncomfortable silence fell over the room until Cam stood up and waved good-bye. "See you soon," she said and blew a kiss as she brushed past Missy and closed the door behind her.

"So, what can I do for you?" Mary asked Missy.

Missy chewed her lower lip and said what she had

memorized. "I know I don't have the best track record, but things are different now. I was going to email you but my mom insisted I come in person. She said it would have a better impression on you."

Her blatant honesty did in fact move Mary.

"I'm looking for a job and I thought I might be an asset to your business. I mean, if nothing else I know how to deal with crazy, entitled brats." She smiled shyly.

Mary laughed. "Indeed you do." A thousand thoughts went soaring through her mind. She glanced at Lina who shrugged as if to say *"how bad can it be*?"

"Well, I suppose it couldn't hurt to talk. Come on in," Mary said as she entered the office. Behind her she heard Lina ask, "Do you happen to know any of the Kardashians?"

ACKNOWLEDGMENTS

No one ever writes a book alone and *She's Dead, Who Cares?* is no exception. The journey of this book, which started many, many years ago could be a story in itself what with twists and changes in plot, title, and characters to the point that the end has no relationship to the start. During the writing of this book, I have lived in half a dozen homes, worked an equally diverse number of jobs, and interviewed so many wonderful, helpful people without whose willingness to give of their time to me, I would have no book.

And herein lies the rub. In one or more of the moves, I lost my notes and unfortunately with it the names of the police officers, artists, and medical professionals who were responsible for She's Dead. I apologize with all my heart and promise you – and myself – that this will never happen again.

That being said, Detective Sergeant Bob Feeney in the Suffolk County Police force was amazing with his guidance, information sharing, and editing. Detective Sergeant Vincent Ward opened a door that became my library of facts. Early reader and editor Joanne Pilgrim kept me steady when I settled on this path.

Eileen Boxer said yes and made magic.

Finally, Charlotte Sherwood, Genie Henderson, Hope Harris, Leah Sklar, Susan Duff, and Tamar Cole are an invaluable group of extraordinary writers, friends, readers, and editors. Thank you

ABOUT THE AUTHOR

Randye Lordon is the author of the award-winning Sydney Sloane Mystery Series that explores family relationships vis-à-vis murder. She presently lives in East Hampton where she is an innkeeper.

BOOKS IN THE SYDNEY SLOANE SERIES

Brotherly Love
Sister's Keeper
Father Forgive Me
Mother May I
Say Uncle
East of Niece
Son of A Gun

Curious about other Crossroad Press books?
Stop by our site:
www.crossroadpress.com
We offer quality writing
in digital, audio, and print formats.

CPSIA information can be obtained
at www.ICGtesting.com
Printed in the USA
LVHW111508070223
738881LV00022B/122

9 781637 898529